Jan McDaniel is the author of over 20 published romance novels. A native of Detroit, Michigan, she now makes her home in Chattanooga, Tennessee, with her husband, Bruce, their two teenagers and an assortment of dogs and cats.

Before turning to full-time fiction writing, Jan worked as a newspaper reporter and technical editor.

DANCE UNTIL MORNING

Claire Woolrich is a socialite, accustomed to the life of privilege which comes from her father's wealth. But dropout Wheeler Scully makes it clear that he isn't at all impressed. Circumstances mean that they must spend the night together, but after that their paths need never cross again. So why is it so important to Claire to make an impact on him?

Books by Jan McDaniel
Published by The House of Ulverscroft:

KEEPSAKES

JAN McDANIEL

DANCE UNTIL MORNING

Complete and Unabridged

ULVERSCROFT
Leicester

First published in Great Britain in 1998

First Large Print Edition
published 2005

The moral right of the author has been asserted

British Library CIP Data

McDaniel, Jan
Dance until morning.—Large print ed.—
Ulverscroft large print series: romance
1. Love stories
2. Large type books
I. Title
813.5′4 [F]

ISBN 1–84395–598–9

Published by
F. A. Thorpe (Publishing)
Anstey, Leicestershire
Set by Words & Graphics Ltd.
Anstey, Leicestershire
Printed and bound in Great Britain by
T. J. International Ltd., Padstow, Cornwall

This book is printed on acid-free paper

1

'Storm's moving in fast,' the surly man walking beside Claire Woolrich reported. 'You should head home.' Distant thunder rumbled across the mountains in confirmation.

Surprised by Wheeler Scully's sudden talkativeness — he'd muttered maybe two words to her in the past five minutes — Claire stiffened her slight shoulders. With a new sense of urgency, she attempted to plod faster through the dense overgrowth. 'This won't take long,' she insisted.

The tall, lanky man flanking her side did not quicken his leisurely pace. The corner of his mouth twitched, hinting at a smile. 'Headstrong,' he observed. 'Just like your old man.'

Bristling at his audacity, she questioned the wisdom of having requested his assistance with her errand. Then she recalled it was Father who had proposed it. 'If you still want that sculpture, have Wheeler fetch it for you. It's out back in the storage shed.'

'Shed's full of junk, Mr Woolrich,' the man in the faded jeans and threadbare once-red T-shirt had objected.

Because Claire couldn't wait all day for the caretaker to sort through Father's cast-offs, she'd volunteered to accompany him.

Naturally, Wheeler Scully had all the time in the world.

At least he moved as though he did. Living on this secluded mountaintop and looking after Father's property, he couldn't have much reason to hurry.

She, on the other hand, had a pressing appointment. Only a few more hours and her engagement to Barre Sutton would be official. All day, she'd been plagued by a premonition something was going to go terribly wrong. Nerves, she supposed, wishing Mr Scully would speed up.

'We'll be off the mountain and out of your hair shortly, Mr Scully,' she assured him, straining to sound pleasant. She was determined to let nothing dampen her buoyant spirits.

Hampered by her cute purple pumps, she trod painstakingly through the dense weeds. Burrs jabbed at her nylons. 'You'll have the place all to yourself again.'

Personally, she'd been secretly relieved a short while earlier to have the charity luncheon conclude so she could relax and abandon her role as gracious hostess to a throng of the area's most prominent and self-righteous citizens. Finally, they were gone.

'No hurry,' he replied. 'I've got nothing better to do.'

His sarcastic tone prompted her to swing her head just in time to catch him turning away. Perplexed, Claire arched her thin eyebrows and bit her bottom lip, wondering if she had done something to offend her father's employee.

His thumbs hooked in his belt loops, Wheeler Scully stared straight ahead and seemed satisfied to forgo further conversation.

Strange man, she reflected. Deciding perhaps he'd chosen his solitary occupation because of difficulty relating to people, she felt a pull of sympathy. All too well, she knew how socially debilitating shyness could be. She'd been struggling since childhood to fit the mold of being Joshua Woolrich's daughter.

An unexpected close glimpse of the caretaker's profile caught her off-guard. She'd been too busy all afternoon to pay much attention to the quiet, unassuming man. In fact, he spirited himself around the grounds like a phantom.

At first glance, he was merely a nondescript tall, muscular, sunbaked individual. Because of his spry, athletic movements and the baseball cap he wore perpetually slanted over his eyes, she'd assumed he was younger than she was. Now, angled beside him, she got a close view of his profile beneath the visor.

Discerning the strikingly handsome face camouflaged by dark whisker stubble shadowing his angular jaw, she strained to look harder. While his smooth features gave him an almost boyish charm, they revealed an unexpected underlying maturity.

Suddenly, she felt peculiar at finding herself alone back here with this puzzling stranger. But at this point, she couldn't think of any excuse to abandon the errand.

He was not a college student earning summer money. He appeared old enough that he should have had too many ties — home, job, family — to live alone up here. Why didn't he?

They were behind the massive stone mansion her father had poured so much money into renovating. Beyond the sprawling terrace and the beginnings of a flower and herb garden that wouldn't be planted until next year, the wooded yard fell into a steep incline. The woods smelled damp and mossy and sweet.

Traipsing through the overgrowth toward the tin storage shed, Claire cast a worried glance toward the ominously darkening sky. The towering oaks and pines swayed under intensifying gusts of wind, cooling the sticky summer air. Wisps of honey-gold hair escaped from her sophisticated French twist. Absently, she pushed back a handful of stray curls from her narrow forehead.

She prayed the weather would hold out a while longer. With an hour's drive ahead of her, she hoped for a relaxing soak in a steamy bubble bath before the party. Tonight, of all nights, she needed no delays.

Claire ventured another furtive glance at the mansion's caretaker. Surely he must get lonely up here by himself? She sensed an aura of solitude radiating from him. Or was it resentment? Because of who her father was, people mistakenly assumed she was different than everyone else. An attitude she'd been fighting all her life.

By allowing him to put her off, she was perpetuating his presumption, she realized. She'd always taken a genuine interest in people. She disliked being set apart. Perhaps with some encouragement, Mr Scully could break free of his shell and discover his full potential. If he cleaned himself up, paid more attention to his clothes and grooming, he might be attractive. Definitely. And Father praised him as a conscientious worker. The condition of the house and grounds attested to the truth of that. Perhaps he was capable of more than menial labor.

Now, while they were alone and he wouldn't be embarrassed presented the perfect time to raise the subject. 'Mr Scully, have you ever read Denver Sutton's *Elevator to Success?*' she asked.

Hearing a funny, muffled sound, she could have sworn he laughed. But when she swung sharp eyes his way, his expression remained deadpan, and he was staring straight ahead.

'Well, have you?' she repeated, slightly vexed.

'Yes.' His answer did not invite an extended discussion.

She clasped together delicate hands. Frosted mauve polish accented the tip of each long, delicate finger. 'Marvelous! Isn't it wonderful? How recently did you finish it?'

'It's rubbish,' he replied, in a low, husky voice, turning to face her. One muscle-roped arm swooped to his head in a swift, fluid motion. He lifted his cap to look her straight in the eye.

His clear, maple-syrup brown eyes shone with mild amusement mingled with annoyance. He regarded Claire with the look he might give a fly he discovered floating in his morning coffee. Through her irritation, she saw he was even more handsome than she'd discerned earlier. His shaggy, sun-streaked blonde hair blew at odd angles around his head as the wind caught it.

His startling, penetrating gaze triggered an unsettling quivery feeling in her stomach. Suddenly, she remembered Father's exact words about Wheeler Scully.

'Takes care of the place like it was his own. Just showed up one day and never says much about himself or anything else. I suspect there's a history of drugs or gambling or something worse, but as long as he does his job, I'm not asking questions. If a man wants to keep to himself, I don't need to know why. So long as he plays straight with me.'

Claire lowered her gaze to the ground, then raised it defiantly. She wasn't accustomed to being contradicted. 'Mr Sutton has changed my life,' she argued.

This time, he made no attempt to mask his deep, mocking laughter. It sliced the air against the faint backdrop of rustling leaves and crows cawing overhead. The corners of his eyes crinkled into twin sunbursts.

'Stinks being an heiress, doesn't it?' he asked. 'What was it about your life needed changing? New car? More credit cards?'

Claire bristled, her jaw clenching. Why shouldn't he assume things came easy to her? Everyone else did.

'I work for my living, thank you. I only thought the book might help you. Obviously, you're beyond wanting self-improvement.'

Wheeler came to a dead stop, towering over her five-feet eight inches with his hands on his hips. With his chest at eye-level, she couldn't ignore its massive span. He was more muscular than she'd noticed.

He addressed her as though she were a stubborn child. 'You can read books by hacks like Sutton from now till Doomsday, Miz Woolrich, but the sad truth is the rich get richer and people like me work for people like you and your father.'

'My father would help you, if you wanted to get ahead, go to school.'

He was studying her intently. 'Why would your old man do that?'

'Well, because I'd ask him to.'

'You're serious, aren't you?'

'Of course.'

'Look, Princess, why don't you stick to your fancy parties and find another drifter to reform? Someone worth your time and trouble? I like this job. Most of the time.'

She stiffened indignantly, refusing to back off as he loomed boldly over her. 'I was only making a suggestion,' she insisted. 'I didn't mean to insult you.'

Shame on her. She hated seeing anyone unhappy and had a bad habit of wanting to butt in and fix everyone else's problems. And she'd sensed he was unhappy. Perhaps she'd overstepped the bounds. This wasn't the first time her compulsion had gotten her in trouble.

But he wasn't finished. 'Denver Sutton insults humanity. He exploits poor working people who scrape by and dream of winning lotteries and will never enjoy the wealth he's accumulated by selling them worthless, overpriced books. Books teeming with vague, time-worn platitudes — I doubt he knows the meaning of genuine success. The only person he's interested in helping is Denver Sutton.'

'And I suppose you do know the meaning of it?' she countered, immediately regretting her impulsive comment as a shadow crossed his eyes. Her benevolent intentions had backfired into an argument. Oh, Lord, she sounded exactly like the snob she was trying to prove herself not to be. But he shouldn't have called her Princess.

'Yeah, what do I know? You asked.' His censuring eyes pinned her where she stood. A sudden blast of wind inflated the full skirt of her white and purple dress like a parachute.

Her face reddening, she quickly pushed down the floral print fabric. But not before she noticed his eyes filter downward and widen appreciatively.

Quickly, she dismissed his appraisal along with the distressing softening sensation his reaction sparked in her belly. After all, any healthy, breathing man couldn't have helped but look. Certainly, a gentleman might have attempted to avert his eyes. But Wheeler Scully defied any pretense of being a gentleman.

Still, she couldn't help admiring his conviction. In telling her off, he'd revealed an intelligence and integrity she found compelling. Most of her father's employees would have refrained from expressing their own ideas simply to avoid arguing with her. How boring. Under different circumstances, she might have liked this man. If he weren't so rude. And arrogant.

He wouldn't dare talk down to me like this if Father were here, she thought, then caught herself. She was twenty-six years old and capable of sticking up for herself. Even against this man who was goading her and enjoying it. If she wanted independence from Joshua Woolrich's long shadow, she couldn't evoke his power every time it proved convenient.

'Denver Sutton is highly respected among his peers as well as a personal friend of my . . . my family's,' she countered, defending her future father-in-law.

'And the wealthy are always right,' he clipped.

Claire huffed. No point in trying to employ logic with this guy. For some reason, he had a huge chip embedded in his shoulder. He was never going to agree with her. Best to leave him to himself.

Anxious to put some distance between them, Claire quickened her pace, a bad move considering she was maneuvering the slope in narrow high heels. As she slipped and wobbled, he came up behind her and nonchalantly caught her by the elbow. For a long, heart-stopping instant, his callused fingers lingered on her delicate arm, searing her flesh as though her finger had been plunged into an electrical outlet. She stifled a gasp at the shock the brief contact produced.

Finally, he released her and moved away, glancing caustically down at the stylish shoes perfectly matching the deep purple hue of the pansy print on her dress. 'Don't you have sense enough to wear boots out here?' he asked.

Certainly, she would have brought boots if

she'd expected to be hiking. Remembering the sculpture of the two lovers embracing came as an impulse. Now she couldn't leave without it — the perfect engagement gift for Barre.

Mr Scully didn't have to speak to her as though she were an idiot. Before she could reply, he ignored her and marched on toward the storage shed perched on a small, level shelf of ground. Removing the large key ring that dangled from his belt, he unlocked the door. She trampled weeds to catch up.

As fiercely as he irritated her, she wondered what she'd ever done to warrant his animosity. Obviously, bashfulness wasn't his problem. Not his biggest one, anyway.

Fearing being told once again to mind her own business, she fell silent. She wasn't going to let anyone spoil this happy day for her, least of all him. She rubbed the elbow that still tingled from his touch.

He'd scoff at the statue. Suddenly, with reluctance she couldn't explain, she didn't want him to see it.

'The weather is turning nasty,' she blurted. 'I should leave the statue until next trip up here.'

'After we've come all this way?' he asked incredulously, flashing her a disdainful look before he turned into the doorway without waiting for her reply.

Claire glanced repentantly at her hands. Now she'd confirmed his opinion of her as some flighty, vain little ninny who had brought him back here chasing wild geese.

Crouching, he leaned inside the low doorway, peering into the dark interior. From behind, Claire found herself absently studying the contours of his male form. His jeans strained interestingly across his rounded backside as he bent. Suddenly appalled to find herself admiring his rear, she tore her eyes away.

'What am I looking for?' His muffled voice drifted from inside the shed. Realizing she'd have to show him, she made the mistake of rushing to his side and squeezing into the doorway beside him. Pressed against his rock-hard muscle, she tried to ignore the tightening in her chest.

But at the forced closeness, he invaded her senses. Surprisingly, he smelled more of soap than sweat. Clean, masculine and musky. His overwhelming raw maleness made her light-headed. But she attributed the wooziness to the muggy air and the brisk walk.

'What was it you wanted out of here?' he repeated. If having her poised at his side bothered him, he didn't show it.

'Excuse me?' Her nerves were tingling,

dancing, spinning.

'Didn't we come here looking for something?' he reminded her. She felt his eyes resting on her with more than casual interest.

She pointed to the statue against the far wall. 'That's it,' she said, gesturing with her head. 'Please be careful.'

He shot her a pointed look. 'That thing?'

'Yes, of course. It's for Barre.'

He continued staring at her skeptically.

'My fiancé,' she added, realizing he couldn't know who Barre was.

'What's his name — Barry?'

'No, Barre. B-a-r-r — '

'That's what I thought you said. Whatever,' he muttered condescendingly. 'Maybe you could ask your old man to spring for a bigger storage shed closer to the house. This one must have been built for one of the Seven Dwarfs.'

Grumpy, I presume, Claire mused cryptically but remained silent.

She felt his breath against her cheek.

'Are you coming in with me?' he asked.

Face flushed, she inched backward. She rose, retreating into the faint sunlight, tossing her head back as she brushed her skirt with damp palms. Whoa, her heart was tap dancing. No reason for it. Except she felt like she'd just escaped from a lion's cage.

Wheeler disappeared inside the tiny shed. She heard clattering. Was he wrestling a grizzly bear in there?

'Ouch!' he grumbled, following that outburst with a sharp, explicit curse that brought color to her cheeks.

'Are you all right, Mr Scully?' she asked. She'd die if he broke the statue. The artwork had been left in the attic when her father bought his mountaintop mansion. She couldn't believe Father had finally agreed to let her have it. But this piece was too modern to fit the Victorian decor he was strictly adhering to in the renovations. Father's mood today was exceptionally good too. His generosity stemmed from his approval of her forthcoming marriage.

After an eternity, Wheeler squirmed free of the shed, the sculpture, intact, cradled in his arms. His face was smeared with grime, and she realized retrieving her prize had been no simple task.

She graced him with an appreciative smile. 'Thank you so much, Mr Scully. I will mention the shed to Father.'

He dismissed her gratitude. 'It's my job.'

For a long moment, he stared down at her so intently that she self-consciously pulled at the scooped neckline of her dress, wondering if he could see over it. His dark eyes moved to study the plaster representation of the passionate, naked lovers, then swung back to her with cool curiosity.

Reading his mind, Claire battled futilely to keep a blush from rising to her skin. No man had ever made such an immediate physical impact on her. Not even Barre, she reflected guiltily.

Barre had never flooded her mind with images of being carried off to a dark cave somewhere and wanting to go! Oh, Lord help her, she pushed the demon thoughts from her mind. What had come over her? Why was she finding a man who openly disapproved of her so ruggedly appealing?

She held out her arms to relieve him of the bulky item. He refused to relinquish it. 'I'll carry it to the car,' he told her. 'It's heavier than it looks. And you wouldn't want *this* broken.'

At his exaggeratedly solemn statement, she met his gaze defiantly. His brown eyes captured hers and held them prisoner for a long, silent moment. Challenging her. Her stomach fluttered and her pulse quickened.

'Better hurry. Weather's about to break,' he decreed finally. He sounded genuinely concerned, she thought, which was unexpected after his earlier tirade. 'The road down the mountain gets mighty slick.'

'Yes,' she agreed, falling in step beside him once again.

She lapsed into silence, and Wheeler Scully seemed content at not having to make conversation. He was right. They got along much better when they didn't try to talk to each other.

As they rounded the side of the house, she spotted Father and Sadie waiting out front by the cars. Joshua Woolrich paced the length of his restored, powder blue, 1957 T-bird convertible. The car gleamed as though fresh from a showroom. Her father stood tall and distinguished, with his black hair graying at the temples and his gray suit a perfect fit over his trim, still sturdy body. At the moment, Claire could almost see smoke billowing out of his ears. Father never liked being kept waiting.

She turned to Wheeler Scully while her family was still out of earshot. 'I'm sorry if I came off as though I were trying to force my ideas on you, Mr Scully. It's hard for me to imagine anyone being happy up here alone all the time.'

'Why the devil should you care?'

She knit her brow. 'Why the devil shouldn't I?' she retorted.

'Maybe you're the one of us who is

confused. I know exactly what I want.'

Her small mouth puckered. 'And what is that?'

'To be left alone.'

Claire didn't need to be knocked over the head to take a hint. She raced on ahead in long, brisk strides.

'Is everyone else gone?' she asked, approaching her father and cousin as the caretaker stepped aside. She couldn't help wondering whether Mr Scully would dare be so outspoken with Father. Certainly not, and yet with one word she could have had him fired in a twinkling. Perhaps it was only women Mr Scully enjoyed bullying, and maybe he deserved to be unmasked.

She didn't know what kept her silent about their confrontation. She was loath to ruin her special evening with guilt over costing someone his job. Or maybe it was her own guilt at having allowed him to rattle her.

Father rolled his eyes impatiently. 'Yes, Claire. No one wanted to stay. There's a severe storm warning out.'

Claire glanced toward the stately stone mansion behind them. Surrounded by woods and shadowed by the gloom of the approaching storm, it reminded her of a haunted castle. Her father had bought it as a plaything

— he loved restoring antiques. But Joshua Woolrich derived even more pleasure from finding new ways to make money. Within the next few weeks, the house would become an exclusive short-term rental property, available for weddings, corporate retreats, and lavish parties.

'I can't go yet,' she lamented.

'Why not? It's going to start pouring any second,' Sadie warned her.

'I won't be long. I've got to take the ferns from the luncheon back to Madeline at the flower shop in town. She needs them for a wedding tonight,' Claire explained.

'Oh, for heaven's sake, Claire,' Joshua Woolrich snapped. 'Why can't you arrange to have these tradespeople pick up their own things? That's part of their business.'

Claire stiffened her spine. 'I only convinced her to let me use them because it was for the luncheon to raise money for the children's hospital. And she's not even charging to let me borrow them.'

'Oh, leave them. She'll understand about the weather. You have only a few hours to get back and get ready for the party as it is.'

'I promised I'd return them,' she insisted, her hands balling into tight fists at her sides as her glance seesawed between her father and the house, then back again. Her father was giving her that familiar look she'd long ago learned left no room for argument. Her stomach began to roil. She'd given her word.

'Now, Claire, if this florist wants them badly enough, she'll come after them. Wheeler will be here.'

Claire didn't want to make a scene. Her father was used to getting his way. But neither could she let down someone who had done her a favor.

To her relief, Sadie stepped forward. 'It won't take long to load them in the car, Uncle Josh. I'll help.'

He looked unconvinced.

'Go on along, Uncle Josh,' Sadie coaxed as though the issue were closed. She boldly shooed him away with one hand. 'We'll see you at the country club in a few hours.'

Joshua Woolrich frowned. 'Bad timing all around to schedule this luncheon today.'

Claire grinned. 'Next time I arrange a charity luncheon, I'll check with Barre first to see if he's planning to ask me to marry him that day. He arranged this party, after all. Besides, I have plenty of time to get home.' She stepped forward and planted a light kiss on her father's cheek. 'I think it went really well — we solicited a lot of pledges. Thanks for letting us use the house. This tranquil setting put all the donors in a generous mood. And most of them aren't easily impressed.'

'Huh,' he grumbled. 'Most of them have more money than they could ever spend on themselves.'

She shook her head. 'Go on back to town. I'll be right behind you,' she promised.

'Don't be late tonight,' he instructed before reluctantly climbing into the T-bird. 'You know how particular Mrs Sutton is.'

She cocked an eyebrow. 'But it's not Barre's mother I'm marrying,' she noted.

Her cousin came up behind her. 'Thank your lucky stars for that!' she exclaimed.

Joshua Woolrich shot Sadie a disapproving glance before closing the car door and driving off. When he was gone, Claire turned to her cousin. 'You shouldn't provoke him,' she scolded, struggling to squelch her own amusement.

Sadie patted her thick mane of wavy brown hair. 'Somebody's gotta do it. Maybe you should once in a while. A little rebellion is healthy and normal. Besides, all of Middle Tennessee knows Aurora Sutton is a conniving biddy. Comes from spending too much time married to a pompous jerk like Denver.'

'Sadie! These are my prospective in-laws you're talking about,' Claire protested. Secretly, she loved her cousin's outspokenness and admired her gumption, even when she expressed opinions Claire disagreed with. Sadie was the closest thing she had to a sister. Claire didn't know how she would have managed without Sadie in her life.

Her cousin, looking as cool in her tailored mint-green suit as if she'd been born wearing it, was everything Claire strove to be. But poise, a flair for fashion, and social grace came naturally to Sadie, whereas Claire wrestled to avoid feeling awkward, blurting the wrong thing, or committing a fashion *faux pas*.

Now, Sadie pulled off her white high-heeled sandals, wriggling her newly-freed toes with their scarlet-painted nails against the hard-packed red dirt. 'I can't help what I think of them.'

'Barre's not like his parents. You seem to get along fine with him.'

'Barre's more subtle. Haven't quite pegged him yet. And are you sure you know him well enough? Sometimes he does strike me as overly preoccupied with himself. The rest of your life is a long time, sugar.'

Claire flexed her shoulders, absently pulling loose the pins from the tight French twist that was giving her a headache. A streamer of curly honey-gold hair spilled down her back to the small of her spine. 'Of course I'm sure. Barre's ambitious, requiring a certain amount of self-absorption,' she shot back.

Sadie studied her intently. 'Okay, don't get uppity about it. Just seems to me your dad and the Suttons have poured a lot of effort into throwing the two of you together. I know you, and if you go through with announcing your engagement tonight, you'll suffer in silence if you realize later you made a mistake.

'There's no mistake. Sadie, what are you trying to do?' Claire demanded. 'I'm happy for once and you're trying to stir up doubts. I love Barre. That's all that matters, isn't it?'

She couldn't help suspecting Sadie might be a tad jealous of Claire having been the first of them to find the right man. Sadie was the elder, three years older than Claire. Since their teenage years, they'd been good-natured rivals as well as best friends. Sadie, with her ample curves, sapphire eyes, and dark shining tresses, never lacked for dates. But she frequently bemoaned her failure at finding a man worth sacrificing her freedom for.

Since Sadie required no less than a composite of Tarzan, Keanu Reeves, and Socrates, she was setting herself up for failure, Claire reflected.

'Just make sure in your own mind you're doing this for your happiness and not your dad's,' Sadie requested. 'You deserve to be adored. Terrific job with the luncheon, by the way.'

'Thanks. Look, I'm not as vocal as Father, but I know my own mind,' Claire insisted. Nodding for emphasis, she glanced sideways and remembered Wheeler Scully was still standing there, mutely cradling her statue. Shame at her thoughtlessness washed through her. The thing must weigh a ton, although toting it hadn't seemed to exert him any more than carrying a loaf of bread. Damn, but the man could make himself invisible when he wanted to. Now he'd listened in on this confidential conversation, and although his expression was flat, her skin heated at what he must be thinking.

'I'll open the trunk,' she told him, keeping her voice even and avoiding his eyes.

Seeming to notice Wheeler for the first time, Sadie eyed him with mild curiosity. Claire had seen that look in her cousin's eyes before — she frequently used it when checking out bartenders, or waiters, or gardeners. Sadie claimed they were more macho and intriguing than the men she encountered within their own social circles. Still, it was the corporate executives, high-powered attorneys and plastic surgeons Sadie dated.

Claire's eyes flickered toward Wheeler. Yes, he was attractive in an unkempt sort of way. Her insides were churning annoyingly as a natural response to that. So what? As long as she didn't act on her feelings, she had nothing to feel guilty about. She'd pledged her heart to Barre.

Without looking at Wheeler, she unlocked the trunk of her four-year-old rose-colored Buick LeSabre. She felt the heat of his eyes on her. Damn him.

Sadie was gaping at the statue. 'You're giving that to Barre?' she asked incredulously.

'Yes, I am,' Claire replied, wary of defending the piece.

Sadie cast her a sly smile. 'Impressive. I wouldn't have thought you had it in you, kiddo.'

Claire noticed the corners of Wheeler's mouth curling upward, and to her mortification, she realized she might as well have hung up a banner announcing she'd slept with Barre. Well, they were practically engaged after all.

Flustered, she yanked open the trunk lid.

As she attempted to take the statue from Wheeler's arms, he moved to set it down. His leather-toughened arm grazed hers, the feathery hair tickling, then burning her skin.

25

Lightning flashed overhead. A booming thunderclap made her jump. Her arm bumped harder against his. The ensuing shock caused her to wonder whether lightning had struck her. Quickly regaining her bearings, she stepped back.

'I'll start bringing the ferns out,' Sadie volunteered.

'Thanks,' Claire called back, relieved at not being left at the house alone with Wheeler Scully to finish the task.

'Are you all right?' he asked.

Humiliated at his sensing her distress, she raised her eyes to his, expecting to see them mocking her. Instead, she found them surprisingly sincere and concerned, and they held her gaze. Her throat constricted and her heart raced. Would his lips be rough against hers? Or tender like the sweet nectar of candy beneath a hard outer shell? Her craving for a taste alarmed her.

'Yes.'

'Sorry. Didn't mean to knock into you,' he apologized.

Relief filtered though her as she comprehended he thought he'd jostled her and wasn't inquiring about the warmth spreading through her midsection.

Lightning splintered the sky. More angry thunder followed.

'Let's hurry, please,' Sadie called from halfway down the snaking brick pathway to the house. 'I don't want to get caught out here in a cloudburst.'

Apprehensively, Claire looked skyward.

'Could you help us, please, Mr Scully?' she asked the unsmiling man beside her. She began to comprehend how remote their location was. The closest neighbor lived a mile or so down the mountain.

With a grim nod, he headed toward the house. As they all made a concentrated effort, collecting the potted ferns didn't take long. Finally, Claire slammed her loaded trunk shut.

Digging in her leather pocketbook, she produced a bill and held it out to the caretaker. 'Thank you for your help, Mr Scully,' she said. Maybe with her tip he could get the haircut he so badly needed. She expected him to snatch it readily, and she was confused when he made no move for it.

His eyes darkened. 'You're welcome,' he grated. 'But give your money to the hospital. It'll be better spent.' Spinning on one boot-clad heel, he headed toward the house.

Incredulously, Claire retracted her hand. 'I was only tipping him,' she told Sadie helplessly.

Sadie shrugged. 'Don't worry about it,

27

Claire. I don't think he's got much use for human beings in general.'

Claire chewed her lip. 'Maybe I offended him. I should apologize,' she whipped around, but Sadie caught her by the arm.

'Forget it, kiddo. He doesn't want to be one of your causes, and if you try to adopt him, he's going to bring you trouble. Kind of intense for a handyman, isn't he? Besides, he's probably wanted by the cops for some heinous crime. Let's get out of here while the gettin's good, as they say.' She cast an anxious glance skyward. As if answering her, the first small, cold raindrops sprinkled them.

'You're right,' Claire agreed with a final nod. 'I suppose I should just leave him be.'

Sadie tucked her head under upraised hands and scooted into her fire-engine red BMW. ''Atta girl. *Ciao!*' she called.

Claire grinned. '*Ciao!*' she called back before climbing into her own car. Once inside, she sank back thoughtfully against the seat. She waved as Sadie took off. Shaking her damp hair back, she took a deep, calming breath. The main house, as well as the small caretaker's cottage off to one side, appeared deserted now. She saw no movement, no sign of Wheeler Scully aside from a single yellow light in the cottage. What was he doing in there?

Nothing that was any of her business. Remembering how she'd trembled inwardly in his presence, she was glad Sadie had stopped her from going after him. Nothing on this earth would have made her go near that unsettling man again. What truly troubled her was no man had ever made her feel before as though she were melting from the inside out, like chocolate in a microwave. Not even — and she would never admit this to a soul — gorgeous, personable Barre Sutton, the man she loved and had given her virginity to.

She was sure some rational explanation existed for her sudden savage urges. Pre-wedding jitters most likely. A test of her loyalty to Barre.

With a heavy sigh, she focused on a vision of herself in her new sling-back dress, dancing in Barre's arms tonight. Yes, once she got back to Barre, she'd know in her heart everything was going to be all right. Except when she tried to reassure herself by envisioning Barre's face, Wheeler Scully's roguish countenance maliciously manifested in its stead.

Her preoccupation with the rough-hewn caretaker and his open contempt for everything she believed in disturbed her. Life came with certain social responsibilities.

People who trivialized obligations hurt others through sheer indifference. Her own experience made that woefully clear. Mr Scully wanted everybody to go away and leave him alone, so he deserved his own miserable company. None of her concern.

She turned the key in the ignition, relieved to feel the strong, steady hum of the engine kick to life. The last thing she needed was to be stranded up here, with nothing to do but beg Mr Scully for a ride down the mountain. How he might love gloating over such a predicament, pouncing on the opportunity to bring her down yet another notch or two. She told herself to forget the ornery man.

Still, she couldn't help wondering why a strong, intelligent, attractive man believed he didn't merit her concern.

Rain sheeted across the windshield, and she half-wished she hadn't bothered with the ferns. Navigating down the mountainside would be rough. But she didn't want to wait out the storm in her car, nor was going back an option.

Stay up here alone with Mr Scully? No way!

By the time she started her car crawling down the road, she could scarcely see two feet in front of the bumper.

Her heart leapt into her throat as a

blinding flash illuminated the car's interior. A deafening crash shook the earth. The mountain fell away beneath the tires.

Praying as she dug teeth into her soft bottom lip almost hard enough to draw blood, she smashed on the brake and felt the car sliding sideways. With a sickening helplessness, she realized she might very well be at one of the many points where the shoulder dropped off into eternity. In her mind, she saw Father and Barre and all their friends waiting in their evening wear at the country club while she lay lifeless at the foot of the mountain.

She closed her eyes. How bad would it hurt to die? Perhaps she could endure the pain, but she wasn't ready for her own extinction. She had things to do, appointments to keep.

At the clattering of metal, she grew absurdly concerned over the sound of Barre's statue shattering in the trunk. Her life smashing into pieces. Her distress lasted only an instant. Then blackness numbed her, and she ceased to worry about anything.

2

The light, persistent fragrance of gardenias tormented him, a mocking reminder of all the joys beyond his grasp — the soft feel of a woman's body tucked beneath his, a tentative, affectionate touch.

Turning away from the window, Wheeler stripped off his T-shirt and tossed it on the threadbare, ugly dark-gold sofa as he crossed through his tiny living room to the kitchen. This had been a bad day all around — first the invasion of the snooty upper crust into his wooded refuge, then spoiled Miss Pollyanna Woolrich encouraging him to better himself.

Wheeler snickered inwardly. Him of all people. Been there. Done that. Had his fill of high-handed wheeling and dealing. Liked it better here with no one to bother him.

Still, her misguided concern stirred something inside him he'd buried along with his past life. As hard as he tried, he couldn't shake the stubborn image of those wide, clover-green eyes, delicate features fringed in golden curls, the small puckered mouth the color of rose petals. She carried her long, slender body with the grace of a deer picking its way through the woods.

He remembered how agonizingly delightful her subtle curves had felt briefly pressed to his torso. Like touching a butterfly's wing. The small, taut breasts straining through crisp cotton and the tiny dip of her waist had triggered fierce male longings he'd repressed for a long time.

Lord, she'd smelled so good he could have taken a bite out of her. His loins had clamped miserably each time she'd come near him. Any other woman, he might have suspected of flaunting herself intentionally, but Ms Woolrich seemed unaware of the exquisite torture she'd inflicted.

For the past nine months, he'd worked at avoiding human contact. People you trusted betrayed you. It wasn't worth the risk. Now, suddenly, a brief encounter with a beautiful woman had him aching for the most fundamental contact.

He'd had to remind himself he was her father's lowly hired hand, and she was off limits. Even if he'd been inclined to pursue her — which he wasn't. Why should he care if she planned to marry a cutthroat like Barre Sutton?

Wheeler knotted his hand into a fist. He'd once mistaken Barre for a friend. He'd learned the hard way Barre cared only for himself. And the thought of gentle Claire Woolrich loving a two-faced devil like Barre until she grew as cold and bitter inside as he was grated on him.

He should have warned her.

No, he couldn't have. Not without explaining where he'd come from and how he knew Barre. And, blinded by love, she wouldn't have believed him. That stupid statue told him more about their relationship than he wanted to know. Picturing her with Barre was like seeing a flower garden steamrolled. Except Barre was too clever to show his true self.

Even back in college he'd had all the professors snowed while he paid brighter students to do his work. Back then, Barre's antics had been amusing. Before Wheeler realized how far his former friend would go.

Again he cautioned himself to mind his own business. But he couldn't forget Claire's concern. For crying out loud, there was nothing he could do about it. She was a grown woman who obviously knew her own mind.

Still, he couldn't help thinking if she never made it back to Nashville tonight, it would be the best thing that could happen to her.

But he realized nothing was going to put Barre off if he'd made up his mind to have her. Joshua Woolrich was one of the richest men on the Eastern seaboard, and even if his daughter had been homely she'd have been a good catch in Barre's greedy eyes.

Attempting to banish Claire from his mind, Wheeler flipped on the kitchen light in concession to the unnatural darkness outside, then swung open the refrigerator door. Locating a lone can of beer on the top shelf, he extracted it, leaning over the door and pausing to roll the cool metal across his forehead before he popped the top. Foam spewed onto his hand, and he wiped the dampness on the side of his jeans.

Tilting back his head, he downed a long swig of the cold, bitter brew. He swiped his mouth with the back of his hand. Too bad he hadn't had time to get to the store. This would be a good night to put away a couple of six packs. Lately, many nights had proved suitable for what was rapidly becoming his favorite pastime. Well, no beer-runs down the mountain in this crap. He'd have to find some other way to dull his senses.

At least he had his wish. Thank God the

last of the intruders were gone. Woolrich seldom came up here, and this was the first time he'd brought visitors.

Soon the place would be constantly overrun with bored, overprivileged city dwellers, who would not only disrupt Wheeler's peace but increase his chances of being recognized. A few more weeks maybe, and he'd have to move on. He regretted that, since he liked it here, and Woolrich left him to himself.

No one had paid much attention to him until this afternoon when Claire Woolrich had appointed herself his mentor. He'd almost liked her before she held out that damn twenty-dollar bill. He hadn't minded helping, admired her determination to keep a promise even when it proved inconvenient. And then instead of a word of thanks, she'd offered money, emphasizing for the second time the inequalities in their positions. She didn't see him for who he was after all. The insult struck him like a hammer blow. Well, her majesty could keep her cash. That bill represented the distance between them. Maybe she was more like Barre than he wanted to believe.

He slammed the refrigerator door so hard the floor shook. He would never get used to acting meek and ingratiating to anyone. But he had to have money to live and a place to stay. He wasn't up to starting over.

Rain pelted the roof overhead. Wheeler assured himself he'd soon drive Claire's distracting floral scent out of his head. And her along with it. He didn't want to give a damn about what happened to her. He'd already failed to watch his own back — he surely wasn't capable of covering anyone else's.

Returning to the cracker-box living room, he was about to pull off his boots and turn on the stereo when the ominous crash shook the cottage. He recognized the sickening, snapping sound. Looking out the front window, he didn't see any downed trees. Still, he had the gnawing feeling something bad had happened, and he couldn't get comfortable until he checked it out. Joshua Woolrich didn't pay Wheeler much. But when Wheeler committed himself to any job, he took his responsibilities seriously.

With a resigned sigh, he set down the almost-empty beer can. After retrieving his T-shirt and pulling it over his head, he went to the hall closet for his yellow slicker.

At least everyone who had been here this afternoon should have gotten safely down the mountain before this hit. As much as highbrows irritated him, he didn't wish anyone harm.

Claire was still on his mind. He'd been watching out the window as she'd gotten in her car and sat behind the wheel, staring into space a long while before finally leaving. For an instant, he'd feared she was going to come back. He wasn't sure he'd have the strength to resist her a second time.

His own dull disappointment when she finally cranked the engine and drove away surprised him. She'd brought him back to life for a short while. Now he felt flat and dispirited. Even that signaled a change from his normal numb resignation.

Fastening the slicker and pulling the hood over his head, he opened the door and was immediately doused by slanting sheets of rain. Shielding his eyes with one hand, he trekked slowly across the lawn. His boot heels sank into the gooey red mud.

He told himself he was checking his boss's property, but he headed straight down the long, snaking drive. Claire had driven off only an instant before the jarring crash, he realized, calculating the amount of time walking from his front window to the refrigerator required. Not much.

The wind howled and shrieked, and thunder ricocheted across the mountains. He was sure he'd end up feeling like a fool for doing this, probably walking all the way to the road to find nothing. Oh well, nobody around to see him doing this. He wanted to be sure she'd gotten off safely.

Scaling the last curve on the drive and heading down the steep incline, he stopped short at seeing, some twenty feet ahead, a mammoth tree lying across the roadway, leaves and splintered branches strewn everywhere. Sticking out of the ditch on the wrong side of the pavement was the deep pink car he'd watched Claire Woolrich climb into. It was turned in the opposite direction, pointed back toward the house.

'Sweet Jesus!' he declared, racing toward the car, flinging the door open and finding it ominously empty. Had she been thrown? No, couldn't be. Windshield was intact and windows were rolled up. Where had she disappeared to?

Sweeping his glance around the perimeter of the woods, he spotted her leaning against a tree a few feet away, perched on one foot like a flamingo. Her wet dress was plastered to her skin, the white background sheer enough now to reveal bra and panties and intriguing contours, a sight that would have keenly captured his interest if he hadn't been scared out of his wits at seeing her car in the ditch, if he wasn't so relieved to find her seemingly unscathed. Muddy red rivulets streamed down her skirt, arms, and legs, as though she'd been crawling on the ground.

Her face was pale and drawn, and she stared past him as he approached her.

'Miz Woolrich?' he asked gently, clasping her shoulder. Gingerly, he looked her over, checking for obvious wounds. No gashes or blood, aside from a swollen bottom lip and bruises on her arms and legs.

'Are you hurt?' he shouted over the rain, leaning close. 'What's wrong with your leg?'

She studied his face, then looked idly downward. 'My ankle,' she said thickly, wincing. 'I turned it. I was trying to walk back to the house and fell. It won't hold my weight.'

Wheeler tore off his slicker, exposing himself to the rain. He wrapped it around her, despite the fact she was already drenched. He scooped her into his arms. Although she was cold and trembling, she made a feeble attempt to wrest free.

'What are you doing?' she demanded.

'I'm only taking you back to the house,' he promised gently, understanding she was shaken from the accident. Did she realize how narrowly she'd escaped being under that tree when it fell? He didn't want to think about that.

She raised her head, her face inches from

his. 'I have to be in Nashville by eight,' she insisted.

Wheeler rolled his eyes. It was all he could do to keep from depositing her in the nearest puddle. A near-death encounter and all she could think of was getting back to Barre on time?

'You're safer here,' he snapped. Taking a last look at the fallen tree across the road, he spun with her still in his arms. There was only one way up or down this mountain. And the downed tree blocked it now.

Clasping her close to his chest, then slanting forward to shield her from the pelting rain, he dashed toward the house.

'I can't be late.'

'Yeah, well, welcome to the real world, Princess. You're gonna miss the tardy bell. It looks like you and I are stuck here with each other for a while. Believe me, I'm not crazy about the idea either. And listen, the room service sucks.'

★   ★   ★

Dazed, Claire listened to Wheeler mutter something about room service, and she thought that sounded good right now — a nice bowl of steaming hot gumbo and a dry blanket and she'd be fine. Colored lights

41

flashed in her head, and she struggled to remember what had happened.

The constant jogging made her realize she was being carried. How odd it felt to be moving along without her feet on the ground. Closing her eyes, she sank back in his strong arms, thinking how secure and tight they felt. She smelled beer, but she hadn't been drinking. She nestled her head against his massive, muscular chest, forgetting in her confusion who he was.

In the back of her mind, panic prodded her as she remembered earlier fantasizing about having this man carry her off somewhere. Now he was, and the prospect excited and scared her.

Through her fog, she realized he was indeed taking her to his lair. In her daydream she hadn't dared to imagine what might happen once they reached it. Ready or not, she supposed she was about to find out.

★　★　★

Standing in the living room of his cottage with the woman in his arms, Wheeler debated over what to do with her. Water, streaming off their clothing, pooled on the wooden floor. He knew she couldn't stand up, but he didn't want to get the furniture wet and he didn't

42

think she'd take too well to being set on the floor. Finally, he decided on the kitchen.

Reaching it, he eased her down into one of the straight-back vinyl chairs at the table.

As he straightened, she stared up at him with those green eyes — as wide as headlights now. Her hair hung limply over her shoulders like a mop, and drops of water peppered her face. Her lips were blue, her teeth chattering. The temperature had dropped slightly after the rain started falling, but he guessed she was chilled more from nerves than the air.

He leaned back against the counter, trying to decide what to do with her next. She was quietly looking over the small, functional room, and Wheeler noted she was the first woman to invade his little hideaway. Entertaining wasn't high on his list of priorities these days.

He towered over her, taking time to appreciate how the wet fabric clung to her chest, two firm mounds straining beneath a lacy white bra as she breathed. It had been a long time since he'd held anything so soft and smooth against him, and the pinching in his loins had eased only slightly since he set her down. Gosh, she needed out of those wet clothes.

He fought to stave off his desire. He couldn't offhand recall the last time he'd even contemplated having a woman. Just his luck to start feeling horny around this particular one. Joshua Woolrich was no humanitarian, but he had given Wheeler a job and a place to stay, treated him fairly, and Wheeler wasn't about to betray the older man's confidence. Maybe the idea of stealing her from Barre enhanced her appeal to him.

Besides, if demure Ms Woolrich knew of his reaction to her, she might run — or hobble — back out in the storm to hide. She wasn't the type to be that grateful for his bringing her in out of the elements. She'd want to reward him with something meaningless to her, like cash.

Staring down at her, he remembered how disoriented she'd been outside. He stooped to peer into her eyes. 'You're in my kitchen,' he told her.

She smiled tentatively. Despite the swollen lip and smeared make-up, she was remarkably pretty.

Restraining his urge to trace her smile with his fingertip, he did it with his eyes instead. 'Are you all right, Miz Woolrich?'

She gave him a worried, blank look. 'No, I don't think so. Just give me a minute, okay?' She dropped her forehead into her palms.

Wheeler stood over her, his brow knit. Allowing her time to compose herself, he explained, 'You were in an accident. Your car ran off the road. You're safe now. Okay?'

She raised her head. Her eyes scanned the room nervously then settled back on him. 'You do have a phone here, don't you?' she asked.

'In the bedroom,' he replied.

Color rose to her cheeks. Then, she raised her chin. 'Could you bring it here? I must use it, please.'

He laughed. 'It doesn't move, Princess. Your daddy didn't equip this place with cordless phones. There's one jack, and it's in the bedroom. And no, I'm not going to limp you in there. I don't care to have my bed drenched, since I plan to sleep in it tonight. You've got to get those wet clothes off.'

The green eyes narrowed. 'I have to get to Nashville — '

'By eight,' he finished for her. 'Tell me the number and I'll make your call for you. Perhaps your boyfriend can have you airlifted out.'

She looked distressed, and he felt a pinch of sympathy. After all, living a privileged life wasn't her fault.

'I was hoping you might know of a back road.'

'The one you were on — that was it. And even if your car is drivable, it's going to take a tow truck to pull it out of that ditch.'

She appeared undaunted. 'Well, I'm sure if there's a way, Barre will find it. He's quite ingenious.'

Ingenious. Wheeler had another word for it. He scowled. The sooner he got her back to her precious Barre, the better.

'Works miracles, does he?'

'Barre can do anything he sets his mind to. As I was trying to explain earlier . . . '

No, Barre gets anything he sets his mind on, Wheeler reflected. 'If you tell me the number, I'll call him for you.'

She looked startled. 'If you have some paper, I'll write it down.'

'Just tell me. I'll remember it.'

She gave him the number, and he stormed off to the bedroom, the wet soles of his boots squeaking against the floor. The last thing he needed was Barre coming up here. He couldn't imagine Barre braving nature's fury for anyone. Ahh, but for a fine catch such as this . . . he'd be here.

Wheeler lifted the receiver of the ancient rotary phone on the nightstand, pressing it to his ear and hearing only a distant snap, crackle, pop.

'Damn!' he muttered, slamming the phone down.

'Mr Scully? What's wrong?'

Wheeler returned to the kitchen, helping himself to another long, admiring look at her creamy cleavage. If he was to be responsible for his actions, he needed to get her out of that see-through garment.

Fast.

'Phone's dead,' he informed her.

The corners of her mouth drooped. 'My cell phone's in my car,' she mused.

In the ensuing silence, the wind whipped at the walls of the small structure. The rain was beating down in a torrent.

'You gonna go get it?' he asked.

She bit her lower lip and looked away from him. 'No, I suppose not.'

If she'd been trying to reach anyone but Barre, he would have felt sorry for her. 'I'll get it for you as soon as the rain stops.'

Her mouth took on a hard set, and for the second time he gleaned something of her father in her. 'That could be hours!' she lamented.

He met her glare with one of his own. 'Look, I don't mind getting wet. But there's lightning and falling trees involved here. It may not have occurred to you, but even though I don't follow the philosophies of Denver Sutton, I do value my meager existence. And the phone's not going to make any difference. It could be days before the county gets up here to clear that tree off the road.'

Her expression conveyed total distress. Oh damn, she was getting to him again. What a joke! Him feeling sorry for her.

'Oh, hell. I'll go.' He reached for his slicker.

Just when he was working up a good mad, she sounded contrite. 'No, don't. I'm sorry, Mr Scully. I don't know what I was thinking. I'm grateful you came by when you did. I'm truly not so selfish I expect you to run back out into the storm. And this must be an unwelcome disruption in your plans. What did bring you out?'

'I heard a crash, and thought I'd better check it out. I'm paid to look after your father's property.'

She looked up at him with a glance so inquisitive and penetrating he felt as though his clothing were transparent.

'I'm no hero,' he denied quickly.

'You're no groundskeeper either, Mr Scully. What are you hiding from up here?'

'It's peaceful, Miz Woolrich. Usually. You always ask so many questions?'

Her look darkened. 'Sorry. I shouldn't pry.'

He regretted snapping at her, but whether he liked it or not, he was obviously going to have company for the next few hours, and the more distance between them the better. The first thing he needed to do was get her properly covered. Maybe then he'd stop contemplating peeling her out of that soggy dress.

'I'll find you something dry to wear,' he offered, turning away.

'I don't want to put you to any trouble,' she qualified.

It wasn't trouble, it was self-defense.

'Trouble's not an issue. I don't need you getting hypothermic on me.'

Once again, he went to the bedroom, rummaging through both his closet and dresser, wondering what in blazes he had that might cover her. Finally, at the bottom of the drawer, he unearthed the cotton pajamas Jillian had given him one Christmas a lifetime ago. His other lifetime. He wondered why he'd kept them, since he'd never worn them and usually slept in the buff or, on cold nights, in his boxers.

He grabbed the PJs and a couple of towels, then returned to the kitchen.

'Best I could do,' he grumbled as he handed her the bundle.

'Thank you,' she said, accepting his offering and setting it on the table. Looking apprehensive, she latched onto the tabletop with one hand and the back of the chair with the other, struggling to get to her feet.

Remembering her ankle, he glanced down, worried to see it badly swollen.

'Need some help?' he asked.

Teetering, she smiled bravely. 'I can manage,' she insisted.

Wheeler stood back. Was she that independent or did she just find his coming near her abhorrent?

On her feet now, clutching the tabletop with both hands, she looked perplexed as she eyed the pajamas and towels.

Wheeler had half a mind to leave her to her own resources, but as it was, more of her slinky, appealing curves were visible now, and he was impatient to remove her from his sight.

He stepped forward, grabbing the towels in one hand and tucking her under the curve of his arm. A flood of unwanted warmth shot through him at holding her slender, fragile form against him. He couldn't help wondering how those rose-petal pink lips might taste. Like cotton candy or strawberry jam maybe.

'Lean against me,' he commanded, feeling her resistance ebb as she did so.

Painstakingly, he began leading her toward the bathroom.

'You are going to be able to dress yourself, aren't you?' he asked.

'Absolutely,' she shot back so quickly,

Wheeler had to smother a laugh. He sensed she'd die trying before accepting his assistance in that area. A wise woman at that. He'd never been the kind of guy who could look at something he liked without touching, and he hadn't seen anything so appealing in a very long time.

Leaving her on her own, Wheeler retreated to the bedroom to shed his own drenched clothing. When he finished changing, she was still in the bathroom, and he considered inquiring whether she was all right. Then he thought the better of it and went to the kitchen to make coffee. This had already been a long day, and if his hunches were right, the night stretched ahead even longer. He'd have to keep his wits sharp to figure out how to get his uninvited guest back on her way and out of his.

3

He can't be such a tough guy if he wears cotton pajamas, Claire decided, studying her reflection in the tiny rectangular mirror over the medicine cabinet. The steel-gray fabric hung over her like a circus tent on a pole, sleeves extending beyond her fingertips and the legs bunching over her feet like the bellbottoms she'd seen in old photographs.

To her dismay, she found her undergarments soaked through, and she couldn't very well put on dry clothing over wet bra and panties. While she felt uncomfortable, she admitted she couldn't expect him to have produced women's underwear. Still, she felt terribly vulnerable this way. She'd never worn anyone's clothing but her own and to have something of his against her skin was disturbingly intimate.

Claire strained to discern whether the pajamas covered her adequately. She'd suffer endless humiliation to think he could see through her clothes!

She felt dry and warmer although her hair was still damp, and it would take hours for the thick mass to dry on its own. If only he had a blow-dryer. She glanced around the tiny, tile-floored bathroom. Not seeing one, she hesitated to call out to him and ask, fearing he'd barge in. There was scarcely room enough for her to negotiate without him climbing over her. And her body warmed so unsettlingly at the slightest contact with that long, lean body. She wondered if a woman responded more strongly to all men once she slept with one. She hadn't experienced this reaction with anyone else though. She read *Cosmo* faithfully and had never seen this phenomenon mentioned.

Her body should be tingling for Barre, not this stranger. She told herself it was. Her reactions resulted from transference, in light of Barre's absence. Why else would she find Wheeler so appealing? Claire closed her eyes. She'd never wondered before whether one man's lovemaking technique might be as unique as the way he put on his socks. Now, she burned with curiosity as to how Wheeler might approach a woman. Purely intellectual curiosity, she assured herself.

'The first time is always awkward,' Sadie

had advised once. 'Believe me, it gets better after you're used to each other. Like breaking in new shoes.'

Claire believed with all her heart that would happen. She was devoted to Barre, the man who would soon become her husband. And she didn't want anyone else. Afterward, he'd apologized for letting things get out of hand and promised her it wouldn't happen again before their wedding night. Claire, masking her bewildered disappointment, hadn't protested.

After waiting over a quarter of a century, was it too much to expect bells ringing and fireworks exploding and confetti falling? Geeze, it was sex not a parade. She'd ruined that first time for herself with her own nervousness, she decided. And Barre, bless him, had been too gallant to mention her failings.

In her early teens she'd resolved to abstain from lovemaking outside of a permanent relationship, never dreaming her own inexperience might someday become a burden. But she'd had good reason to wait, unconventional as her decision sometimes seemed.

With a heavy sigh, Claire raised a tentative hand to the medicine cabinet. She wasn't snooping, just looking for a hairbrush.

What was a man like Wheeler doing up

here all by himself? With his cool handsomeness, he should have had no problem finding someone to love him. He wasn't even really as rude as he tried to pretend. His modest quarters were clean and spartan — the bathroom smelled of pine cleaner, and the chipped porcelain, although bearing ancient stains, sparkled.

Father should have fixed up this cabin if he expected a human being to inhabit it. Why hadn't a man as assertive as Wheeler insisted on improvements? Hmm. Father could be intimidating. Hadn't she relied on Sadie's intervention when she'd argued with him about the ferns earlier?

With her hand on the medicine cabinet's door, she scanned the shelves. Not much here — no condoms or prescription drugs, just a bottle of generic Ibuprofen, a razor, shaving cream, a box of bandages, toothpaste and dental floss. On the top shelf sat a half-full bottle of the same rich musky aftershave her father was so fond of wearing, 'Static'.

This stuff came at no small price, a strange indulgence for a man who lived so sparsely. Perhaps an admirer had given it to Wheeler. He had to have had a life before he came here. Or maybe Father had left it behind in the main house after one of his visits and Wheeler had pilfered it.

Was he a thief? She remembered what Father had hinted about his shady past. For all she really knew, he could top the FBI's most wanted list. And here she was in Wheeler's jammies and nothing else, far removed from the safety of civilization.

Heaven above, into whose whose hands had she fallen? Considering her limited options at the moment, she'd have to hope he was a decent, honorable man.

As she remembered, his were firm yet gentle hands that had held her securely. Wheeler Scully didn't seem overly fond of her, but intuitively, she sensed he wouldn't hurt her. She'd felt a respectful restraint in his touch. Of course, as he pointed out, he received wages for safeguarding Joshua Woolrich's property, and she supposed, in his mind, that must include her.

The sudden pounding on the door made her jump, and she nearly fell as she landed full force on her injured limb. She caught hold of the sink to brace herself, then slammed the cabinet shut.

'You all right in there, Princess?'

She wished he'd stop calling her that. 'Yes,' she replied. *At least, I was, anyway.* 'I'm just brushing my hair, thank you.' She'd been delaying emerging and facing him again. Her hand was shaking, and not just from the cold.

Still, he didn't go away. 'You're not sick, are you?'

'No,' she answered.

'I made some coffee.' Coffee. So that's what that wonderful smell was. 'Need any help?'

'No.' She fired back her answer before she stopped to realize he was baiting her again. Damn it. Through the door, she could have sworn she heard him snicker.

Carefully cleaning her stray hairs out of the brush she'd found, she replaced it in the cabinet. Shame crept through her at poking through his belongings and automatically assuming he'd steal from her family. Awkwardly, she gathered her wet clothes, then took a deep breath and swung the door open, half expecting to find him standing there.

He wasn't. He'd disappeared. One hand against the wall, she swung herself toward the kitchen.

Standing at the counter, Wheeler turned suddenly, looking startled to see her approaching. Before she could protest, he rushed toward her, taking the wad of wet clothing from her hand and depositing it atop the stereo cabinet. She glanced uncertainly at the personal items he was taking charge of.

'Here,' he said, his voice oddly smooth and, for once, kind. 'Settle in on the sofa. Put that leg up.'

He guided her toward the sofa, and once more she found herself leaning against his hot, hard muscles, soaking in his scent. Her unbound breast mashed against his side, spearing heat through her chest. Claire shivered at the unexpected surge, and apparently mistaking her reaction for a chill, he gripped her more tightly, fueling her distress.

When at last he deposited her on the sofa cushions, she sank back in relief. As she attempted to situate herself, he disappeared, returning quickly with two pillows.

'Here,' he offered, his hand searing her back to cinders as he wedged the pillows behind it.

Gratefully, she relaxed. Such a small effort, and she felt truly exhausted.

'Thank you,' she said, embarrassed at the fuss.

His face hovered over hers briefly, and she found herself locked in his gaze. She liked his clean, male scent and the warmth that radiated from him. His jaw was cut in a fine square line, and his nose slanted at a neat angle. Up close, his face was even more compelling than she'd imagined earlier. His breath grazed her cheek, and she realized that was where the smell of beer was coming from.

'You've been drinking.' Her thoughts spilled into words.

He shrugged. 'Not much else to do up here. Don't worry, Princess, I only had one beer and my brain is still functioning.'

'I can see you're not drunk,' she countered. 'And if we're going to spend any length of time together, I'd appreciate it if you'd not call me Princess.'

She longed to turn her eyes away, because she feared he might guess her reckless thoughts of wondering how his kiss might feel.

His eyes danced, and she grudgingly admired how the smallest things delighted him.

'Excuse me — Miz Woolrich.'

'Claire is fine.'

'Claire.' He said her name as though describing a new flavor of ice cream he'd tasted, and the sound rippled through her unsettlingly.

Finally, she did look away.

'Has the storm let up any?' she asked, longing for the comfort of home and familiar faces.

'No,' he answered, jolting her as he

dropped to his knees, then swiftly and none too gently took hold of her tender ankle.

'Youch!' she protested.

'Sorry,' he muttered, neither looking at her nor releasing his hold on her ankle, squeezing her flesh in a distracted way that made her want to kick him. Hot flames licked the inside of her leg at the intimate contact, despite the soreness. Her midsection churned with a fierce, incomprehensible ache.

'No broken bones,' he announced happily. 'Just wrenched.'

Scowling, Claire knit her brow. As if she couldn't have told him that without his prodding and probing. 'I should think I'd have known if there were,' she clipped.

Ignoring her, he disappeared, returning in a few minutes with a rolled cloth bandage. Refocusing his attention on the ankle, he used both hands to raise her pajama leg without stopping to ask permission. Claire squeezed the sofa cushions at the intense sensations moistening her in the most private of places.

'I can do that,' she insisted, bowing forward to snatch the bandage from his hands. God, if she allowed him to finish, she'd have been moaning and writhing on the sofa before he was done.

He gave her a hurt look, then quickly

hardened it and dropped into the armchair beside the sofa.

'I suppose my bedside manner could use some improvement,' he conceded.

'Mr Scully, you have no bedside manner. What did you do before you came to work here?' she asked. 'Meat-packing comes to mind.'

'There you go with the questions again. What difference does it make?' he asked defensively.

'I was making an observation, not expecting an answer. Your secrets remain safe.'

She finished wrapping the ankle and pulled the pantleg down. She looked up to find him plunging his bare foot into a white cotton sock.

He glanced up before she realized she was staring.

'What's wrong?' he asked.

'Do you always put your socks on in the living room?'

'Yeah. As a matter of fact. Sometimes I put them on in the kitchen. Look, if it offends you . . . '

'No, no. Just pretend I'm not here.'

He did.

After a long, uncomfortable silence, Claire relented. 'Since it appears I'm going to spend the duration of my engagement party with you, I don't think I'm asking too much to know a little of your background.'

'Just because we're stuck here right now doesn't mean we have to get chummy.'

She swung her glance around the cabin. 'There doesn't seem to be much space here to avoid each other.'

'Isn't,' he agreed.

She stared at the sofa cushion. 'This is an odd color upholstery,' she noted. 'Amber, I'd say, wouldn't you?'

'Mustard's more like it. Your old man's interior decorator must have been wearing sunglasses the day she picked it out. Or else she wanted to stay true to the pre-twenty-first-century don't-care motif.'

Claire ignored his ranting. 'Actually, I expected you'd say it's green for the sake of argument.'

He cast her a low, grudging smile. 'All right. You made your point. I'll play. You get one question. Then I ask you one.'

'Well . . . '

'Look, Miz . . . Claire. I put in a full day catering to your rich guests. I'm on my own time now, not yours. I'm not obligated to answer any of your questions. Especially if you're not answering mine.'

She eyed him evenly. 'All right. I have nothing to hide, as I'm sure you don't. I'll answer your question. I'll even let you ask yours first if you like. So you'll know I'm not going to back down.'

He shook his head. 'Ladies first.'

Typical male chauvinist, she assessed, bristling. 'Why do you want to stay up here?'

'Because I don't trust people anymore, and maybe if you took those lollipop glasses of yours off for a while, you'd start seeing people for what they really are.'

'I feel sorry for you, being so bitter. Something terrible must have happened to you . . . '

'The last thing I want is your sympathy, Princess. And I believe it's my turn now.'

She held her neck stiffly, sure his question would be rude and invasive. She braced herself for it.

He didn't fail her. 'Why are you so afraid to stand up to your father?'

'I am not afraid of Father!'

'I saw you with him. You leap through flaming hoops to win his approval.'

She turned away. 'My father has high expectations of the people close to him. You should know that — you work for him.'

'I do my job. I would for any employer.'

'And for your own father? Haven't you ever wanted to please him out of respect?'

'My father died a long time ago.'

'Oh. I'm so sorry.'

His expression set like concrete. 'No need. He really didn't much give a damn what I accomplished, as long as I stayed out of his way. Anything I did, I did on my own.'

She couldn't believe he cared as little as he professed. 'He was still your father. You must miss him, no matter what kind of man he was.'

'Like I said, he's dead. It was your old man we were discussing. You act plenty like him. Must be the genes.' He had not meant it as a compliment.

Claire's eyes narrowed, then her chin jutted out. 'Despite his faults, my father lives by his principles, and I admire him for that. But any similarities you see in us are definitely not hereditary. The Woolriches are not my biological parents.'

'No kidding? You're adopted?'

'It's no secret.'

'I wondered why you didn't look like your father.'

She raised an eyebrow. 'Did you?'

'Ah, no secret, but still a touchy subject?'

'You owe me a few more answers.'

He rose, stretching his long form. 'Considering our extenuating circumstances, why don't you just call me Wheeler, Claire? And no one forced you to answer. I don't owe you anything. Coffee?'

64

She gaped indignantly. 'P-please,' she stammered finally, outraged by his arrogance and trickery.

As he disappeared into the kitchen, she took a long, deep breath. What could anyone have done to wound a man so physically powerful so deeply that he retreated from society? Because he had saved her, she yearned to offer him some hope, some comfort. But obviously, he'd locked away the part of himself willing to accept anything from anybody. And he seemed especially hostile toward the rich.

He returned briefly, a mug of steaming black coffee in each hand. Gratefully, she accepted the one he gave her. She carefully avoided touching his hand.

'Thank you.'

'I would have asked you how you take it,' he ventured. 'But I don't have milk or sugar anyway.'

She blew on it and took a sip. 'This is fine,' she insisted. It wasn't gumbo, but it was warming.

He stood looking down at her. 'Is something wrong?' she asked.

'No. I'll go throw your clothes in the washer out back.'

'You shouldn't bother. The dress is ruined. The red mud never comes out of white things.'

Reaching for the clothing, he shrugged. 'Somehow, I'd rather have you wearing a dry, stained dress when your old man comes for you than my pajamas. Do you really think he might not jump to the wrong conclusion?'

Her face flushed. 'Of course not. I'll explain everything.'

He shook his head. 'Sure. Look, I like this job. I don't want to lose it just now.'

He left the room, and a few seconds later she heard the distant churning of a washing machine.

He returned, and she studied the length of his blue jeans, his olive-colored cotton shirt. 'I realize I've disrupted your plans for the evening, Mr . . . Wheeler. Please, just do what you'd normally do if I weren't here. And if you have something to say about my father, perhaps you should say it to his face.'

For an instant, he looked almost remorseful. 'I'm sorry. I was out of line,' he agreed. 'As for my plans . . . ' He reached over and turned on the television. The screen was blank. 'Sh — ' He glanced at her, biting off his epithet. 'Cable's out.'

Claire cradled her forehead in one hand. 'What next?' she declared.

'We wait.' He gestured her way with his head. 'How long did it take you to grow your hair that long?'

She tossed a handful of it aside. 'I don't remember.'

'Why didn't you tell your father how angry I made you earlier?'

'Well, I . . . what makes you think I was angry?'

'You were burning to tattle. What kept you from it?'

'Because he would have fired you.'

He studied her evenly. 'Listen, it may take a while, but I will get you out of here one way or the other, Prin — Miz Woolrich.'

'Claire,' she reminded him. 'Ms Woolrich is a tad formal for someone wearing your jammies.'

'I've never worn them — in case you're worried about fleas or anything.'

Deliberately, she scratched at her sleeve. He watched her, then turned his eyes away, but not quick enough to hide the flicker of amusement playing behind them.

'Why do you have clothes you've never worn?'

'Somebody gave them to me. Listen, why don't you just keep them? That should remove the stigma of your wearing my pajamas.'

'You might get cold some night.'

He averted his gaze. 'Cold doesn't bother me much.'

'What does bother you?

'Shh.'

At first she thought he was about to swear again. Realizing she was being shushed, Claire stiffened her spine defensively. Then, seeing him crane his neck as he listened intently and his mouth burrowed into a deep frown, she perceived something was terribly wrong.

Rapid-fire lightning strikes illuminated the room like a short-circuited strobe light. Claire heard no accompanying thunder. The rat-a-tat-tat of hailstones battered the roof like machine-gun fire. But it must have been the lower, mournful wailing Wheeler was tuned in to, the sound of a big train approaching rapidly in the distance. Confused, she realized there were no railroad tracks up here.

Her ears perked up, and her insides froze.

'Come on,' he ordered.

When she failed to move, he swung his eyes at her injured ankle as though suddenly remembering it.

Leaping forward, he lifted her by her underarms, half dragging her into the bathroom, slamming the door shut, then stuffing her into the tub.

Her heart galloping, she held her breath as he climbed in after her, making a close fit.

Time ceased. She didn't dare move.

She understood all too well this was no game.

'Stay down,' he commanded. 'Lock your hands over your head.'

Too frightened to argue, she slid down against the cold, hard porcelain, feeling him easing himself over her, covering her with his body for protection. As cramped as he was, she felt him straining to keep his full weight off her. One large hand reached around the back of her head to cushion it from the hard porcelain.

She recoiled at the sound of a loud snap, but it was only Wheeler yanking the shower curtain free. It fell over them like a blanket, fashioning a dark, momentarily safe cocoon.

No one in her whole life had ever gone to such lengths to protect her, as he instinctively had.

She blinked back tears. Here she'd been feeling cocky about having eluded death and then comes a damn tornado. Wasn't she destined to ever have just one thing work out perfectly in her life?

One side of her face pressed into his shirt front, she felt the movement of his breathing against her, his staccato heartbeat hammering in time with her own. His body was warm and strong and hard, and if she had to die right now, she was grateful she wouldn't be alone.

She gasped aloud at the sound of lumber ripping overhead. The cottage shook as though caught in a giant electric mixer.

Wheeler held her closer against him.

She trembled as the tub shook and she heard crashing from above.

'Dear God,' Wheeler muttered. He glanced down at the quaking angel he held in his arms, fully aware her face might be the last he ever saw. He'd been longing to kiss her all day, and at the moment who she was ceased to matter. He wanted his final moments on earth to count for something. Maybe to compensate for hours and days that hadn't. At least this once, he'd claim what he desired.

Relegating consequences to hell where they belonged, he pressed his grizzled face against her satin cheek and nearly groaned at the soft, comforting feel of her.

When his lips came down seeking hers, it seemed the most natural thing in the world for Claire to turn her mouth to his and forget this might be her last act in life. He kissed her frantically, fiercely at first, like a man lost in the desert drinking from a well of cool, clear water. Still, he considerately diverted the pressure away from where she'd bumped her lip earlier. Deeply grateful to be alive, to feel anything at all, she responded more eagerly than normal caution warranted.

Then, as he got his first urgent fill, his lips gentled over hers, melting into a sweet syrupy warmth. Languidly, she drifted into the soothing flow of it, pressing her body along the length of his firmer, harder one, nibbling at his lips and teasing them with her tongue. The exotic, manly taste of him intoxicated her. Never in her life had she acted so boldly, but she wanted only to numb herself to the danger by flooding her senses with the scent, taste, and feel of him.

And by God, something was exploding! It was the house cracking to pieces around them.

Each heartbeat struck like the ticking of a clock as she withdrew more deeply into the comfort of the kiss and waited for oblivion. She kissed him urgently, with all that was inside her, and to her startled delight, she felt his insistence, his power. The force of him stunned her.

His hand slipped under the loose pajama top, skating across her tight, bare midriff and sparking such shivery sensations, she quivered beneath him. Her hips mashed to his of their own accord. As he cupped her breast and began, slowly, deliberately kneading it with his fingertips, she gasped softly, closing her eyes at the unbearable heat coursing through her. Relentlessly, he teased her nipple until it hardened beneath his thumb and the damp ache below her belly begged for a relief she couldn't fathom. Her legs were parting as though by his command.

A low, tortured moan escaped from the back of her throat. Wherever he was taking her, she wanted to go.

Abruptly, he pulled up. Claire blinked her eyes open, cold water slapping her back to reality.

She found herself staring past Wheeler up into the open sky. The roof was gone. Rain poured in.

Wheeler, also looking up, raked splayed fingers through his shaggy blonde hair.

Discomfited and still smoldering from his touch, Claire straightened the upraised pajama top, her face scalding at the memory of her impetuous behavior with a man she scarcely knew.

Barre, she remembered, aghast at her lapse.

'Damn,' Wheeler muttered, staring up at the dark sky, then looking back at her blankly as if he had no memory of what had just transpired. Rivulets of water trickled down his face. But his lips were dark and slightly puffy. From her kiss. The taste of him lingered in her mouth. She hadn't been hallucinating. Maybe she would have been better off if she had.

He climbed out of the tub, tossing the ripped shower curtain aside. *Good God*, could he reduce her to flaming embers then feel nothing? The man was inhuman!

What could have possessed her to respond to him so? Obviously, he'd intended only to prove his effect on her. Mow her down to his level. That done, he was finished.

She knelt in the tub, watching him. He seemed unconcerned as to how she might feel about him at this point.

Finally, he leaned over her, offering a hand. 'Come on, Princess,' he directed. 'We're going to have to move to the main house — if it's still standing.'

Shunning his outstretched arm, she struggled to maneuver out of the tub and avoided meeting his eyes. This storm could spin them both off to Oz before she'd allow him to touch her again.

4

Sadie reached the outskirts of Nashville before guilt sent her down an exit ramp searching for a pay phone. Once again, her mother was right. She should carry a cell phone when she traveled. But normally Sadie enjoyed her brief interludes away from ringing telephones.

Unable to concentrate on the audio book she'd been trying to listen to, she shut off the cassette player.

On another day, she would have driven faster, been home by now. But on this gray afternoon, passing suburban shopping plazas and tree-lined side streets, she was dawdling intentionally, dreading a party she should have been looking forward to.

Barre Sutton adored Claire. Outwardly, he seemed everything Sadie wished for her younger cousin. Dashing, intelligent, ambitious. Too solicitous for Sadie's liking — if anyone had asked her.

But as hard as she'd scrutinized Barre, she couldn't pinpoint exactly what about him she didn't trust. *Face it*, she told herself. *No one will ever seem good enough for Claire.*

'Keep an eye on Claire, Sadie,' her parents and her uncle had been telling her for the past twenty-some years. By now, her protective mode kicked in automatically even though Claire was plenty mature enough to look out for herself.

Mom always told Sadie she'd been born middle-aged, dangerously precocious even as a little girl. Ever since they were children, Sadie had been trying to fill in as Claire's big sister, mama . . . guardian angel.

Sadie smiled softly, remembering Claire as an impish three-year-old who always seemed a little lost. Sadie had just turned six when she'd drawn her little cousin under her wing, believing God had finally brought her the next best thing to the little sister she'd been praying for. Mom certainly hadn't accommodated her repeated requests, she recalled, grinning now at her own naïveté.

Small wonder, as much time as Dad spent in his office. She knew now her parents had wanted more children, but had failed to conceive any.

Claire had been a cute kid, half-moon grin

peeking out from beneath drifts of golden curls, but woefully scrawny and frail. Years had passed before Claire began filling out, gradually blossoming into a tanned and athletic normal kid, although even now she stayed thin without trying. Claire could look stunning in rags, while Sadie painstakingly spent hours applying her make-up exactly right, wearing clothes tailored to her figure and coloring.

The first few times Uncle Josh and Aunt Anita brought Claire to Sadie's parents' house, she'd sat quietly between her parents or hidden behind their legs, too bashful to even talk to anybody. Sadie had brought out every doll and stuffed animal in her collection before she and both sets of adults finally coaxed Claire into venturing into the playroom with Sadie.

Nobody had ever explained to Sadie back then where Claire had come from, but she'd caught snatches of Uncle Josh's whispered concerns to her father. *Sketchy background, abandoned, neglected. God only knows for sure . . .*

Uncle Josh would speak calmly but grind his teeth and ball his fists. Sadie understood something terrible must have happened to Claire.

Until now, nobody had loved her. Sadie

had understood that intuitively. With the easy wisdom of a first grader, she considered Claire to have fallen into awful good hands — Uncle Josh meticulously salvaged and restored damaged valuables.

When Sadie asked one day where her aunt and uncle had gotten Claire, Mother had told her from the hospital. Sadie had accepted the answer without question, because she'd known that's where parents went to get their babies. At the time, she'd missed her mother's evasion. Ready-made three-year-olds didn't come from hospitals. Later, she'd assumed her mother meant an adoption agency but at the time hadn't wanted to try to explain what that was.

Through the years, Sadie and Claire had shared countless long soul-searching talks, and if Claire ever remembered anything of those years before the Woolriches had adopted her, she'd never once mentioned them. Sadie had never asked. Still, Sadie wished she knew. Nothing could be worse than the images her imagination conjured.

When Aunt Anita died shortly after Claire arrived, Sadie had resolved anew to shield her cousin from any more heartbreak. It never occurred to Sadie that might prove impossible.

Left to raise Claire alone, Uncle Josh

brought her frequently to the house to stay when he traveled on business, and Mom was always happy to have Claire around. But it was Sadie who took charge of the solemn younger girl. Sometimes Sadie marveled how Claire never cried unless she fell off a swing or something. She was incredibly brave for someone so small. Tough to the core.

It was long past time to let Claire soar or fall on her own, and Sadie owed her an apology for planting doubts about marrying Barre. Claire could orchestrate a successful fundraiser or marketing campaign in the blink of an eye. Few people could say no to her. Claire knew her own mind. If Barre was wrong for Claire, Claire was going to have to just figure it out on her own. But Sadie had never been good at holding back her opinions.

And as Claire had pointed out back on the mountain, Sadie hadn't done such a hot job of lining up her own ducks. Sadie examined her own motives. Was she jealous because Claire was about to settle down, leaving Sadie — on the threshold of turning thirty — behind to continue knocking around in her supposedly carefree, single existence?

She should be worrying about her own future instead of obsessing over her cousin's happiness. Her little art gallery was more hobby than a career, a place to mingle with friends and people whose talent she admired. She made a little money, but she could close it tomorrow and not particularly miss it. Not as much as the unknown local artists whose work she show-cased might.

But if she kept silent now, would she wish she'd spoken out later? Sadie couldn't help worrying her cousin had endured in her early years more than enough unhappiness for one lifetime. And damn it, she'd glimpsed her own skepticism reflected in Claire's eyes. Couldn't Barre back off, give her some breathing room? He'd wooed her with the speed of a space shuttle climbing into orbit.

Sadie gripped the steering wheel tighter, slowing as she passed an outdoor phone booth, then accelerating past it. God only knew what people did inside those enclosures during the dead of night. None of the phones inside ever worked anyway. She scanned the roadside for a restaurant that might have a phone. She could use a cup of coffee.

There was that nasty business with Claire and Sam Murray. Sadie should have stayed out of that. Claire probably would have shot her if she'd known.

Keep out of Claire's life, she warned herself.

If having children caused anywhere near

this much worry, Sadie certainly never wanted any. Not likely to become an issue soon at the rate she was going. With a heavy sigh, she braked in front of a flat, rectangular building set off by itself. Neon glowed before a lace-curtained window, proclaiming it 'Ned's Place', and the pale light inside beckoned her from the gloomy overcast beneath the nickel-plated sky. She'd beaten the rain, but she suspected the storm was at her heels.

As she pulled into the parking lot, she spotted a vinyl 'For Sale' sign posted by the curb, and she took a second look at the place to make sure it was open. The sign on the door proclaimed it was, and a few other cars were scattered around the gravel lot.

Reaching for the running shoes she kept on the passenger-side floorboard, she came up with a fistful of air. Now, she remembered. She'd worn them while she'd helped Claire with the last-minute luncheon preparations, kicked them off in a corner, then forgotten them in the rush to gather the ferns. Wriggling her bare toes, she reluctantly reached into the back seat for the dress shoes she'd so happily shed earlier.

She got out of the car and entered the diner. A middle-aged man and woman sat at a booth along the wall eating sandwiches.

Sadie saw no other customers. She approached the counter, leaning over the Formica. A reedy man standing with his back to her was fumbling with the coffee machine.

'Terrific,' she announced loud enough to get his attention. 'Fresh coffee. You must be the man of my dreams.'

Sometimes she didn't stop to realize people who didn't know her might take her offhand comments literally. She'd probably offended him.

The man turned, looking flustered, eyeing her quizzically. Then slowly, he smiled. Something about the way he smiled immediately captured her attention. He was clean-shaven, with dark blond hair, darker eyebrows and effervescent blue eyes behind brown-framed glasses. Tall and straight with broad shoulders, he exuded strength despite the white apron tied over his jeans and plaid cotton shirt.

Businesslike, he cleared his throat and wiped his hands on the apron. 'Be a few minutes for the coffee,' he informed her.

'What about that in the other pot?'

He eyed her ruefully. 'Sludge,' he admitted. 'Been there for hours.'

She raised one palm. 'Okay, I've sworn off sludge this week. I'll wait. Do you have a pay phone?'

He nodded toward the back.

Sadie walked in that direction, wondering if she'd lost her touch. She seldom encountered men unwilling to flirt with her. This one had wanted to, then changed his mind. What difference did it make? He had been wearing a gold band — yes, she'd checked out of habit — but she'd only been making conversation, not seducing him. Mom always told her to be more careful about the things she said, warning her people might take them the wrong way.

Sadie called Claire's cell phone, but wasn't particularly worried when she didn't get an answer. Claire didn't like to mess with the phone while she was driving and sometimes wouldn't answer calls, especially if she were stuck in heavy traffic or bad weather. Sadie just hoped Claire hadn't lingered at Madeline's flower shop, gossiping about residents of Blakesville, people Claire didn't even know.

Sadie tapped a red nail on the receiver. She'd stopped for nothing. Oh well, she'd call Claire's apartment from the house. She couldn't explain her nagging sense of uneasiness, and she told herself once she set things right between her and Claire again, she'd could relax and enjoy tonight's party. Honestly, she didn't see why Barre had to make such a production out of their engagement. A quiet dinner, a bottle of champagne and a declaration of undying love seemed far more romantic.

As Sadie turned and headed back into the main dining area, she inhaled the smells of fresh coffee brewing and food cooking. The good-looking guy behind the counter was standing with a phone tucked between his shoulder and his ear. When he saw her, he waved one finger to indicate he'd be right with her.

Swinging her gaze around the restaurant, she realized the other two customers had finished their meal and left. Sadie sat on a stool at the counter. Once she was settled, she discovered she couldn't help overhearing his conversation.

'I don't care if Shelly's mother can come and get you. Stay put and get that room clean. I'll drive you to Shelly's myself when I get home . . . No, I can't come right now. You know that, Lisa.'

He hung up and flexed his shoulders, shaking his head. Sadie read the frustration in his eyes.

'Kids,' he decreed into the air around him. 'You try to do the best you can, and bingo — they think they're beyond parental guidance.'

He seemed to be awaiting celestial intervention. Sadie saw she was the only one around to answer him. 'You wonder if they really know what they're doing,' she empathized, thinking of Claire.

He quirked an eyebrow, craning his neck to peer more closely at her.

Sadie felt a bubbling in her stomach. She wondered what he thought of her.

'I must be older than I like to think. Excuse me for saying so, but you look awfully young to have teenagers.'

Sadie laughed lightly. 'That's a relief, since I am. I just understand the feeling. It's a long, complicated story. How many children do you have?'

'Two girls, one thirteen and one fourteen.' He was shaking his head. 'We've been through a nightmare. My wife was killed in a car accident two years ago, and the girls and I kind of pulled in close, kept each other going. Now all of a sudden, they act like they don't need me. Just want to spend every minute with their friends.'

'Hmm. Leaving you behind? I recall a time when nothing struck me as more boring than Saturday night with Mom and Dad. Dare I suggest it's typical?'

He chuckled, then extended an open hand. 'Obviously, you do dare. Thanks. I'm Ned Quince.'

She liked his grip, light yet solid. Her

fingertips tingled in his grasp. 'Sadie Woolrich. So why're you selling your place, Ned?'

He poured her coffee. 'Just feel like I'm stalled here now. I'd like to start over someplace new, maybe up around Gatlinburg. Might be easier to keep track of the girls in a smaller place. Like it or not, they have some remaining years under my supervision.'

'Gatlinburg would be a beautiful place to live.'

He ladled a bowl of vegetable soup and set it in front of her. The steam rising from it carried an irresistible spicy aroma.

'I didn't order this,' she protested.

'You look like you could use it. Go ahead, it's on the house. Just like your free advice.'

She eyed him skeptically. 'Do you always give your food away?'

'Do you always dole out counseling to total strangers?'

'Only when I'm nervous.' She eyed him as she sipped a spoonful of soup, tasting beef and tomatoes and a hint of chilli powder. 'This is . . . wonderful. Do you have somebody's grandmother shackled to the stove?'

He chuckled. He had a pleasant laugh. 'My wife's parents used to run this place. We bought it from them when they retired. This is made from Greta's mother's recipe. I'm not much of a cook, but I can follow instructions.'

Sadie nodded. 'Too many memories here, huh?'

'Way too many memories. Too much time away from the girls.'

'And now they're abandoning you?'

'For tonight anyway. Too many changes too fast. Did you get your call through?'

'No.'

'Need to try again?'

'No. My message should probably be delivered in person anyway. I just . . . I have this nagging feeling something's wrong with my cousin. Silly. I just left her an hour ago and she was perfectly fine.'

He laughed lightly. 'Sounds like me and the girls.' He took a hard look at her and pressed splayed hands on the countertop, seemed to be steeling himself. 'You wouldn't happen to be free tonight, would you, Sadie?'

So, Sadie had misread him. And he her. Flirting came so naturally sometimes . . . She felt very tempted.

'No, I'm not,' she confessed.

He lowered his eyes. 'Sorry,' he muttered, openly dejected. Then he shrugged. 'I'm rusty at this kind of thing. Look, if I offended you — '

There was something genuine in his

manner she couldn't resist. 'No, I'm flattered you asked. But I have to attend my cousin's engagement party.' Inspiration struck. 'Would you like to come?'

'I . . . you're serious, aren't you? I'm sorry I put you on the spot. I don't know what came over me.'

'Can you meet me at the country club?' She pulled a business card from her gallery and a pen out of her pocketbook, scribbled a few notes on the back, then slid it across the counter. 'Eight o'clock. Show them this card at the gate.' She studied his features. His lips parted, his eyebrows working together as he silently read the name of the posh club, and she hoped he wouldn't be put off when he realized how prominent her family was. For the first time in her life, Sadie viewed her social status as a drawback. Something about this man appealed to her, and she didn't care that he ran a diner or was probably ten years older than her, or had two daughters. In five minutes, she liked Ned more than any man in recent memory.

'My cousin's marrying Denver Sutton's son. You know, the king of psycho-babble?'

'Oh yeah, the guy who recommends playing with plastic submarines in the bathtub?' he asked.

Sadie laughed brightly, liking him more.

'Who's going to argue with someone giving everyone license to be a kid again? Claims it shaped him into the man he is today.'

'I'll bet.'

She set her fingers lightly on his wrist, his warmth and strength making them tingle. 'Look, if you decide not to show, I'll understand. It's not like we'll ever have to see each other again. But I'd really like for you to be there. It'll be fun. And to tell you the truth, I wouldn't mind some moral support tonight myself.'

'Sure, I'll see you later then. And I hope you get in touch with your cousin. Be careful going home. There are storm warnings out and I caught something on the radio about a tornado touching down somewhere.'

She thanked him for the soup and left him studying the card as if he were trying to decipher an ancient scroll. She doubted he'd show. His wife had died two years ago, but he was still wearing his wedding ring.

★   ★   ★

The cottage had been reduced to a pile of sticks. Claire stood frozen in the pouring rain, knee-deep in shredded timber.

'Dear God,' she lamented, sweeping her gaze over the rubble. Disbelieving her own eyes, she shook her head. Had Wheeler not pulled her into the tub, she'd be viewing that pile of wood from the bottom up right now. She felt a scream building inside her.

Wheeler grasped her shoulders and shook her rudely. 'Spilt milk, Princess. C'mon.'

'All your belongings — ' she protested against the downpour.

'I'll get what's left later.' He glanced down at her feet. 'No shoes. I'll have to carry you to the house.'

She shrunk back. 'That's not at all nec — '

He lifted her easily out of the timber before she could complete her objection. His strength astonished her, even though she'd experienced it before. By now, she liked the feel of it far too much for comfort.

Wheeler plowed through the debris, kicking aside boards and shingles in his path. He circled around a broken tree. Claire clung to his neck. His longish hair was plastered to his skin, water streaming down his face, droplets sticking in his eyelashes as he blinked rain from his eyes.

The Tennessee clay had turned to thick red goo, sucking at his boots as he stepped free of the cottage's foundation. Gray mist shrouded the landscape, and Claire looked wildly around, losing her sense of place as she failed to make out the house. She balled her fingers into a fist behind his neck. What if it had been destroyed too? Where would they find shelter?

But Wheeler seemed to know exactly where he was going, battling fierce wind and sheeting rain, proceeding in a straight line until the mansion materialized before them.

Claire sagged with relief at the welcome sight. 'Oh, thank God!' she exclaimed. 'It's still here.'

Wheeler snorted, and she wasn't sure how to interpret that. He wasn't completely up the porch steps when she began wriggling to free herself. But in his unyielding iron grasp, she realized she'd be free only once he got ready to release her.

He set her down against the porch railing, standing at her toes. Heart thrumming, Claire gripped the railing with both hands behind her and fought to steady her ragged breathing. Not an easy feat with him standing so close, his whisker burn still stinging her chin and cheeks.

She refused to think right now about his kiss. Or her fierce reaction to it. For the moment, she'd pretend it hadn't happened. The world was crashing in around them. No time for an argument.

Raising her chin, she blinked raindrops from her eyes and met his gaze, discomfited at how it held her despite the furies of hell raging around them. She had to think of what they were going to do now.

But the vision of the demolished cottage filled her whirling mind. Not a single wall of the living room they been sitting in just moments before the tornado struck remained standing. She felt queasy, gripping the railing tighter to control her trembling.

Wheeler's breath came in spurts too. 'Any damage, Princess?' He propped a hand on the pillar, leaning against it, slanting over her.

Not yet. His body pinned her to the rail. Her heart was catapulting, slamming inside her chest as hard as the rain beat against the ground. Each labored breath pushed her closer against his muscled frame.

She resisted a wild impulse to put her arms around him just because he was here and solid and standing in front of her, hold on until her heart slowed to normal. By some miracle, they'd both escaped the same disaster. Like it or not, their unlikely survival welded an intimate bond between them. Mutely, she blinked up at him, still too numb to know whether she was hurt.

In an oddly touching gesture, he reached out and pushed a long strand of wet hair off the side of her face. His hand moved slowly, deliberately, as if he too sensed the uncanny link. Her pulse accelerated as his roughened fingers grazed her smooth cheek.

'Hey, it's over now.' His tone was almost kind. 'You okay?' He seemed oblivious to the effect his positioning was having on her. For a split-second, she feared he was going to resume kissing her. Hoped? Nothing was making sense.

Well, yes, just ducky considering you've got me doubting everything I believed about myself until a few hours ago. She had to get a grip.

'Take a deep breath,' he ordered, eyeballing her like he expected her to flee screaming into the woods any second.

Feeling foolish, she realized he wouldn't be happy until she complied. She filled her lungs with air, then slowly exhaled. Amazingly, the action did soothe her.

'I'm all right,' she reported. A stabbing pain in her toe indicated the presence of a splinter, but under the circumstances, the wound was too minor to complain about. She'd yank the thing out once they were safely inside. And of course, her ankle still throbbed. 'But your house — '

'Is gone. Nothing's bringing it back. Forget about it.'

'What about you?' she asked, concerned despite hating him for the way he made her body feel, hating herself for liking it. But he was more likely to have taken a blow when the house fell apart, having been, well — on top.

His eyes narrowed, his brow crinkling above the bridge of his nose. 'Me?' he replied, the corner of his lip hinting at a smile. 'Bounced a couple timbers off my head, but otherwise, I'm fine.'

Without thinking about it, she smiled back at him, imagining two-by-fours rebounding off that thick skull of his. Things couldn't be all that bad if he could manage a joke on himself, even a bad one. Realizing he might misinterpret a smile stemming from sheer relief and gratitude, she smothered it and shifted her gaze.

Forcing down her rising hysteria, she calmed slightly. She tried not to wonder too hard how they were going to get out of here. Panicking wouldn't help their situation. Father always prided himself on his ability to stay cool even during the most cutthroat business negotiations.

Finally stepping back and turning away from her, Wheeler reached by reflex for his key ring. Claire tipped her head over the railing and wrung her hair. The wind nipped her skin through the wet pajamas. She hugged her chest and tried to get warm. Her poor bare feet felt like blocks of ice. Hard to believe she could feel so chilled in summer. Glancing down, she noticed blood dripping from her toe.

She saw Wheeler staring at the heavy wooden door, rubbing his chin thoughtfully. She wondered what was the matter, then realized he no longer had the key ring he'd carried earlier — must have taken it off when he'd changed his clothes back at the cottage.

'How are we going to get in?' she demanded.

He cast her a low glance.

Immediately she regretted snapping. He couldn't know any more than she did. She was just so cold. She couldn't stop shaking, and her teeth were chattering.

'Stay here,' he ordered, sprinting down off the porch before she could stop him, darting into the rain and disappearing around the corner of the house.

Honestly, where did he think she might go?

Muscles tensing, she looked out across the rain-shrouded landscape, wondering what she would do if he failed to return. Served her right for barking at him. She was just so darn scared. Had he run off to some secret shelter in the woods and left her to herself?

She leaned over the railing, rain peppering her face. 'Wheeler?' she called tentatively.

No answer.

She leaned farther. Through the blinding rain, she couldn't see anything.

He rounded the corner, treading cautiously in deference to the ax he cradled in both hands. Claire remembered having seen it earlier by the wood pile.

'So, you do remember my name,' he commented as he scaled the steps.

Claire had been so infuriated at his refusal to call her by her first name, she hadn't stopped to consider she'd avoided using his.

Facing the door, he turned to her, waving her back. 'Look out,' he ordered, making a sweeping gesture with his hand. He didn't have to warn her a second time. Claire scurried backward to the far end of the porch.

She watched in fascination as he hoisted the heavy ax, muscled arms rippling as he hurled the blade into Father's custom-carved door. The porch shook under her feet with each swing, wood chips flying.

Father would be unhappy about the expensive door. But even Father couldn't expect them to camp in the woods all night. And if he'd provided Wheeler a suitable structure to live in instead of a shack, it might have withheld the storm.

After chopping the better part of the front door into kindling, Wheeler kicked in what was left. Wood crumbled under the powerful thrust of his boot sole. Claire watched dumbfounded. His brute strength awed her. Nodding with satisfaction, he set down the ax and propped it against the wall. With an outstretched hand, he gestured for her to enter. 'Your lodgings, Miz Woolrich.'

Her brief admiration fizzled. So it was back to that was it? Just as well. Considering their situation, the less she found to appreciate about Wheeler, the better. Nice of him to remind her of his contemptuous attitude.

Casting him a sidelong glare, giving up on trying to read his mind, she brushed past him. His wet pajamas stuck to her like papier mâché. How could he be so detached? Wasn't he even human enough to be afraid?

She turned around, expecting him to have followed her inside, astonished to see him running down the porch steps instead. Where was he going?

'Wheeler?' she called after him. He was already back out in the storm, running in the direction of the cabin.

She pushed down her sense of abandonment. The man had just lost everything he owned; he was probably going back in hopes of salvaging some irreplaceable memento.

Stepping inside the darkened mansion, she hit the lightswitch. Nothing happened.

Leaning her back against the wall, she closed her eyes and shook her head. Was anything ever going to go right for her again? Annoyance rippled through her. Why had Wheeler deposited her in this darkened house and left? Whatever he hoped to recover could have waited until the rain stopped. Out in the storm, something awful might happened to him. As worry set in, she stepped into the doorway and tried to see through the sheeting rain.

When his large frame materialized between the raindrops, she refused to acknowledge what a welcome sight it was.

'Where did you run off to?' she asked.

He paused to catch his breath. Water streamed down his forehead, running into his eyes. He swiped at it, pushing back a handful of dripping hair. 'Missed me, huh? Thought it might be a good idea to shut off the gas valve at the cottage now. Before the place blows up. Storm could have broken the line.'

Properly admonished, Claire grudgingly marveled at his prudence. She'd never have considered the gas lines, nor known what to do about them barring a call to the gas company. Maybe she did take many things for granted.

Wheeler reached for the lightswitch.

'The power's off,' she warned him.

He glowered at the switch. 'Figures. Go on in the basement,' he ordered. His voice echoed through the empty rooms. 'We'll stay there until the storm's over. Maybe if we're lucky, we'll find a flashlight.'

'Obviously neither of us is lucky today.'

'We're both still here, aren't we?'

Regretting her impatience, she realized he was right. She should be rejoicing at being alive instead of cursing temporary inconveniences.

Standing beside him in the dimly lit foyer made her anxious enough to shift her stance. She softened her tone a notch. 'You can't honestly believe there'll be another tornado.'

'The way this day is going, I wouldn't bet against it.'

'There'll be dry clothes and towels in the master-bedroom suite upstairs,' she argued, suddenly resenting his bossing her. By rights, she was in charge. Her father owned this house, paid Wheeler's wages. The time had come to get her wits about her and assert herself, or he'd be running roughshod over her until help came, which might be hours yet. And taking command of both herself and the situation would keep things on track, remind her Wheeler was her father's employee doing his job. Right now, she didn't want to think about him as the man who'd been kissing her as though tomorrow would never dawn. Who had in the span of a single instant pushed from her consciousness the man she was going to marry.

He leaned closer. 'You don't need to be wandering around up there in the dark, not before this storm's over.'

'We both need dry clothes.'

'All right. You go downstairs, and I'll see what I can find up there.'

She shook her head. 'I'm not an invalid, and I've troubled you enough for one evening. Besides, I know where Father keeps things.'

Wheeler's expression tightened, then he relented, shrugging. 'So we each go our separate ways now? Fine with me. But try not to get killed, okay? It'd really wreck my résumé. I'll be in the basement if you need me.'

'At last we agree on something.'

He shot her a murderous glare.

She was chilled to the core, and the damp, cold basement was the last place she wanted to go. Especially with him. What harm could there be in running upstairs for the few minutes required to change?

And after what had happened, she didn't want to rely on him for anything. The kiss she was struggling not to think about had changed everything. She'd never again view him solely as her father's hired man, and she would do whatever it took to distance herself from him for the duration of their confinement.

Leaning against the wall, he pulled off his mud-covered boots and set them down on the linoleum. His white socks were stained copper, and he pulled those off too, draping them over his boots.

Glancing from her own dirty feet to the expanse of ivory carpet, she hesitated. Tracks of red mud would be hard to get out.

She gaped as Wheeler stripped off his wet shirt. She could sympathize with the discomfort of wearing wet clothes, but how much did he plan to take off?

Glancing down at her, he seemed amused by her stunned expression. Shamed, she realized she'd been ogling him. He probably thought she'd just crawled out of a turnip patch and never seen a man undress before. She repressed the observation she'd never seen a man like him. He pressed the wadded mass of wet cotton into her hand.

'Here. Wipe your feet, Princess. Best I can do at the moment.'

Her cheeks scalded with embarrassment. 'I asked you not to call me that, *sweetie*.'

He pushed down a smile. 'Wipe your feet,

Claire.' The intimacy with which he spoke her name didn't sit any better with her.

'On your shirt?'

'I'm not going to wear it again.'

She struggled to refrain from staring at his bared chest, the fringe of fine golden hair over tanned skin and tight muscle. 'You need your shirt. There's no heat in here.' She tried to hand it back to him.

Not reaching for it, he shook his head and waved her off. 'It's soaking wet anyway. I can't afford to pay your daddy's carpet-cleaning bills. And I'm responsible.'

'I'm sure my father's insurance will cover any damage as well as your belongings.'

'I'll work that out with him.'

Desolately, she wiped her feet with his shirt. Since it too was sopping, her feet stayed wet, but she did manage to clean off some of the mud.

Revealing her lack of sophistication must be making her look childish in his eyes, which wouldn't help her maintain control of the situation. She realized she'd have to feign worldliness, as though she consorted with half-naked men on a regular basis. Easy enough to pull off. She'd just imitate Sadie's breezy manner of discussing sexual matters as casually as she might describe buttering toast or reading the newspaper.

'You've got a nasty splinter,' he observed.

Reflexively, recalling how he'd grabbed hold of her ankle back at the cabin, how his touch had shot flaming arrows up her leg, she swiped her foot back. 'I'll see to it.'

He took the shirt back from her, wiped his own feet, then tossed it atop the little laundry pile he'd started with his socks.

Needing to get away from him so she wouldn't be thinking of how he'd kissed her senseless a short while ago, Claire stepped into the dark living room, astonished by how different this place felt now, empty without the tables and chairs the rental company had hauled away earlier.

Set so far off from the everyday world, on first sight this house had made Claire think of castles and fairy tales, fantasies she'd refused to believe in even as a child. She didn't set stock in anything she couldn't see. Father had taught her not to. The imagination deceives, he always said. Believe in what's real, and you can't go wrong.

Padding across the carpet, she missed the conversation, laughter, and music of a few hours ago. A few hours that felt like a lifetime. The smells of ham salad and marinated cucumbers lingered in the air.

She recoiled as a quick flash of lightning illuminated the room briefly. Loud thunder rumbled. Wind and rain hammered the walls, wind shrieking mournfully. The storm had transformed her castle into a bleak prison. How long would they be stuck here?

All day she'd been plagued by a premonition of tonight's party being ruined. Thinking more along the lines of runs in her hose, a spill on her dress, or Aurora Sutton making another tasteless comment, she'd never imagined this.

A deep thirst and a pang in her stomach reminded her she'd been too busy greeting guests and soliciting donations for the hospital to eat properly earlier and she was hungry now, a fact she didn't dare mention to Wheeler. He already saw her as spoiled and weak. She would have happily relinquished the balance of her checking account for a glass of ice water. Wistfully, she thought of the mug of steaming black coffee she'd left in Wheeler's living room. The twister had probably carried it halfway to Canada.

Shivering, she folded her arms over her chest.

Sensing Wheeler at her back, she spun. 'I thought you'd gone to the basement,' she charged. She hadn't for a moment believed he wouldn't give in and go upstairs with her.

'Rather go without breaking my neck on the stairs,' he replied as he passed her.

Reaching the stone fireplace, he plucked a tube of long matches from the hearth and one of two crystal candlesticks from the mantel. 'Here.' He pressed her father's antique candlestick into her hand and proceeded to strike a match. 'My kingdom for a flashlight.' A circle of yellow light illuminated his features.

'I'd have thought you'd keep one up here.'

'Excellent idea. Unfortunately, along with everything else, it was in the cottage.'

Despite her efforts to hold the taper steady as he touched the match flame to the wick, her hands were trembling. 'There's dry wood in here. We could stay in the living room and light a fire,' she suggested.

He clasped a hand over hers to brace the wobbling candle. His palm felt hot and firm. He had a nice grasp, steady but not rough. 'Once the storms have passed, I'll start one. Too risky right now.'

'This is a sturdy old house. It held up through the tornado.'

'The tornado missed it. Just barely. Didn't you see the path it sliced through the trees?'

The candlelight flickered in the small space between their faces. Even as he withdrew his hand, she felt its imprint against hers. 'Afraid of the dark?' he asked, reaching on the mantel for the other candlestick.

'No more than you are,' she replied, gritting her teeth. The light of the second candle haloed his fine features. A spark ignited inside her as well as she remembered his warm breath against her cheek, his lips against hers. Wheeler Scully was a drop-dead attractive man, and a woman more like, say, Sadie, might have been delighted to find herself stranded on a dark mountaintop with him. Claire pushed the wanton thoughts from her mind. Beneath the macho good looks lurked nothing but crudeness and sarcasm. In a moment of desperation, she'd already compromised her good judgment, her loyalty to Barre. Because of the storm, not because she couldn't resist Mr Scully, she assured herself.

It meant nothing. Only that she'd been very scared, startled into responding. Barre would understand that when she confessed her indiscretion. Besides, technically, she didn't belong to him yet, not forever. Belonging to him — what an odd way to think of it. For so many years, she'd belonged to her father, cherished and protected like all his possessions — the restored cars, this mansion, the house in Nashville, his companies. Maybe something inside her was rebelling at the prospect of being possessed now that she was finally on her own. That mutinous part of her had jumped out and enjoyed Wheeler Scully's kiss. She'd been testing herself so to speak, perhaps needing to do so before she took that final step.

Wheeler probably assumed she was hot for him, a notion she must set him straight on as soon as the opportunity arose. Without wounding his ego, of course. She guessed it was made of kryptonite anyway. Their kiss in the cottage had been spawned from the same cosmic upheavals that produced the tornado itself. A fluke.

'Well,' he said, saluting before he turned to the stairwell, 'sure you don't want to change your mind? You're going to be awful lonely up there by yourself. Just you and the wind. And the ghosts.'

Obviously, he had no intention of changing his mind. Mule that he was, he really wasn't going with her. 'I don't believe in them. Hope you enjoy being wet and cold,' she shot back.

He rolled his eyes. '*Ciao*, Princess.'

Claire bristled, sure he'd overheard her and Sadie earlier and was mocking them now. His head and the orange circle of candlelight disappeared into the stairwell. She watched incredulously as he left her standing alone. She jumped as lightning bleached the room and thunder cracked loud enough to shake the house. Nearly chasing after him, she came to her senses before taking any rash actions. If Wheeler were trying to scare her, he couldn't have timed his exit any better. But backing down on her plan would only fuel his highhandedness.

Rush back to his side now and he'd endlessly gloat over it. No, she wouldn't endure that. She'd had her fill of his browbeating. Wheeler was obviously capable of looking out for himself, and so was she. Why would she want to sit dripping and freezing in a dark, musty basement when she could make herself more comfortable upstairs?

In this situation, Father would sort his priorities, then tackle them one by one. And she would do that now. Mentally, she erased appeasing Wheeler Scully from her list. First order of business was getting dry and relatively comfortable, second was tending to the splinter.

Squaring her shoulders and drawing a deep breath, she cupped the candle flame with one hand as she headed for the stairs.

Leaning heavily on the the railing while holding onto the candle took some doing. She navigated partially by feel, favoring her injured ankle, several times stubbing her already wounded toe. Hitting it hard against the stair for the third time, she refused to cry out in pain. Climbing the single flight of stairs to the second floor took forever. Several times, she paused to look back down, half-expecting to find Wheeler watching her. Laughing. But if he was there, he remained well-hidden in the shadows.

Pausing to look out the window in the hall, she watched water sheet over the glass against a backdrop of black and gray silhouettes, branches and leaves dancing eerily in the wind. Something was beating against the roof, knocking as if demanding to be let inside.

With an involuntary shiver, she hurried toward her father's bedroom suite. Since the work on the house wasn't finished, his was the only bedroom furnished. It contained a few functional pieces — bed, dresser, bookcase, desk, and an easy chair flanked by a reading lamp. Claire smiled slightly as she imagined Father here, sitting by the window, reading. Joshua Woolrich wasn't a demonstrative man, or a man who had ever intended to raise a daughter alone. Claire often suspected he'd consented to her adoption to please his wife, indulging her as he might give a child a puppy.

But in his own, albeit sometimes maddening, way, he'd always been good to her. She understood his protectiveness, how he conveyed his love with gifts or privileges rather than open affection, and she loved him dearly. Suddenly, recalling how he relaxed with his reading, how absorbed he got in his favorite books, how sometimes he would doze with an open book in his hand, she wished she had told him that this afternoon. Instead of arguing with him.

You're not going to die, you ninny. You're safe now. You should have been pondering this philosophical stuff earlier, instead of throwing yourself at the groundskeeper, heh?

Uncomfortable at the jabbing of her own conscience, she set the candlestick atop the dresser. Overcoming her instinctive hesitance at invading her father's privacy, she pulled open the bureau drawer, praying he'd left something behind she might wear. This was an emergency. Father would understand. And she'd find something for Wheeler too, since he was afraid to come up here and she didn't especially want to have to contemplate his bare chest all night.

All night? Would they be stranded here that long?

Surely Father would send help the second he discovered her missing. But no one really knew she was still up here. She and Wheeler were alone. No one outside would know a twister had struck. Was weather radar equipment set up out here? When she failed to show up for the party, Father and Barre would figure out she was still on the mountain. She pressed down her concern at how wild with worry Father would be. Sadie, too. If only she could somehow get word to them.

She thought of the cell phone sitting out in her wrecked car. If she'd been acting rationally, she would have grabbed it. Too late now. But the racket outside squelched her faintest hope of retrieving it anytime soon. Maybe not before morning.

Closing her eyes, she focused her mind on Nashville, attempting futilely to key in on first Barre, then Father. He kept his high blood pressure a closely guarded secret. Otherwise, his rivals might take advantage of his condition. Normally he monitored it carefully, taking his medication. But under great stress . . . ? She gnawed her lip, not wanting to think how her disappearance might affect him.

She shifted her concentration to her cousin. As she envisioned Sadie's face, heard her voice, the mental connection snapped in, like a radio locking in on a station. *Take care of them, Sadie. Let them know I'm all right.*

Thunder exploded like a torpedo, jolting her into opening her eyes and abandoning her foolish telepathic experiment. All she could think to do, considering. Besides, no one would ever know of her ridiculous, desperate measure.

Spurred into action, she inspected three partially full drawers of carefully folded and sorted rows of clothing, straining to see in the faint light. Finally, she unearthed Father's gym clothes — shorts and T-shirts. He liked to unwind, dress casually and walk in the woods when he was up here. These would have to do. They were dry at least. Wouldn't keep them very warm, but she intended taking the blankets off the bed as well.

Grabbing a handful of clothes, she limped into the bathroom where she began stripping off the wet pajamas. Slipping out of the heavy clothing was a relief. Taking a plush bath towel off the rack and adding another to her stack of clothing, she dried herself, gleaning small comfort in the luxury of the soft cotton against her skin. Such a simple, yet welcome relief. Oh, for a hot bubble bath. And a mug of hot, buttered rum, the kind Father served his guests at Christmastime.

On a sudden impulse, she opened the medicine cabinet. Father's aftershave centered the top shelf. She closed the door quickly, ashamed at her need to look.

111

Wheeler wasn't a thief. How quick she'd been to assume he was. Maybe his favorite, pricey aftershave was one thing he splurged on. Trying to figure him out was a dangerous game she had no business playing.

Or had she been overanxious to find some damning evidence? Something concrete to prove him unworthy of her consideration? Justification to extinguish her mounting curiosity about him?

Listening to the storm raging outside, she suddenly felt intensely alone inside the silent, dark mansion. Maybe she should have stayed with Wheeler, disagreeable as she found his company.

She reminded herself she lived alone. Being up here wasn't so different than sitting in her own apartment.

With an unexplained need to hurry, she pulled on a pair of shorts, the loose elastic band securing them precariously as they ballooned over her hips baggy as a clown's drawers. But they were dry, and they covered her. Deciding to rid herself of the annoying splinter before Wheeler — kamikazi medic — got at it, she propped her foot awkwardly on the sink beside the candle, leaning over to inspect the wound.

A sharp crash shook the floor. Claire fell

back screaming. Wood snapped overhead and her heart rose into her throat, choking her. A gust of wind extinguished the candle flame and slammed the door shut, leaving her in total darkness.

5

Barre straightened his bow tie, thinking he might as well have been wearing a noose around his neck for how it was strangling him. Impatiently, he swung another glance around the section of the ballroom roped off for the party. Surrounded by fountains and foliage, he felt like he was on safari in a tropical rain forest instead of walking around inside a country club. Why not just hold the damn bash outside?

The tinkling of piano music and clinking of glasses blended with the cacophony of scattered conversations. The room was rapidly filling with guests, many whose faces were unfamiliar. Joshua Woolrich would be introducing his prospective son-in-law to the business associates he'd invited tonight. Good contacts with people who ordinarily wouldn't have given Barre directions to a bus stop.

The fake shrubbery made him claustropho-bic, but he chalked it up as a concession to the kind of novelty Claire liked. And he'd do anything to hold on to his bride-to-be. Now, if he could just find her. He scanned the crowd again. Where the hell was she? He checked his gold wristwatch.

Looking up, Barre cringed at the sight of his old man approaching, grinning, stopping to shake everybody's hand, a cocky bounce in his step. The usual floor show. Barre marveled people fell for the old man's sham. To Barre, his father came across with the sincerity of an appliance salesman on a late-night television commercial. Barre shifted uneasily, surrepti-tiously seeking a convenient escape route and finding none.

Denver Sutton was a plain man who gave himself a distinctive, intellectual air by wearing a goatee, tweed jackets, and keeping his graying hair dyed jet black. Fortunately for Barre, he had not inherited his father's nondescript features. By some genetic phe-nomenon, two plain parents had produced a striking son who resembled neither of them. Barre took deep satisfaction in having escaped being a clone of his old man. He'd learned years ago how to use his good looks to his advantage.

Reaching Barre, Denver Sutton glanced to

both sides to ensure no one stood close enough to overhear before he spoke. Still, he kept his voice low and his broad jester's smile in place. 'You haven't screwed this up, have you, son? I don't see your beloved.'

Hello, Dad. Good to see you too. 'She'll be here,' Barre grated, flinching with embarrassment.

'You two didn't have an argument, did you?'

'I haven't even seen Claire today, and I'm not an idiot, Dad. Quit badgering me.' Defiantly, he looked his father in the eye. Just once he wished the old man would have a little faith in his competence.

'You should have gone to the mountain with her.'

'I would have been in the way. Besides, I was working all day.' Actually, Claire had asked him to attend her luncheon, anxious to show off her father's renovated house and her fund-raising abilities. Barre had declined, begging off to work. Actually, nothing bored him more than high-society gatherings teeming with women his mother's age, showing off their designer clothes and gossiping about each other. Traveling way out in the sticks didn't ring any bells for him either.

Denver relented. 'Sorry, son. Everything rests on this.'

Barre nodded desolately. He'd learned everything he knew from his old man, who had started out packing boxes in a farm-equipment factory, married the factory owner's daughter then settled into the executive offices. Dad knew how to dress, where to dine, the right place to live. He was a magician who'd learned how to create illusions people grasped readily in a world where few things made sense. He'd created the image of his own fame, then forced people to believe in it until he'd actually made a reputation for himself. But the books and the speaking engagements weren't enough. He wanted television production, wanted to open a school and retreat for suckers longing to mirror his success. Sometimes, lately, Barre feared his father was actually starting to believe himself motivational guru to the middle classes. Only problem was, Dad didn't have any money. He spent twice what he earned maintaining his lavish, impressive lifestyle. He needed serious backing, the kind Joshua Woolrich might gladly extend to his son-in-law.

Denver had hinted strongly to Claire her prolonged dependence on her father had kept Joshua Woolrich from remarrying and glean-ing some happiness in his sunset years. Once the doubts were planted, he'd overcome her protests that she was independent by speculating Joshua would probably never stop feeling responsible for her until she settled down with a husband and family of her own. Then, his timing precise, after he'd primed her, he'd introduced her to Barre. And making her fall for him hadn't been as easy as the old man promised. Claire might look fragile and unassuming, but down deep she had the spunk of a barracuda, just like her old man. Winning her affection had proved the hardest task of his life, and he prided himself on his conquest.

Barre supposed he should thank the old man for finding Claire for him. Her sweetness and innocence provided a welcome contrast to his affair with Jillian. A bungled entanglement he'd sooner forget.

Now, with Dad glued to his back again, Barre felt tired. Pretending to be some superhuman Sir Galahad to impress Claire was wearing on his nerves too. He wanted to drop the pretenses and be himself, but he feared losing her affection. He had to dazzle her until at least after the wedding.

Steadfast, dependable Claire would be here. Not marrying him would never occur to her, especially once they'd slept together. He pushed that memory from his conscience too. She might have warned him she was still a virgin instead of catching him by surprise. Burdening him with a disturbing sense of obligation.

'Claire will be here,' he insisted.

'Stop standing around and muster some anxiety,' his father hissed. 'Unless you want to end up working in the factory.' He yanked Barre's tie straight, and Barre's face burned. He prayed no one was watching. Barre couldn't recall a day of his life Dad hadn't dangled this threat over his head, even though he'd never set foot in any kind of manufacturing facility.

After shooting Barre a warning look, Denver transformed his expression to a beatific grin, then turned and stepped off to clasp a newcomer's hand between both of his. One day soon the old man would stop browbeating him. Real soon.

Looking across the room, Barre spotted Sadie stepping up to the bar. The exchange with his father had made him thirsty. And if anyone knew where dear Claire was, Sadie did.

Following the old man's example, he pasted his smile in place as he approached her. Her gold off-the-shoulder gown scarcely concealed her ample bosom, and his gaze locked automatically on the intriguing display of ivory cleavage.

Reaching Sadie, he caught her by the waist, pulling her against him and planting a kiss on her cheek.

She stiffened and stepped out of his grasp. Her eyebrows dipped into an inverted V. 'Where's Claire?' she demanded.

'Exactly what I was about to ask you,' he retorted, still studying the swell of her breasts. Claire had a nice body, solid round breasts, but of the two cousins, Sadie had been more amply blessed.

Sadie shrugged. 'Surely you've been stood up before, Barre. Maybe she had an attack of good sense. You have been rushing her. I don't think she's ready for marriage. If you care about her, you'll give her some breathing room.'

Barre scowled at her without realizing it. Sadie protected Claire like a mama bear guarding her cub, an annoying stance considering Claire was a mature woman in control of all her faculties. 'No one's holding a gun to her head. Maybe it's time you stopped mothering her and concentrated on your own affairs.'

Sadie shot a pointed glance toward a tall, blond-haired stranger in a blue suit, slanted over the hor-d'œuvres buffet. 'I'm managing fine, thank you.'

He shifted his gaze to scrutinize her escort.

'I've never seen you with him before.'

Sadie glanced toward her date and smiled proudly. 'Actually, we only just met this afternoon.'

He shook his head sadly. 'Sadie, honey, you should have called. I'd have arranged an escort for you.'

Sadie rolled her eyes. 'If I didn't have a date, I would have come alone. Ned may not fit in with the usual crowd, but he's a sweetheart. *Trés* refreshing.'

'Looks *trés* rough around the edges. Not an academic, is he?'

She laughed. 'Shows what you know about people. He's a successful independent businessman. Introduce yourself, Barre. I've heard rumblings about you and your father wanting to branch out.' She cast him an accusing glare from beneath mascaraed lashes.

Barre feigned uninterest in her pointed remark. What was she getting at? Had Dad boasted prematurely about their plans? Or was Sadie fishing? Testing his reaction? The Woolriches were all as smart as they were rich.

But she was speaking again before he had to produce an answer. 'Honestly, Barre, I'm seriously worried about Claire. This isn't like her. I expected she would have phoned you as soon as she got back into town.'

He'd nearly forgotten Claire's mysterious absence. Now, he was starting to worry. He'd assumed Sadie would know exactly where her cousin was. If she didn't, no one did. 'I was out all afternoon, but she didn't leave a message on my machine.'

Sadie appraised him darkly. 'Something's wrong here.' She clicked her tongue nervously. 'Very wrong. But don't worry. If she were backing out of the engagement, her style would be to tell you.'

Joshua Woolrich appeared beside her. He shot an inquiring glance at both of them. Turning toward her uncle, Sadie instantly ironed her scowl into a smile. 'Hello, Uncle Josh,' she greeted him.

He gave a preoccupied nod. 'It's damn near eight-thirty. What's keeping Claire?' Joshua directed his question to Barre.

Barre groped dumbly to supply an answer. Why did everybody assume he kept Claire under surveillance? She was a grown woman, for cripe's sake.

'Nobody's seen her since immediately after the luncheon, Uncle Josh,' Sadie explained. 'She'll be here any minute. She left right behind me.'

'You saw her leave?' he asked.

Sadie blanched. 'I saw her getting into her

car as I was driving away.'

Josh shook his head. 'That old car of hers. I've been telling her to trade it in.'

'She hasn't mentioned having any trouble with it. And you know Claire runs to her mechanic at the slightest thump of the engine. She must have something going with him.' Her weak attempt at a joke didn't raise any smiles.

'I don't like this,' Joshua asserted, staring distractedly into a marble waterfall. 'You should have waited for her, Sadie.'

'You didn't wait for anyone, Uncle Josh.'

'Well, there wasn't any reason to . . . '

'Exactly. Claire's probably had some last-minute problem to fix — a wrinkle in her dress, a missing earring, a scuff mark on her shoe. She must be on her way. Try calling her on the cell phone.'

'I have,' Joshua barked. Barre shifted uncomfortably. He should have been the one to call her. He should have picked her up and made sure she showed on time. Like Joshua, she could be headstrong about wanting to do things her own way.

Sadie took a deep breath. 'Look, she had to stop at the florist shop in town. We can call the owner and find out what time Claire was there. But let's give her a little more time. She had a lot of things to do this afternoon. Or she may have just been exhausted and taken a nap when she got to her apartment.'

Joshua looked at Barre. 'Have you called her apartment?'

'I was just about to,' Barre assured him. 'Again,' he emphasized.

Sadie chewed her lip. 'Uncle Josh, she was ready to leave right behind me, but she may have . . . '

'May have what?'

'She may have gone back to speak to the caretaker.'

'What business would she have with him?'

'Well, you know how Claire is. She thought she might have offended him and wanted to set things right. I doubt she went back. She told me she wasn't. But if she did, she could have decided to wait out the storm on the mountain.'

Barre saw his mother approaching, wearing a frilly baby-blue dress that would have been charming on a ten-year-old. Her rounded features were puckered into a deep frown.

Sadie, turning, followed his glance. 'Oh, oh,' she mumbled under her breath.

Barre expected a tirade over Claire's late arrival. His mother disapproved of their relationship and pounced on every opportunity to illustrate how Claire simply wasn't good enough for her only son. After all, she'd told him privately, everyone knew Claire was adopted, not really Joshua and Anita's daughter. God only knew her real background. Even to Barre, his mother sounded chillingly fascist. As far as Aurora was concerned, Claire may as well have been raised by werewolves.

But as Aurora reached them now, he realized her grim expression for once wasn't associated with Claire. 'Joshua, isn't Blakesville where your mountain is?'

'He doesn't own the whole mountain, Mother — '

Josh answered as though Barre hadn't spoken. 'Yes. What's wrong, Aurora?'

'Well, I just overheard some people talking about tornadoes near there tonight. Part of the town has been leveled. I don't want to alarm you, but with that grand old mansion of yours so nearby . . . '

Joshua Woolrich went white as chalk, wobbling slightly.

Sadie reached out and set a hand on his forearm, bracing him. 'Claire may have stopped to take shelter somewhere, Uncle Josh. She's too sensible to take foolish risks.'

Joshua's hands balled into fists at his sides. He glanced blankly at Sadie. Barre had never seen Woolrich look so distraught.

'My God. She's all I have,' Woolrich professed.

'Well, I assume you're adequately insured, Joshua,' Aurora professed cheerfully. 'It's not as though you live in — '

'Claire may still be in Blakesville, Mother,' Barre informed her quietly, dumbfounding her into silence. Her mouth still hanging open, Aurora turned purple from the neck up.

Barre set his drink down, clasping the glass to still his shaking hand. As Sadie had said, Claire probably was all right, dozing in her apartment or standing in front of the closet debating over what dress to wear.

Joshua turned, heading for the door.

Sadie rushed after him. 'Take it easy, Uncle Josh.' Her tone remained level, but she looked peaked herself. 'Where are you going?'

'To the police.'

'They won't search for someone who's half an hour late for a party.'

'Then I'll find her myself if I have to drive all the way back to Blakesville tonight. In fact, that's exactly where I am going.'

'If the storm was bad, they may not even allow you into the town.'

'Let them stop me.'

'Please, stay calm, Uncle Josh. Sit down while I go make some phone calls. I don't know where Claire is, but I have this weird gut feeling she's okay.'

'And I have this gut feeling she's not here!'

Sadie clasped polished fingertips to her forehead. Barre came up beside her and set his hand on her smooth, bared shoulder. Leaning against her back, he poised his lips close to her ear. 'Stay with him, Sadie. I'll start making calls.'

Sadie turned to look up at him over her shoulder, her eyebrows raised in surprise. 'Thanks, Barre.' She patted his hand. 'Look, I mean it, I know she's all right.'

For the first time, Barre considered Claire might not be. She never played the games some women indulged in, showing up late intentionally. In fact, she'd kept him waiting only once when she'd gotten an important long-distance phone call just as she was leaving her office. And even then, she called ahead to the restaurant to alert him she was behind schedule. She was too consider-ate and predictable to be playing hide-'n-seek.

Barre watched his father, working the crowd on the other side of the room. Like a clown without a costume, Barre thought.

'She has to be,' Barre agreed, his distress genuine now. No bride, no wedding.

Joshua leveled a sweeping glare, condemn-ing them *en masse* for Claire's absence.

'Do what you want,' he charged Barre and

Sadie. 'I'm going to Blakesville to bring my daughter home.'

He moved toward the door.

'Wait, Joshua,' Barre called after him. 'I'll drive you.'

★   ★   ★

Not even bothering to bring the candle, Wheeler scaled the steps two at a time, sailing through the darkness more by instinct than sight. Sweat poured from his temples. He didn't know which had sounded more ominous — the crash or Claire's scream.

Why had he let her majesty jaunt off on her own? Well, he couldn't force her into the basement, could he? Still, he blamed himself. He could have made her go downstairs, refused to share the candles with her so she wouldn't have been able to wander away from him.

Remembering her warm, pliant female body meshed beneath his in the bathtub, he admitted he'd made a big mistake losing control back at the cottage. But he hadn't expected following his impulse was going to matter. At that moment, he'd never imagined later would come. Now, he acknowledged he'd given her reason to be wary of hiding in the basement with him.

How was he going to explain to her an action he couldn't justify to himself?

She was different than what he'd expected of formidable Joshua Woolrich's daughter. And she acted different when her father and his stuffy friends weren't around. Hot. Geeze oh Pete. He'd kissed her anticipating guarded acquiescence at best, not a volcanic eruption. For those fleeting moments, he'd lost himself to her. If the cottage hadn't blown away, he couldn't swear he could have stopped himself from making love to her. All sense of reality had blown away with the twister. Just as well nature had intervened. He must have been crazy to kiss her, but he'd assumed they were both about to die anyway. Was there a temporary insanity plea for making reckless advances? Now, he couldn't get his mind off wanting more. One taste of heaven wasn't enough.

Obviously, the woman was in shock and he must keep her safe. Including protecting her from him? Worrying about her made him stay in control, kept him from dwelling on his own plight. Finally forced to step outside himself, he suddenly felt more human than he had in a very long time. But unleashing feelings repressed for so long proved dangerous. Everything boiled to the surface at once, and suddenly he longed for everything Benjamin

Wheeler Scully had once possessed.

But all that would wait. For tonight, he had something to live for beyond his own needs — getting Claire Woolrich out of here unharmed.

Sending her later straight into the conniving arms of Barre Sutton was an inevitability he'd have to swallow. Claire's problem, not his. He'd trained himself now to consider only the present, never to think in terms of the future. And he'd be better off for maintaining that outlook.

He swung open the door of Joshua Woolrich's bedroom to find its confines exposed to the night and the storm, rain pouring in where the roof should have been. A massive tree limb reached across the bed like a giant, gnarled claw, filling the room.

He didn't see her. Alarm gripped him. 'Claire? Claire!'

The bathroom door opened, and she shot out, hobbling past him clad in nothing but a pair of loose basketball shorts and clutching a wad of clothing over her bared bosom. His fleeting glimpse of all that creamy skin triggered a reflexive tightening inside his jeans.

He discerned a muffled sob as she shot by. Turning, he viewed her bared back in retreat, a mantilla of yellow hair draping her spine almost to its base. A light floral scent lingered in her wake.

Cold water dashed his face. Cursing, he stepped back and slammed the door. If she hadn't been in the bathroom, the falling limb probably would have killed her.

Shaking off both astonished relief and his disturbing physical reaction, he chased after her. She was already at the bottom of the stairs, a T-shirt tented over her head as she squirmed to work her arms into the sleeves.

Angrily, he made his way down the stairs. He took hold of the sides of the shirt, pushing it down until her head popped out. What he had to say needed to be said to her face. 'Damnit, why couldn't you stay in the basement?'

She pulled her mane of hair through the neck hole. While her chin jutted defiantly, he read the fright in her eyes. 'Point made, Mr Scully. I'm going downstairs now.' She pressed a folded towel into his hands, then limped off without waiting for him.

Wheeler stood thoughtfully, staring at the towel and wondering absurdly whether this was the same fabric she'd hugged to her naked breasts seconds ago. Knowing she could find the way without his assistance, he pressed the cloth to his wet face, noting how warm it felt against his cool skin. Smelled like her too. He closed his eyes. Dear God, how would he get through the next few hours? She was headstrong and willful, yet even in fear for her life she had brought him a damn towel. Such innocent consideration was near more than he could tolerate.

By now, her father and Barre would be missing her. Her prominence, the storm damage, the story of her narrow escape would bring law enforcement and reporters up here in legions. Would his name be mentioned in the media? Someone would recognize it, tell Woolrich who he really was. Woolrich would start asking a lot of questions.

Whatever happened tonight, the refuge he'd found on the mountaintop was gone. For him, there'd be no going back to the reclusive life he'd fashioned for himself here, and he had no other life to go back to.

Immediately, he resented that now. Even resentment was more than he'd allowed himself to feel in ages.

But the time had come to move on. As soon as he delivered Claire to her father, he was out of here before life spun itself into another web. Or could he wait that long? What if Barre or the press showed up first?

Stowing the towel under his arm, he made his way downstairs through the darkness. The unfinished basement was strewn with stored work materials, sawhorses and tools hidden away so as not to assault the aesthetic sensibilities of the luncheon guests with signs of work underway. Furniture arranged in no particular order, some new and some to be discarded, was draped with sheets.

He'd found an old mattress earlier and pulled it up against the wall. Having left his burning candle on the floor beside it, he was thankful now it hadn't caught fire. Hadn't enough gone wrong for one night?

Claire paced the tiled floor, dragging her injured leg.

'Get off that ankle before you make it worse,' he advised. 'I can see it's hurting you.' She kept pacing. Unfolding the towel and spreading it out on the mattress, he sat on it with his back to the wall, watching her as he reached for one of the cartons he'd brought down with him from the kitchen. Without speaking, he let her burn off her anxiety. Calmly, he scooped ham salad onto a cracker, then popped it into his mouth.

She looked real cute, a little wild with her long hair mussed and bushy, her long legs bared. He traced the outline of her hardened nipples through the T-shirt. From the cold, he thought. Felt like a deep freeze down here.

He knew a good way to keep warm, nearly

suggested it just to provoke her. As long as she stayed mad at him, she wouldn't think so much about being afraid. And she'd hate him enough to stop making these considerate little gestures, stop working herself into his veins.

'You're making me dizzy,' he decreed finally, tired of watching her. 'Like a wind-up toy with a broken spring. Why don't you sit down? Please.'

She halted, apprehensively eyeing him, then the mattress. After what had happened back at the cottage, he couldn't blame her for assuming he meant to pin her down on it. Wasn't like the idea hadn't occurred to him. Appealed to him. Make love to her real slow while the rain beat against the windows.

Pleasant distraction from the storm. Yeah, in his dreams. Or some other lifetime maybe. Ha! And he thought the furies of hell were descending upon him now.

He peered up at her. 'Save your energy. You might need it later.'

She looked indecisive.

'Walking down the mountain may be our only way out of here,' he added. He dangled the carton of ham salad in the air. 'I have food. You can sit on the floor if you're afraid to get too close.'

Finally, Claire, careful to distance herself from him by a wide gap, slipped down beside him on the mattress, pressing her back against the wall. Crossing her legs in front of her, she began rummaging through the cartons.

'Is there anything to drink?' she asked. 'I'm so incredibly thirsty. I was going to get some water upstairs, but there wasn't a glass.'

He reached for a half-filled plastic bottle of lukewarm fruit punch. 'Should have used your hands.'

She looked so appalled, he nearly laughed. Obviously, she'd never known a moment's inconvenience, let alone deprivation.

Pulling off the top, he offered her the punch. 'We're fresh out of crystal goblets down here too. Damn.'

Narrowing her eyes to glare at him, she hoisted the bottle and took a long swig, wiping the mouth of it with her fingertips before handing it back to him. 'Thank you,' she said, meeting his gaze with eyes so green they reminded him of Christmas trees. The punch had stained her lips vampire red.

He raised the bottle to his lips, surprised as the smell of alcohol assaulted him. 'Spiked punch?' he asked, sniffing.

Claire grinned mischievously. 'Champagne. Puts the donors in a festive mood.'

Wheeler took a generous drink. 'I could use a couple more gallons of this stuff myself.

Somewhat of a double standard, isn't it? Guzzling champagne punch all afternoon is acceptable where having one beer makes me a drunk?'

'I admit I overreacted. You flatter yourself to think I'm afraid of you.' Happily, she popped the lid on a styrofoam carton of cheese dip and sniffed the contents. Her hands were trembling, and she was so cold her lips looked blue. Tear tracks around her eyes glistened in the candlelight. Her refusal to acknowledge them moved Wheeler. Under the circumstances, she had every right to be terrified. He repressed his urge to console and comfort her.

She'd come through a car wreck and a tornado without a whimper — now she'd been upstairs weeping? Wheeler wanted to hold her, calm her and warm her. Not a wise gesture, considering the pull in his loins as he recalled how he'd felt in those arms in those brief seconds when they'd both thought of nothing but each other.

Besides, she'd obviously enjoyed being pampered all her life, and he refused to indulge her.

Pausing, she shot him a suspicious glance. 'Please tell me you didn't resurrect this from the garbage,' she pleaded. He realized she didn't know he could tell she'd been crying.

'Maybe you don't want to know,' he challenged. 'If I say yes, there's more for me.'

Her gaze swung indecisively between his face and the food. Mentally, he kicked himself for being such an ogre. Maybe he was pushing the goading too far. Getting stuck up here wasn't her fault.

He relented. 'I'd have to be way hungrier than this to start eating out of the garbage. Your caterer stashed the leftovers in the refrigerator for me to take over to the cottage later,' he explained. 'I probably would have thrown the stuff out.'

Claire eyed him thoughtfully. 'You prefer steak and potatoes to this type of food, I'd bet.'

'Hmm, T-bone marinated in Jack Daniel's, medium rare. But right now, I'm damn glad to have even this rabbit food.'

She opened another container, extracting a miniature quiche. She popped one into her mouth, grimacing as she chewed.

'That's got to taste like glue,' he commented.

She finished chewing, then swallowed. 'Not so bad actually. Try one?' She offered the container.

Shaking his head, he warded her off with crossed palms. 'Not on your life.'

'Listen,' she said. 'I suppose it might be a

while before we can get out of here, and I want you to know I appreciate all you've done. Once I tell my father how you kept me safe, he'll give you anything you ask for. Don't minimize your request, Wheeler. You deserve a generous reward.'

Something came immediately to mind, but nothing he'd ever mention to her father. 'The less you say to your old man about me, the better I'll like it.'

'Consider what he might offer you, so you can think hard before you automatically decline out of pride. Would letting him help you get a new start be so awful? My father has money and connections. He can get you anything, and you'd be doing him a favor by accepting. Once this place opens, for example, he'll be needing a manager.'

'Your father's already paying me to look after the place. I don't expect any bonuses from him.'

'Why must you be so stubborn, Wheeler? I'm explaining this to you because I know my father. He'll respect you for specifying what you want and see you get it. If you say nothing, that's what you'll get. You're familiar with the myth about cats having nine lives?'

'Sure, but I don't get the connection.'

'Maybe people sometimes have two. Something terrible happens yet you don't die.

It's a warning. You have a second chance to change, do things differently. A responsibility to improve your life.'

'Not that again. Maybe I like my life just the way it is. Why does all this philosophy apply to me and not to Claire?'

She pressed a hand intriguingly to the center of the tented T-shirt. 'Me? Why, I . . . '

'Look, I just want to see to it you get home safely.'

'My safekeeping is beyond your realm of responsibility.'

'Not at the moment. You'd have been home by now if you hadn't insisted on retrieving that ugly statue.'

She stared off into the darkness, a faraway look in her eyes. 'Well, that 'ugly' statue is broken to pieces now, I'm sure. Believe me, I'd rather be dancing with Barre tonight than here putting a damper on your evening.'

Wheeler fended off the pull of sympathy he felt toward her. She really cared for Barre, for the man she believed Barre was, and grieved at not being with him. Anger rose in him. Barre Sutton had never felt an honest emotion in his life, yet he had somehow touched this angel where she was most vulnerable. Barre would destroy everything natural and genuine Wheeler glimpsed in her.

'My evening's pretty much a washout

anyway,' he said pointedly. 'Why do you always fall back on your old man to take care of your business? Or is this your way of reminding me I work for him so I'll behave myself?'

The color rising to her skin confirmed this. 'I handle my own affairs. Although I didn't notice your being as rude to him as you were to me.'

'He doesn't nag me to better myself. As long as I keep up this house, he's happy. He doesn't meddle.'

'Oh, for heaven's sake. I sensed you were unhappy is all.'

'Sorry, Princess, but for the time being daddy's not here to look after you. As nature's wrath demonstrated twice already, his being the King of France couldn't matter any less at the moment.'

'France has a president, not a king. And not that it's any of your business, but I stopped relying on my father to take care of me years ago.'

'Yeah? Then why is it driving you nuts he hasn't arrived with the cavalry to get you out of here?' Leaning back, he rested his head against the wall, wincing as he jerked his head forward and set one hand atop it.

'You are hurt!' Claire exclaimed.

'It's nothing,' he insisted, immediately

lowering his telltale hand.

She shot up on her knees, leaning over him. 'Let me see,' she demanded, cautiously parting his hair with her fingertips. 'Oh, Wheeler.' Her soothing tone massaged his heart in a disturbing way. He heated to her closeness, her scent teasing his nostrils. Miserably, he gazed down at the swell beneath her T-shirt, swaying inches from his face. Groaning, he clamped his muscles to resist lassoing her slender, curving, body into his arms.

'You really did get clobbered.' She leaned closer, the tip of one breast pressing against his muscled shoulder, long hair brushing skin he was about to jump out of if she didn't back off. 'Stop wiggling so I can get a look.'

Ironically, she broke the spell, pressing the tender knot rising from his scalp.

'Ow!' He bucked.

She retracted her probing fingertips. 'Sorry. You said it didn't hurt.'

'It didn't until you poked it, thanks.' Wheeler moaned inwardly, and not just from the pain in his head.

'Okay.' She held splayed fingers in the air. 'I won't touch it again. I'm just moving back the hair around it.' She continued hovering precariously close, breasts rising to within scant millimeters from his shoulder.

He couldn't take his eyes off her slender torso poised beside him. How infinitely soft her body had felt. How he'd like to hold her skin to skin, submerge himself in her warmth. Gently, he eased her away. 'Leave me alone. Please.'

'You might have a concussion.'

'I don't. I bumped my head.'

She backed away slowly, coiling into a sitting position again, as though she'd suddenly comprehended she'd gotten too close. Maybe she'd felt his skin sizzling.

If she noticed her effect on him at all, it had taken her by surprise. He'd bet money she hadn't intentionally flaunted herself. For a woman who held a high position in business and society circles and packed statues of naked lovers in her trunk, Claire struck him as fundamentally naïve about her own sexuality. He couldn't figure it. She hadn't been shy or awkward in the bathtub. But a knockout attractive woman would be careful to avoid massaging a guy with her breasts unless she was coming on to him. And he was convinced Claire wasn't trying to come on to him.

Wheeler inhaled deeply.

Beside him now, she plastered her back to the wall, raising her eyes to the ceiling. Mercifully. She'd be outraged to know how she'd affected him.

He ought to tell her, just to get a rise out of her and make her a tad more cautious.

'Do you have the time?' she asked.

He glanced at his watch, then eyed her skeptically. Why she'd asked suddenly dawned on him. 'It's after nine,' he informed her gently, hating his own secret glee at her being late for the ball.

Her glum expression heightened his guilt. 'Oh.' She studied the concrete wall, composing herself. Hell, it was only a party, he wanted to tell her. Wanted to tell her she was better off for having missed it, but she wouldn't have believed him. 'How long do you suppose we'll be here?' she asked.

'All night, I expect. When the storm dies down, we can go upstairs and build a fire.' Small consolation, but the most he dared offer.

'I'd kill for an electric blanket.'

'Still cold?'

She nodded.

'Don't count on the power coming back on. Lines will probably be down for days. And the heating unit hasn't been connected yet.'

She handed him what remained of the bundle she'd been carrying earlier. 'I brought you some of my father's clothes. If you'd like to get out of those damp jeans.'

'Thanks, but you shouldn't have gone up there.'

'I realize that. But I'd already gathered the clothes, and I wasn't about to leave them behind.' Color rose becomingly to her cheeks. 'I'm grateful to have them.'

'You going to tell me what happened?'

'As you saw, a tree ripped through the roof.'

'No. What happened to you?' He touched a fingertip to a tear stain on her cheek. 'Were you out in the bedroom when the tree fell?'

She swung her head back, her blush deepening. 'No. I was in the bathroom, changing. A gust of wind blew the door shut.'

'And you were terrified.' He clasped her wrist. 'You're still shaking now.'

She stared at him indignantly, blinking. 'Being in the dark has always bothered me since I was a little girl. I mean, I don't let it bother me now. Upstairs, I got caught off-guard. One of those childhood phobias that never completely vanishes.'

'There's no shame in being afraid. Lightning, falling trees. The danger is real.'

'It's not fear exactly. Not like I'm expecting monsters to leap out at me. I feel like I've done something terribly wrong and if I just don't move, it'll be all right finally. I should have been out of that room before you got up the stairs, but I couldn't move until I heard you calling. Barre's father says I have to face it. I've tried sitting in a dark room.'

'What fun.'

She shot him a caustic look.

'Barre's father's a nitwit. He's not even a psychologist.'

'You're quick to draw assumptions about people you don't know. His method does seem to help.'

'Seems like you could sit in the dark from now until the turn of the millennium while the only thing that would help would be facing why you hate it so much. Your old man lock you in the closet when you were a kid?'

She gasped. 'My father would never do anything inhumane. He punished me by taking away privileges, and if he was angry he wouldn't talk to me much until he got over it. Or worse, he'd lecture me in that ominous tone he uses sometimes. No, he never stuffed me in any closets, thanks. My father can be single-minded and unyielding but never cruel.'

'Dark woods, stormy night, big house and the power out must be your worst nightmare. Stop worrying about it. Everybody's scared of something. Even your old man.'

'Were you afraid? When the cottage collapsed?'

Wheeler laughed stiffly and swept his hair off his forehead with his palm. 'What do you think? I'm not a robot.'

'Yet you shielded me without thinking of yourself.'

He shrugged. 'Everything happened fast. I reacted by instinct. It's not worth mentioning.'

'You saved my life.'

'You would have been all right anyway. I was.'

'I wouldn't have thought where to go for cover. Why are you so uncomfortable admitting you did a good deed?'

'Because it was less than you're making it out to be.'

'I intend to tell my father about your selfless actions. He'll be indebted to you.'

'If you're really set on doing me a favor, forget about it.' He didn't want Joshua Woolrich looking too hard at him, probing into his past.

She eyed him curiously. 'What would you do now if you were alone here?' she asked.

'Wait out the storm, then hike down the mountain to find someone with a working phone.'

'But we won't have to go that far. There's

the cell phone in my car. I have to get word to my family that I'm all right. I don't want to worry my father.'

Somehow, Wheeler imaged Joshua Woolrich stayed too busy issuing orders to worry about much of anything. He cast her a dubious sidelong glance.

Claire shrugged. 'He wants everyone to think he's invincible. The hard-driving tycoon. Believe me, his outlook is very different when it comes to family. I know he's overprotective, but shortly after my mother died, a close friend of his lost his son. Scared him, I think.'

Wheeler was noting how she hadn't mentioned her beloved Barre's concern. His former friend would be rushing around like a man hunting for the lost stub of a winning lottery ticket.

Wheeler pulled the T-shirt over his head. It fit him snugly. He inspected the pair of shorts she'd handed him.

She set her head back against the wall, staring at the exposed insulation in the ceiling. She sighed heavily. 'We need to get straight about what happened back at the cottage.'

Wheeler studied her upraised, delicate features, the exposed hollow at the base of her throat. At the thought of her breasts hanging free beneath the loose cotton T-shirt, he felt a pinching inside the damp denim.

You can't always have what ya want. Sort of makes life one big joke, don't it? He could almost hear his dad spouting his favorite adage. His father had suffered one disappointment after another. Failed businesses, a farm he barely held on to, then even his secure day job had ended in a permanent layoff. Dad knew all about wanting, nothing about getting.

Good God, was Wheeler becoming just like him, shrinking back and wallowing in bitterness? For years, he'd struggled to prove he could succeed. How ironic everything had fallen apart, fulfilling his old man's prophecy. The obvious parallel jabbed him.

He looked Claire in the eye. 'I thought we just did.'

'You know exactly what I'm referring to.'

He needed to hear her acknowledge it. 'Fill me in. My mind-reading's a little rusty.'

Her voice shrank, but she didn't dodge his gaze. 'I only kissed you because I panicked, and I suspect your motives were the same — I wasn't reacting rationally. We both know it didn't mean anything.'

She seemed waiting for him to confirm this. Wheeler suppressed a laugh. She pressed her shoulders to the wall, her gardenia scent intensifying. The thought of her skin warming inflamed him.

He couldn't help goading her. 'Does it ever have to?'

'Well, yes. I mean no, not for us. For me . . .'

'Took your mind off the storm, didn't it? Maybe we should try it again and see how it goes without the special effects,' he suggested. 'Weather's not gonna let up for a long while.' He said it in jest, but as he watched her eyes darken, he began to acknowledge how much he wanted to do exactly that.

He knew what he wanted. He wanted to take her to bed and watch the shades of green deepen in those eyes, feel the temperature of her body rise, find the point on her skin from which the flowery scent originated.

'I enjoyed kissing you. I'm going to do it again.' He waited an eternal ten seconds for her to say no, elated and confused when she failed to utter a protest.

Her brow furrowed. 'You're a kind man, aren't you, Wheeler? Why do you work so hard at pretending you're not?'

Without thinking about what he was doing, he reached out and pressed his fingers to the smooth skin of her throat, as he'd been longing to do for several minutes now. He felt both her pulse and her breathing under his hand, the very life of her.

'I've never been good at pretending much of anything,' he said. Bowing over her upraised mouth as if to drink from a fountain, he forgot he'd intended to prove nothing astonishing would happen this time.

6

Claire, still numb with regret knowing she'd missed her own engagement party and anticipating the reactions her disappearance would spark, awakened from her fog and was startled to see Wheeler's face looming closer over hers. She liked his features, loved his eyes, and wondered fleetingly about the man behind them. This was happening so quickly, she didn't have a chance to change her mind, nor anywhere to escape if she'd wanted to.

Her eyelids fluttered shut, and she parted her lips like a hungry baby bird awaiting food. Wheeler's mouth covered hers with the same urgency as when the world was falling apart. His lips were warm and as bold as the man himself. Heat rippled through her, chasing away her chills, and she felt wobbly, as though the floor beneath her were crumbling away. She tried to blame the swig of champagne punch, the fear, but the random excuses shattered into fragments inside her head.

His whisker stubble bristled against her cheek, sandpaper on satin. He felt so hard and rough, yet with an underlying tenderness irrepressibly compelling. He smelled of rain and musk — primitive and male. He tasted of fruit punch and champagne. She braced herself by clasping the sides of his head, weaving her fingers through his silky hair.

She parted her lips wider, welcoming his tongue as he slipped it inside her mouth. She met it with her own. As she gave herself up to the sizzling sensations, the hot shivers igniting her desire pressed her closer to him. Her expectation of feeling less this time vanished. His powerful aura permeated her senses, mesmerizing her.

She offered no resistance as his hand lit on her T-shirt, and he planted his open palm solidly against her middle, caressing her belly, warming her to her core. Hot sensation jolted her, and she pressed herself into its source. The heat spread lower, making her squirm in his embrace. He skated his palm upward to clasp her breast through the loose cotton. She heard a startled squeal and realized it had come from the back of her throat.

Stunned by his daring, she moved her hand to push him away, but instead her fingers curled around his wrist. His pulse raced beneath her fingertips. Still sucking the breath from her, he rubbed circles around the hardened nub of her nipple with his thumb. Fire spiraled through her chest. Too late, she realized she'd delivered herself into the hands of a man who knew exactly how to inflame her in ways she'd never imagined possible. How expertly he confused her. All she could do was mew like a kitten in his arms, her defenses slackening along with her body. He was definitely not timid about getting what he wanted, as she'd foolishly assumed earlier. And what he wanted grew plainer with each heartbeat.

Dampening between her legs, she ached to experience the full thrust of his power. How different lovemaking might be with a man so forceful. Feeling selfish and greedy, she could only wonder about it.

She continued kissing Wheeler as though nothing existed but here and now. A vague notion warned her this should have felt wrong, but she couldn't immediately remember why.

Wheeler pulled back, shifting his head sideways to take her earlobe gently between his teeth. Claire squirmed at the quivery sensation tickling down to her midsection. Pushing aside a handful of her long hair, he buried his face in the curve of her neck, hot breath tickling her skin. His scaring tongue traced the curve of her ear, and she forced back a sob at the tremors he shot through her.

To her astonishment, he suddenly drew away.

Left burning and tingling, she missed his touch instantly. The reality of her reckless, urgent reaction to him set in, triggering shame. She'd practically ravished the man. And she had no excuse. She'd sooner endure torture than admit to him she'd never been kissed this way before.

'Bad idea,' he muttered, twisting away from her.

Stunned, Claire wondered what she'd done to initiate this turnabout. She had not wanted him to stop. But she should have.

With Barre, she'd felt an obligation to give, to please. Wheeler consumed her. Made her want to be consumed. She entertained a longing to travel as far as he could take her.

Barre. She snapped guiltily. He was probably moving solar systems to get up the mountain at this very moment. And here she was on the verge of giving herself to a sullen stranger who didn't want much to do with her beyond kissing her witless. Simply because she found him exciting. A man she couldn't get along with for more than five seconds without an argument erupting. Surely the twister had scrambled her brains.

She and Barre would have that wild abandon she craved. Barre had held back out of consideration for her. She'd ruined it that first time. Once she was more experienced, once they were married, making love every day at least . . . If he could ever forgive her once she told him about this. One kiss born of panic he might get past. But a second? How could she explain that?

She didn't need to pick up any additional experience here. If she betrayed Barre, they would never have a life together. Even if he could accept it, maybe she couldn't. Perhaps she had gone too far in betraying him already. To feel tempted at all confused her deeply.

She shook her hair back, still dazed from Wheeler's caresses and struggling to collect her wits, afraid to look directly at him. Because she couldn't shake from her mind wondering how his lovemaking might feel. Unthinkingly, she pressed her fingertips to her slightly puffy lips. 'This is wrong,' she blurted. 'I'm nearly engaged.'

He flashed a look of surprise. 'Is the nearly part what made it take you so long to remember? Anyway, you're off the hook on that score. Blame me. I was the aggressor.

And I'm not spoken for.'

'Then why did you say it was a bad idea? Because you suddenly remembered who my father is?' she asked without thinking, immediately wanting to kick herself. Shame on her, falling back on Father's authority to warn him away.

His low glance indicated he wasn't afraid of anyone. How different he struck her from the man who'd hidden in the shadows and fielded orders from Father all afternoon. Instantly, she knew the forceful man she faced now was the real Wheeler Scully. But why the charade? Yes, Mr Woolrich. Right away, Mr Woolrich. She recalled what Father had said about Wheeler's past. This mountaintop made a good hiding place. He could be desperate, dangerous. But no matter what he might have done, she already trusted he wouldn't harm her. He'd bypassed too many chances to do so. Realizing this, she refused to be bullied by him.

He was still staring at her. 'You got it,' he said.

'You're lying,' she challenged.

His mouth slanted in a wicked grin. 'We finally agree on something, then you accuse me of being a liar. If you insist, we can pick it back up . . . ' he suggested, moving toward her.

She shrank from him, sure she'd be lost if he touched her again. 'No.' So much for not showing fear. The danger lay not so much in his hurting her as how good he could make her feel.

He backed off. 'Entertaining you isn't part of my job.'

Claire's face scalded. 'You're not exactly Chuckles the Clown.'

'You know what I mean. Kissing you in the first place was my mistake. But I figured we'd both be dead by now so it wouldn't matter anyway.'

'Well, surprise, we're not dead. So we both have to deal with it.'

'And you missed your little party and you're bored and blue, so you're playing around to console yourself. Consorting with the hired help? What would Daddy say about that? It must excite you to defy him behind his back when you're too scared to do it to his face.'

'I am not scared of him. You honestly think that's what this was about?'

'What else? You're obviously accustomed to getting everything you want. I'm not one of your playthings, and I'm not biting.'

Strong words for a man who'd been happily chewing on her ear a second ago. At his outrageous accusation, Claire didn't know whether to laugh or cry. She couldn't imagine herself using this hulking, capable man as her toy. She wouldn't have known how. But her pride ran too strong for her to admit she'd wanted to kiss him. Be akin to boasting her brain was missing a few gears.

'What could I have been thinking? Do you actually believe I find this entertaining? Now I'm going to have to go back and face Barre with what I've done.'

'You're going to tell him?'

'To be fair, yes.'

'I don't see a ring on your finger.'

'If I can't be honest with him, how can I expect him to be open with me?'

'This guy must be a saint to tell you everything about about himself. We both know those kisses didn't mean anything. But telling him sounds like a terrific idea.'

'It's nothing to joke about. I'm sure he'll be hurt and angry. Regardless of how meaningless the action was.'

He flashed her a scathing look. 'Listen, Claire, we're probably going to be here together all night. We didn't choose each other's company and, after tonight, we'll probably never see each other again. Circumstances forced us together in close quarters. Nothing is real right now. Everything will shift back exactly the way it was. If we keep experimenting, it might become a little too tempting to do something you really don't want to do. I've been up here alone long enough I could prove way too willing to help you out. Then you'd have one dilly of a confession to spill to this guy you're so anxious to give up your freedom for.'

She gasped. 'I have no intention of doing anything I'd regret later. How dare you assume I would. I'm not so impulsive I'd . . . '

'Wake up, Claire. I wasn't doing all the heavy breathing here.'

'I didn't mean to — '

'Then why were you kissing me?'

'Because I needed to know — '

'Whether your toes would curl? Don't use me for your lab rat because you're getting cold feet about getting married.'

'I do want to get married. I've always wanted to be married and have a house of my own, with several little geniuses running around — '

He spluttered a laugh, breaking the tension. 'You're convinced they'll be geniuses?'

She hugged her knees. 'Naturally. Terribly bright at the least. Well-behaved and charming.'

'These are trained chimps you're describing, not kids. You should spend some time with my nephews if you want to experience the real thing.'

'I wish I could. As an only child, I'll never

have nieces or nephews of my own. At home, it was just Father and me. Not that he neglected me, but he went away a lot, and business kept him preoccupied. I always missed having that sense of family.'

'You shouldn't get married just for the company.'

She squinted at him. 'You're one of those men who doesn't believe marriage ever really works, aren't you?'

'I was married once, and it didn't.'

'What happened?'

'She took off with a guy I'd thought was my best friend.' His expression was hard as ice.

Twice betrayed, she thought, as sympathy tugged at her. And guilt. If she truly loved Barre, how could Wheeler Scully stir such mindless passion in her? Doubt nagged her. Maybe this absurd interlude came as a godsend. Not being trapped here with Wheeler, of course, but having time to measure whether she was capable of honoring the commitment she was about to make. In her eagerness, had she overestimated her own infallibility?

'It must be difficult to trust anyone after losing the two people who should have been closest to you.'

His jaw tightened. 'Who needs to? People

don't always do what they should. They break vows, give up their children . . . '

Claire bristled. 'I can't condemn my biological parents when I don't know their circumstances.' But he'd struck a nerve. She secretly feared as hard as she tried to act like a Woolrich — mirroring her father's unflinching integrity — some basic element in her duplicated her biological parents' irresponsibility. Normally, she implemented extreme caution to avoid acting impulsively, doing anything crazy. Until she'd kissed Wheeler. That ranked as insanity. Especially when she'd allowed it to happen a second time.

And now Wheeler had proven her flighty and unfaithful. Not fair, when he'd caught her in a weak, desperate moment. But the world hadn't been crashing in just a moment ago. She had no excuse.

She realized he was speaking to her. 'Then why does being adopted bother you so much?'

'I didn't say it bothered me.'

'You didn't have to say it. Do you know your real parents?'

'How do you define real? Father's always been there for me when I needed him, although I'm sure he never would have wanted to adopt if he'd anticipated he'd be raising a daughter alone. I suppose I complicated his life in a way he never planned. Nothing gets more real than that. The Woolriches could have had any child they wanted, and they chose me, even though I was already three years old.'

'You've never wanted to contact your birth parents?'

She shook her head. 'Why would I? They're strangers. Father is not. Why should I betray him after he's been good to me? As you so eloquently put it, why should I concern myself with people who didn't give a damn?'

'I'd sure want a peek at 'em.'

'I don't remember them at all.' She shivered.

'You sure you're not just afraid to find out who they really are? Afraid to know you might be someone your father wouldn't approve of? Do you ever wonder if they might come looking for you one day?'

'I pray to God not.'

'You see, you do hate them — you just won't admit it.'

'Hate has nothing to do with it. When I think of them or try to remember them, there's nothing but a void. I don't feel anything. Joshua Woolrich is my father, and after all these years, the sudden emergence of strangers claiming to be my parents would make a mockery of all he's done for me.

Besides, I would never allow them to upset him.'

Wheeler mowed a hand through his shaggy hair. 'Your old man can hold his own against anyone.'

Claire remembered Wheeler, like everyone else, was unaware of her father's physical condition. Wheeler viewed Father as an invincible, unyielding tyrant.

'My father's a human being, and I'm all that's left of his family. He wouldn't appreciate anyone trying to interfere with that. Besides, he's one of those people who hide feelings they believe unacceptable deep inside, where they kick around and inflict the most damage.'

Wheeler rubbed his jaw. She wondered if the stubby whiskers make his skin itch. She wished he would change the subject.

'What happened to your mom — Mrs Woolrich?'

'My mother, Anita Woolrich, died shortly after she and Father adopted me. She had a brain aneurysm, and no one knew until she just collapsed one day. It was too late then for anyone to save her.'

'So you don't remember her either?'

'Yes, I do. I adored her. I was three when I was adopted, not an infant.'

'Seems like you would have remembered

your other family too. I remember things that happened when I was two or three.'

'Good for you. I don't.'

'Seems your old man wouldn't be too keen on your getting married.'

'Oh, no. Father approves. He's devoted so many years to raising me alone. I think it's a relief to him. He finds it settling, I think, to know I won't be on my own if anything should happen to him. That's rubbish, of course, since I manage fine on my own. I don't need to be taken care of, but he has these archaic ideas that go along with his generation, I suppose. And he took to Barre from the start. They share similar attitudes about a lot of things. Almost eerie, in a way. Maybe now Father will stop feeling responsible for me and get married again.'

'Your dad's not all that old that he's about to keel over into his grave,' Wheeler observed. 'And maybe if he wanted to remarry, he would have done it by now. A man like your father decides what he's going to do, then makes it work.'

'Maybe he hasn't had time to consider the possibility.'

'Or doesn't want to. Maybe he still loves your mother.'

Claire was taken aback. Such a romantic notion from a man with such a coarse exterior and jaded outlook. She tilted her head, studying him closely. 'Memories make poor company,' Claire said. 'After all this time, he must be terribly lonely.'

'Why don't you just ask him why he's never remarried?'

Claire's shoulders sagged. Obviously, Wheeler didn't understand her father. 'Pry into his personal affairs? I don't think so. Besides, he'd never tell the truth if he suspected it might hurt my feelings.'

'You're his daughter, not his secretary. Why are you two so formal with each other? He seems like a straightforward guy to me. Since you're basing your whole life around an assumption about him —'

'I am doing no such thing. I want to marry Barre.'

'What if your old man disapproved?'

She raised her chin. 'Well, I'd marry Barre anyway.'

He laughed. 'No, you wouldn't.'

Claire felt vaguely forlorn. Fortunately, Father was nearly as fond of Barre as she was, so Wheeler's scenario loomed as mere speculation. If she defied Father's wishes, he would react with hurt and anger, and when wounded he could be inflexible. He was still upset with her for moving into her own apartment, and he'd never accepted even one of her repeated dinner invitations. She was glad her choice of a fiancé had not estranged them.

How would Father react if she called off the wedding? She could hear herself trying to explain . . . well, you see, Father, I couldn't resist the caretaker, so I doubt I'd make a very respectable wife . . .

Cringing, she was beginning to doubt whether she could go through with the wedding in December as planned. Not that she entertained illusions about what had happened with Wheeler. But how could she ever make love with Barre without thinking of the profound excitement Wheeler had stirred in her?

She needed time to sort this out.

'I respect Father's opinion, if that's what you mean. He's an astute judge of character.'

Wheeler cleared his throat. 'So if you ran off with, say, a well-mannered garbage collector or a dog catcher, your old man would give you his blessing?'

Father would implode if she befriended a garbage collector. 'That situation has never arisen,' she replied.

Wheeler howled. 'Not by coincidence, I'm sure. Your friends are probably screened more thoroughly than CIA job applicants. You are sharp, Princess, I'll give you that. My take is

166

this garbage collector might be visited by thugs in the night who would usher him away to a safer location.'

'Father is not involved with the underworld or any thugs, thank you. He's an honest businessman. You're quite presumptuous for someone who knows so little about him, or me for that fact.'

He swept his hair back, then lowered his voice. 'Sorry, you just didn't strike me as being all that devoted to your fiancé a while ago. Are you sure your parents are all you're hiding away in that dark little cellar of yours?'

Claire pushed down Aurora Sutton's astonished inquiry ringing in her memory. *You must know something about your people, dear.* As if she were lying about it. Barre had quickly ushered his mother away, apologized for her, but the sting remained. 'You changed the subject. We were discussing you. Are you still in love with your wife?'

'Obviously I never was, or she wouldn't have left, would she?' he asked. His voice lowered. 'The guy she ran off with only used her to get to me. She should have been smart enough to know that.' He cast Claire a pointed look she didn't understand.

She wondered whether Wheeler was too unyielding to forgive or whether such a betrayal was simply too much for anyone to conquer. Obviously, he was transferring his disappointment in his wife to all women. To Claire herself, at the moment, since she was the only one here.

She attempted to console him. 'You'll fall in love again someday, Wheeler, with someone who will appreciate you and stay with you forever.'

He laughed. 'Thanks, Tinkerbell. But spare me. Can I stop clapping my hands now?'

Fuming, she reminded herself some woman had broken his heart, made him bitter. 'Make fun if you must. But I believe most people are good deep down inside, and they can make incredible things happen. I was the child nobody wanted, and yet loving parents came and gave me a life with advantages most people only dream of. Real-life miracles do happen, Wheeler, if you open yourself to the possibility then work at making them come true. I used to have trouble believing, until Denver made me see how much I already had — ' Remembering Wheeler's opinion of Barre's father, she broke off her statement.

He shook his head. 'Thanks for the pep talk, but I know better than to repeat my mistakes. Keeps life uncomplicated. When I think of her, there's that same dark void you associate with your parents.'

'What are your plans? Staying up here and

shutting the world out? Drinking beer and watching TV? Feeling sorry for yourself? Until you actually become as indifferent as you profess you are?'

At her last statement, he recoiled visibly, and she knew she'd hit home.

'Whatever works. I like it up here. Nice and quiet. No one to bother me except a deer once in a while. Normally, anyway.'

'Someplace safe where no one expects much of you? Where you don't have to demand much of yourself? What did you do for a living when you were married? Where did you live?'

He stared hard at her, and Claire's chest constricted as she absorbed his piercing gaze.

'And how much do you demand of yourself, Princess? What risks do you take?'

She stiffened her spine. 'I have a job. An apartment. My own life. I hold my own, Wheeler.'

'With your daddy and his money always cushioning you like a great big net? You'd never have very far to fall, Princess, as long as you stay safely over that big air bag he provides. Face it, you'll never have to contend with the hard realities that dominate most folks' lives.'

Claire loathed his being right. The hard-won independence she took such pride in faded into a thin veneer. She worked for a company Father owned and was free to move back into his home any time. 'I have advantages. They're part of who I am. Why would I want to give them up?'

'No reason. Except it proves you're in no position to badger other people about shying away from their potential. A person who isn't hungry doesn't walk the extra mile to the store. And she hasn't a clue what the trip is like.'

She met his steely gaze. Looking into those intense eyes, she suddenly realized he lashed out at her each time she began getting too close to his heart and mind. Distracting her. How difficult he must find trusting anyone after what he'd been through. 'Perhaps you've brushed the truth. You must have loved your wife very much to feel so hurt still.' Without thinking, she reached out to take his hand between hers, but he pulled it away. She stung as though he'd slapped her.

'Save your pity,' he decreed, getting to his feet.

'You don't mind kissing the socks off me, but you won't let me hold your hand? I see what you're about, Wheeler Scully. Maybe I should pity you, but not for the reason you think. Oh, never mind. What became of the man — the one your wife went away with?'

He hesitated. 'He's found another woman, last I heard.'

'Maybe he won't be able to deceive this one so easily.'

'Yeah, well, he's a chameleon. He had me believing he was my friend for years, and I don't consider myself stupid. I think this one might be smarter, but maybe too naïve to see through him. The only reason I told you what happened to me is because you seem to think getting married will open another chapter in your charmed life. You envision these glittery little scenes filled with young Einsteins in starched white pinafores and a husband meeting your daddy's requirements. Seems you overlooked the reality check. Take it from me, you have to know someone inside and out, see into their soul before you link your existence to theirs. The closer you let the wrong person in, the worse they can hurt you.'

She shivered involuntarily, imagining those penetrating eyes looking into her soul. His eyes. 'You said you never loved her.'

He hesitated, a rabbit startled by oncoming headlights. 'I never should have.'

'Naturally, you're resentful. Divorce is a painful process. I've seen it. Who hasn't nowadays? The walking wounded like yourself. You let someone get close, and she let you down. But with Barre and me, it's different — '

'Everybody thinks they're different going in, Princess. Do yourself a favor and take a hard look at this Barry guy. And yourself.'

She pressed a hand to her chest, still rising and falling rapidly from the physical excitement Wheeler had stirred inside her. Why was he intentionally mispronouncing Barre's name?

'Me?' she asked.

'Face it, Princess, if you were all that crazy in love with him, you wouldn't have needed that second kiss to find out what you need to know. The first one was an accident, something neither of us could ever explain. But this time, we both knew what we were doing.'

He stood up, staring down at her.

Suddenly, one corner of his mouth twitched, leaving her to wonder what he was thinking until he muttered, 'Knocked your socks off, huh?'

She hesitated. She saw no advantage in trying to deny it. Wheeler knew the truth about that as well as she did. 'If I'd been wearing any, yes.'

'Nothing Denver Sutton's books address.'

'Or his son? Is that what you're trying to say? You don't even know him. Besides,

Barre's nothing like his father.' She swallowed hard, determined to sound experienced in such matters. She was thankful now, she'd read so much. 'You and I reached out to each other in shock, and what we discovered isn't so remarkable. Lust is commonplace from lower animals on up. Maybe devotion and consideration are far more important than atomic meltdowns.'

He lowered his gaze triumphantly, and her skin smarted as she realized what she'd inadvertently acknowledged. The chemistry between her and Barre, despite his suave good looks and the ambition she admired so, was as volatile as cream poured over oatmeal. How could she love Barre and melt like wax in Wheeler Scully's arms?

'All I'm saying is it's good reason to keep away from each other. Everything's a little crazy tonight. If you've got jitters over getting engaged, don't use me as your testing board.'

'I didn't mean . . . Quit twisting this around. I agree we mustn't let this happen again. I couldn't agree more, in fact. Obviously, you blame all women because one disappointed you.'

He shot her a challenging look. 'You're a beautiful, alluring woman, and I'd enjoy making love to you. Is that what you want? Because — '

'No!' she snapped indignantly, cheeks flaming.

He nodded. 'Then let's leave it alone. I've been up here by myself for a long time. I wouldn't turn you down.'

'I wasn't trying to give the impression . . .' Geeze, now he thought she was a tease. She bristled indignantly. He'd started it by kissing her first. She hadn't initiated that contact! All at once, she realized he was bullying her into keeping her distance because he didn't want it to happen any more than she did. What was he afraid of? Her father? No, she doubted even her father could keep Wheeler from going after anything he really wanted. She'd seen him defy nature, climb unscathed from the ruins of his home, and pulverize the front door into mincemeat.

At least she knew what she feared — scrambling a life that had fallen into perfect order since nursery school. That's when bad things happened. When life stopped falling into sequence. But not him. She wasn't afraid of him, even if she should be.

Mercy, was he warning her away from him because he felt something he didn't want to feel? As if he needed to. The prospect of having nudged any degree of affection from Wheeler's frozen heart delighted her far more than reason dictated.

Yes, okay, she must be losing her mind completely then.

Ignoring her, he stepped off into the dark recesses of the basement.

'Where are you going?' she called.

'Just far enough to get out of these wet jeans. No peeking, please.' From out of the shadows, his voice trailed back a few minutes later. 'I liked it too.' And she knew exactly what he meant.

Listening to rustling noises from the direction where Wheeler had disappeared, Claire stared at the mattress as though praying. Damn him, now he had her wondering, imagining how he might look naked. Wondering how much he'd enjoyed her kiss. Imagining making love with him.

Why did he scowl every time she mentioned Barre's name? And why so opposed to her marrying him? Something more was going on here than Wheeler's disapproval of Barre's father and his philosophies.

She wasn't so vain as to assume Wheeler madly in love with her and jealous, although he might be thinking if not for Barre she'd be down on the mattress with him right now. No. Wheeler didn't impress her as that superficial. If he meant to have her down on that mattress, he'd get her there. An unsettling revelation.

What was with him? A man who should have had everything going for him now quite literally had nothing. In good conscience, she couldn't leave him behind this way. She owed him.

He came back, carrying a rumpled Army blanket. He presented it to her. 'Not much, but you still look cold.'

'I am. Thanks.' Unfolding the blanket, shaking dust from it, she pulled it over her legs while Wheeler stood watching.

The shorts she'd brought him proved a better fit than the T-shirt he wore, although she tried not to let her gaze linger on the long muscle-roped legs moving at eye level. She thought of the brute force with which he'd pulverized the door.

'Thoughtful of you, Wheeler.'

He grudgingly lifted a corner of his mouth. 'Don't read too much into it.'

He caught her covering her mouth midyawn. 'We won't be going anywhere for a while. Why don't you catch some sleep?'

She eyed him skeptically. 'What are you going to do?'

'Keep an eye on the weather.'

'You must be tired.' He'd been working on the grounds since long before the guests arrived. She remembered being greeted by the smell of freshly mown grass as she'd stepped out of her car this morning. Lord, only this morning? Light years ago.

'I'm okay.'

She was exhausted. 'So am I.'

He shook his head. 'I won't bother you.'

'I just don't think I can sleep. I'm too keyed up. It's not you. It's everything else.'

'Sitting up all night won't banish the storm or clear the road.'

'Sure, I know. But I'd like to be awake when the storm ends. Surely someone will come looking for us then.'

Resigned, he sat beside her, propping his back against the wall. The gap between them was half the span she'd left when she'd originally sat down.

She lifted the edge of the blanket and drew part of it over him. He turned to her questioningly.

'You must be cold too,' she ventured.

'Thanks,' he murmured, turning away to stare into the darkness. Her nerves jangled in deference to his proximity. She didn't doubt if she gave him the slightest excuse he'd make good on his offer/threat to make love to her. She couldn't shake the way he'd made her feel inside. She couldn't pretend any longer she didn't know what she was dealing with.

Surreptitiously, she studied his profile. The silence spinning between them felt almost comfortable, as if they'd exhausted now all possible arguments and had resigned themselves to waiting.

Claire realized Wheeler was right. Once they left this mountain, she'd go back to her old life and he to whatever was left of his. Wheeler was different than any man she knew, rugged and raw and at times honest to the point of agony. Yet those strong hands, capable of splintering wood, had touched her with a reverence she got goosebumps remembering. Wheeler had more dimensions than any of the men she'd met in business and at social functions. As annoying as he could be, the prospect of his disappearing from her life as abruptly as he'd invaded it saddened her.

If she were going to learn anything about him, she'd have to do it before help came, before he turned back into a zombie in her father's presence. If she trusted him, maybe he'd realize he could begin to trust people again, regain his self-confidence outside his wooded sanctuary. Love someone again someday. It suddenly occurred to her being trapped up here with him presented the biggest challenge of her life.

Barre fit in so well, accommodated both

their busy schedules. He never came by unexpectedly, never took her out for a hamburger in the middle of the night, never got so caught up in her he couldn't keep himself from making love. Except that one time.

When they went out, they attended social functions or ate dinner at a restaurant. She'd accepted this as normal, because he lived the same kind of life as her father always had. She loved her father, but she did not want her married life to be a continuation of her childhood existence.

The heat of Wheeler's body warmed and relaxed her.

She envisioned her and Barre, once married, doing things together she enjoyed — lounging in pajamas on Sunday mornings and reading the paper in bed, exploring sleepy little mountain towns off the back-roads, packing a picnic lunch and going sailing on Father's boat. Claire loved simple, private outings more than elaborate galas where she usually felt she was as much on display as a dolphin in an aquarium. She and Barre had never actually done any of those things he'd declared such enthusiasm for. They went only places packed with business people and Father's friends. 'Humor me this time. I love showing you off,' Barre would say in that engaging way of his.

Sadie's advice invaded her consciousness. *Take any man's failings and multiply them by ten, because chances are once he stops being polite, that's how bad they are.* Familiar with Sadie's jaded outlook, Claire seldom took Sadie's observations seriously. Now, she wondered. Did Barre share her inclinations? If he did, wouldn't he have made a point of trying harder to please her?

She squeezed her eyes shut. If she kept thinking this way, she'd end up like Sadie — alone with her lofty ideals.

Still, doubt crept in and left her cold. If Barre really loved her, how could he resist coming back to her bed? She'd seen no reason to wait any longer. Even if she got pregnant despite precautions, they'd soon be married any way, ready to start their family.

But, liberated woman of the nineties that she was, she didn't know how to tell him. Sometimes she wondered whether having remained a virgin so long hadn't left her sexually retarded. Or had she let it slide because she wasn't as convinced he was the man she wanted as she tried to believe? Was she afraid a second encounter might confirm what she already suspected?

Was she transferring the emptiness Barre had left inside her to Wheeler, a man who meant nothing to her? Maybe finding sexual abandonment came more easily with a stranger. No worry over whether afterward he'd love her more or less or at all. She gnawed her lip. Dear God, she was in trouble then. Was she one of those women who would never be satisfied by one man? Something in her genes maybe? Was she as irresponsible as the two parents who had created an unwanted child?

Wheeler left her breathless. Made her experience everything she should have felt with Barre, except for the security, the promise to make her dreams of a home and a family real, her father's blessing. God, she was so confused. Barre was the man she needed, yet at the moment Wheeler the one she wanted.

Even now, her heart fluttered at the memory of how he'd made her feel — warm, womanly and desirable. She'd waited so long for the right man, a deliberate and difficult resolution she'd made back in her teens. Many times she'd been tempted to abandon her principles. Yet she'd remained chaste. Until Barre. Not because she was a prude, but because she believed in commitment and obligation. She'd expected when a man finally made love to her, everything would be perfect. Especially after waiting so very long.

181

But something had been missing. Something in her, she'd assumed. But now, Wheeler had her wondering . . .

Her body rhythms glided into sync with Wheeler's even breathing, his heartbeat. Without realizing it, she let her head drop against his sturdy shoulder.

Closing her eyes, she drifted into a light slumber, striving to think of Barre and unable to banish Wheeler from her thoughts. How could she with his scent, his heat, his hard muscle, permeating her senses? Whatever had happened to her tonight, she could not go home and pick up her life where she'd left off. She dreamed of their stolen kisses, savoring them over and over in her mind.

$\star$ $\star$ $\star$

When she awoke, stiff and cold beneath the blanket, she was lying on her side on the mattress — alone. Pushing herself up, she fought off the inevitable queasiness. The single remaining vivid memory of her previous life, awakening alone in a strange, dark place, haunted her. Each time she woke up, she experienced a sense of dread before she got her bearings and assured herself she was not lost. After so many years, she anticipated it, automatically fighting it down.

Fear weakened a person. Ever since she was three, she'd looked to Father as the strongest person in the world and resolved to be just like him. He must have experienced moments of isolation and doubt, especially after her mother died. But he never revealed that about himself. Nor would she.

Throwing back the cover, she sat up and rubbed her eyes. 'Wheeler?' she called tentatively, her voice echoing in the vast, dark basement.

No answer came. And something else had changed. She no longer heard the rumble of thunder. Everything up above was calm and far too still.

She tried to rise, a stab of pain reminding her of her injured ankle. 'Ow!' she cried, sinking back.

On her second attempt, she got up more carefully, boosting herself by clutching the wall.

She shuffled toward the stairs. 'I'd hike down the mountain for help,' she remembered Wheeler saying. Had he waited until she was asleep and left her here? He'd been so anxious for her to rest.

A fleeting panic set in. In the back of her mind, she saw her mother crumpling into a heap in the garden, falling asleep standing up. Father rushing up to Mother, standing over her wearing a stricken, crushed expression, screaming at Claire to get inside the house, even though no one was inside. She'd tried to tell him, and he'd snapped at her again.

She remembered turning toward the huge, deserted house, feeling as tiny as an ant. Her small palms sweating as she marched toward the glass doors. Something horrible had happened to the sweet, kind woman who said Claire could hug her neck and call her Mommy, and Father must think it was Claire's fault to be screaming at her and sending her away. They would send her away forever now.

Claire pushed off the memory. She was no child. Father had been trying to spare her watching her mother suffer and get her out of the way so he could tend to her. Still, the memory of total despair had left an indelible imprint.

But if Wheeler was leaving, he should have told her rather than abandoning her here asleep and defenseless. She would have gone with him . . .

Exactly why he might have left without telling her. With her weak ankle and no shoes, she'd have held him back.

She climbed the stairs, favoring her sore leg. Reaching the top, she felt a blessed warmth. A fire roared in the hearth. 'Wheeler?'

He wouldn't have left a blazing fire unattended with her asleep downstairs. Still . . .

Shouting his name, she rushed onto the porch, embarrassed to realize he was standing right by the railing, staring out across the wooded landscape into the drizzly rain before he turned to look at her. Gray mist shrouded the night.

'Something wrong?' he asked.

She took a moment to compose herself. After racing out here like a wild woman, pretending she hadn't panicked at his absence would be ridiculous. 'I thought you'd gone for help and left me behind.'

'It's dark and raining. I'm not going anywhere tonight.' Even as he reassured her, she read guilt in his eyes and knew he'd thought about it.

She stood beside him and leaned on the railing. 'How's your head?'

He rubbed the knot. 'A little sore. I'm fine. He glanced sideways, warmth flickering in his eyes, fading so quickly she knew he hadn't meant to show it. 'Are you okay? I thought you were settled for the night.'

She flexed her shoulders and shook her head. 'I'm surprised I fell asleep at all. I'm spoiled by my own comfortable bed.'

'Yeah.'

Realizing she could go back to hers when this was over and his was probably wedged in a treetop miles away, she regretted her unthinking words. She drummed her polished fingertips against the railing.

'What are you drinking?'

'Instant coffee. Carpenters must have left it.' He held the mug out to her, and she took a sip. It was lukewarm and bitter, but she was grateful for it.

'How did you heat water with no electricity?'

'Over the fire. I found a couple cans of soup too, but we'd better save those for later.'

'Do you think it'll be safe to stay upstairs now?'

'Yes, but stay off the second floor. If another storm rolls in, it's back to the basement.'

'These trees keep falling like matchsticks.'

Wheeler swept his gaze across the landscape. 'These trees are old.' He continued stroking his jaw.

'It bothers you, doesn't it? The beard.'

'Yeah, I could use a shave.'

Either his beard grew exceptionally fast or he'd neglected to shave this morning. If walking around unshaven bothered him, why do it unless for some reason he'd intentionally tried to look scruffy for the guests? Disguise himself?

'Father's razor is upstairs. I'm sure he wouldn't mind — '

He shook his head adamantly. 'I feel guilty enough wearing the man's clothes. I can wait.'

'Wheeler, a razor is nothing to Father. He could buy the company that makes them.'

'That doesn't give me license to use his personal belongings. I wouldn't be wearing his clothes except you might be uncomfortable watching me parade around in the buff.'

'Do you have to be so unyielding you can't accept anything from anyone?'

He flicked an eyebrow. 'Yes. I've always taken care of myself. I don't want to be trapped into the kind of gratitude where you feel obligated to live by someone else's rules.'

'As you assume I do?'

Wheeler ignored her question, staring back out in to the haze. 'The storm's letting up. Just raining now.'

'Help should be coming soon.'

'I found something you might be able to use. Those yours? Found them stashed in a corner of the kitchen.'

She followed his gaze to the door frame. Walking over to it, she peered inside. Sadie's old running shoes lay in the foyer. Affection for her cousin surged through her, quickly followed by distress at what Sadie must be thinking right now.

Bending, she reached for the shoes, blinking back tears. She refused to cry over a pair of tennis shoes. Wheeler would think her a lunatic. 'God bless you, Sadie. She must have forgotten them,' she murmured.

Stepping back out on the porch, she impulsively grasped his shoulder, pulling herself up on tiptoes to kiss him on the cheek.

Caught by surprise, he didn't resist. Nor did he respond. 'Will they fit?' he asked finally.

Embarrassed, she stepped back, directing her interest in the shoes. 'We're not exactly the same size, but I think they'll do.'

'Some small progress.'

She sighed heavily. 'I've got to let my father know I'm all right. As soon as possible.'

'Know how to send smoke signals?'

'You don't understand.'

'I think I do. You answer to your father for everything, and it's driving you wild you can't report into him. Your father's a smart fella, Claire. He knew there was a storm system coming. He'll figure out you got stranded up here. Naturally he'll be worried, for only for a short time. You are safe. He'll learn that soon.'

'My father's not as strong as he makes everyone believe. If he thinks anything could have happened to me ... He never completely recovered from the shock of losing his wife so suddenly. I don't want to deliver any more jolts.'

Wheeler studied her expression.

She could tell he didn't understand her ravings. 'He suffers from high blood pressure. If it gets out of control he could have a stroke or a heart attack.'

'I'm sure in his position he knows how to deal with stress. But, look, the rain's nearly stopped. I can probably make it to your car.'

She shook her head. 'It's dark, raining, and too foggy to see. Probably trees and powerlines down. We shouldn't go out before the rain stops at least. I'm just trying to explain so you'll understand why I'm so frustrated about not being about to get word to him. You must have people wondering about you.'

'He's a reasonable man, Claire. There's no reason for him to assume the worst.'

'About me, he always does. I told you his friend lost a son shortly after my mother died? Well, his friend's son was kidnapped and held for ransom. Murdered instead of returned safely as promised.' She shivered. 'Father felt very threatened and security conscious, especially where I was concerned. He installed elaborate security systems, and there was always some muscled bodyguard lurking around our household in the guise of a chauffeur or a gardener or even a nanny. Perhaps that explains why he's always been so cautious about whom I associated with.'

'Hell of a way to grow up.'

'He did it subtly. My aunt warned him his precautions alone might scare me. He usually trusts her advice, where I'm concerned anyway.'

'What happened to his friend's family was tragic. But wasn't he overreacting to assume his would become a target?'

'I suppose his wealth and prominence automatically made him vulnerable.' She rubbed her bare arms, folding them across her chest. 'Not knowing what kind of background I came from probably didn't help him feel more secure.'

'Even when agencies don't give out names, they provide some kind of background, don't they?'

Claire laughed lightly. 'About people who would abandon a child at the roadside like an unwanted kitten? I'm afraid they didn't fill in any questionnaires.' Swallowing hard, she looked off into the gloom. She felt the heat of Wheeler's astonished gaze.

'Claire?' His voice hung in the thick air. She felt his hand fall lightly on her arm.

Involuntarily, she lifted her gaze to meet his. The harshness had faded from his eyes.

'I didn't know that. I am sorry.'

She mustered a brave smile. 'How could you have known? Forget I mentioned it.' She was anxious to change the subject. She never told anyone her blood relatives had been so eager to get rid of her that they hadn't had the patience to place her in even the state's custody. Had she been such a horrible child? She must have been since those people had started out keeping her, not giving her up at birth, later changing their minds.

He moved closer. 'For taking his chances, he didn't do half bad.'

'Do you have any idea how wearing it is, trying to be the kind of child he would have wanted, someone like him? Sometimes I doubt I have it in me.'

'Where did you ever get the crazy idea you're supposed to be just like him? Every kid turns out to be his own person, not a smaller version of his folks. That's why they drive their parents so crazy. Me and my old man were about as different as water and gasoline.' He sounded kind of astonished as he made this last statement. 'We never got along so hot because of it. Couldn't convince either one of us we weren't right about everything.'

She swept her gaze across the misty

landscape, attributing her blurred vision solely to the rain. 'You like being in charge up here when my father's not around, don't you?'

He narrowed his brow. 'I work best on my own.'

'Some people find Father difficult to work for. And believe me, I sympathize. I'm all too well-acquainted with his standards and his peculiarities.'

Wheeler shrugged. 'He's hardly ever around.'

'But he has the utmost faith in you. When he calls and asks you to arrange something, once he hangs up, he's confident whatever he's requested will be taken care of efficiently. There are few people he relies on so instinctively.'

'So what? I could do this job in my sleep. Anybody could.'

'I'm not doling out backhanded compliments. It's an observation. You understand my father, how he thinks. You're strong and self-reliant, the way he is. I can tell he doesn't intimidate you, as he does most people. Yet you pretend he does. You've been my father.'

'Excuse me?'

'In his position. Maybe not literally. But you're used to being the one in authority, you've handled business deals, maybe even run a business.'

He eyed her darkly enough to indicate she'd hit pay dirt before sidestepping past her to go into the house, but she caught hold of him by the arm. 'We both know you had a life before you came here. I've told you my darkest secret. If I'm going to spend the night here with you, I have a right to know who you really are.'

He brushed her off, going for the door. 'Does that make it easier for you, Claire? Believing I'm more than just your father's caretaker? You're looking at who I really am. I work for your father because I need the money, need a place to live. I'm exactly who you thought I was when we walked out to the shed. Not everyone has to cater to your whims like your daddy's always done. What I left behind could be something you'd rather not know.'

'Whatever kind of trouble you're in, refusing to face up to it won't make it go away. We can help you, Father and I . . . '

'I don't need anyone's help. I'm going to make more coffee now. Want some?' He went inside before she could answer.

Claire stomped her foot, reeling with pain as it slammed against the wood. He wouldn't have acted so skittish if she hadn't been getting very warm.

Who needed his insolence anyway? She was tired of idly standing around waiting for help that obviously wasn't coming. She was going after her phone.

7

Two blocks of downtown Blakesville, nearly all of it, was leveled. Red and blue flashing beacons sliced the dark, wet night, making Sadie queasy as she gazed beyond them into the sea of debris and listened to crackling radio messages ricocheting between rescue workers. Finding Claire amid this chaos would be like looking for a marshmallow in a blizzard.

Standing here in the drizzly rain by the roadblock, the group of them in their party clothes must look to these country folks like the castaways from *Gilligan's Island*.

The uniformed sheriff's deputy, his face clean-cut and boyish, gaped at Joshua Woolrich as though he'd encountered an escaped lunatic. 'Nobody's getting up that mountain until morning, sir. Maybe not even then. Road's closed. We've got trees and powerlines down. High winds hit all over. It's a mess. I've got my hands full here, if you'll excuse me . . . '

He tried to sidestep Woolrich but, unaccustomed to being brushed off, Joshua skirted in front of him, blocking his path. 'I'll drive up there myself, if your guard will let me through.'

'We wouldn't have closed the road if it were passable, sir. The barricade's for your own safety.'

'My daughter's missing,' Joshua implored. 'She's up there somewhere.'

The officer looked mildly sympathetic but diverted his gaze quickly. 'Sorry, sir. We can send searchers at daylight. No one's going to find anybody tonight.'

Joshua contorted his face in fury. 'I don't care what it costs,' he shot back. 'Do you know who I am?'

The deputy eyed him with the disdain he might show a busted drug dealer. 'I'm granting you're under a lot of stress, sir. So I'll pretend I heard you wrong.'

Terrific, Sadie reflected. Just Uncle Josh's luck to bump up against a cop with scruples. But even her uncle couldn't bulldoze his way up an impassable road, one treacherous under normal conditions. The officer was right.

She noticed a casually dressed man

standing off to one side watching them. For all the frantic activity underway, he looked suspiciously idle, staring off into the distance when she looked his way, hands tucked in the pockets of his chinos. Under the circumstances, he appeared particularly detached, but he seemed to have taken special notice of the exchange between Uncle Josh and the deputy.

Sharing her normally stoic uncle's distress and frustration and hoping to keeping him out of trouble, Sadie came up beside Joshua and set a hand on his shoulder. Last thing any of them needed tonight was Uncle Josh landing himself in some county jail. She smiled prettily for the broad-shouldered officer. 'What can we do?' she asked sweetly. 'My cousin may have been driving down the mountain when the storm hit.'

Concern flickered in his by-the-book eyes. 'Sorry, ma'am. There's nothing I can do. She may have reached town. There's a shelter set up over at the high school.' He hesitated, cleared his throat, avoiding Uncle Josh's eyes. 'Or, you might try the hospital.'

Aurora Sutton, standing behind Sadie, gasped. Sadie cast her a dark look, annoyed with her and her husband's presence. A small caravan had driven up here behind Uncle Josh, the Suttons tagging along in their

Mercedes as though off on a scavenger hunt. Even Sadie's parents, gravely concerned, had recognized the wisdom of staying behind, out of the way.

The deputy marched off. Joshua moved to stop him again, but Sadie restrained her uncle by tightening her grip on his shoulder. 'A lot of people need his help tonight, Uncle Josh,' she urged. 'He's following orders. I'm sure if he could help us, he would.'

She studied Barre, who'd gone unusually quiet. When she glanced over at Ned, for whose silent presence she was grateful, his reassuring smile warmed her flagging heart. *Some first date.* She regretted dragging him into all this. Most other men would have bailed out by now.

'There's no point in all of us staying up here,' she declared, gazing pointedly at Barre's parents.

Barre looked up as if just noticing their presence. 'Why don't you take Mom home, Dad?' he suggested. 'I'll call you when we find Claire.'

'I won't be able to sleep,' Aurora protested.

Typical she'd be thinking of herself, Sadie reflected uncharitably, balling her fists.

Aurora babbled on. 'Well, the idea of poor Claire all alone and possibly injured on that desolate mountain, wandering in the dark amongst wild animals and . . . '

Joshua blanched.

Denver Sutton locked arms with his wife and guided her toward their Mercedes. 'Home would be the best place for you right now, dear. Barre will call us.'

Sadie sighed heavily with relief as the Suttons drove away. Now only the four of them remained — her, Uncle Josh, Barre, and Ned.

'Best thing to do,' Barre suggested, 'is split up. Two of us check the shelter and the other two the hospital.'

'Ned and I can check the hospital,' Sadie agreed quickly. She did not want to do this, but even more she didn't want her uncle to have to.

Barre nodded. 'We can meet back at that hotel we passed on the highway a couple miles back.'

'Sure,' Sadie agreed. She had no intention of going home without Claire. Ned was probably anxious to get back to Nashville.

The man Sadie had nearly forgotten approached, ignoring everyone but her uncle.

'Mr Woolrich,' he greeted Joshua by name. 'What a grueling ordeal you're going through tonight.' He pulled a skinny notebook from the back pocket of his trousers, and now Sadie understood. 'What exactly is going through your mind right now?'

Uncle Josh's normally cool demeanor shattered. He flashed a look with the unspoken answer, *murder*, and for an instant Sadie feared he might punch the reporter. The man, seeming not to notice her uncle's reaction, kept on talking. 'When did you last see your daughter?'

'Get the hell away from me,' Joshua growled.

Barre caught the bewildered journalist by the arm, leading him aside. Sadie watched Barre's solemn expression deepen into one of bereavement. 'I'm Barre Sutton, Ms Woolrich's fiancé,' she heard him introducing himself, his voice trailing off into the night.

She looked at her uncle. 'Barre will get rid of him,' she promised quietly, not adding Barre seemed overly eager to make his relationship with Claire public when his immediate concern should have been finding her. 'The guy's just doing his job.'

Her uncle watched as Barre spoke to the reporter, who scribbled furiously in his notebook. Uncle Josh made no comment on Barre's actions. He stood silently watching until the reporter finally left.

Sadie waited until after Barre and her uncle had driven off to the emergency shelter before turning to Ned.

'I'm so sorry to put you through this,' she apologized. 'You're a tremendous sport.'

'I'm just hoping your cousin is found quickly, Sadie.'

Sadie folded her arms across her chest and shivered. She was getting wet, and the air was cold. 'Amen. Just please not where we're going now.'

He looped a strong arm around her shoulders, and Sadie liked the comforting feel of him, solid and strong against her. She seldom allowed herself to lean on anybody, and Ned didn't seem to mind her indulging herself in this luxury. She had such a powerful feeling about him. Crazy, but nothing she could analyze in the midst of this crisis. Plenty of time later? She hoped.

'Take my car back whenever you're ready to leave, Ned. Just park it at the club, and I'll catch a ride back with my uncle and Barre. I know your girls depend on you.'

'No rush. I'm a free agent until late tomorrow morning,' he assured her. 'And you've been too busy holding everybody together to realize you shouldn't do this alone. Come on, let's get it over with.'

They reached her car. 'Do you want me to drive?' he volunteered. 'You could probably use the break after driving all the way here.'

She mustered a half-smile. 'This your way

of saying my driving scared you?'

'No way. We were only hanging upside-down for . . . oh . . . less than fifteen seconds.'

Relinquishing her keys, she headed for the passenger door. 'Sorry. All the way here I thought once we arrived, we'd know right away what has happened.'

He followed at her heels, opening the door for her. She brushed past him as she got in. Instead of closing the door right away, he leaned down close, locking her trembling hand between both of his.

'Tears, Sadie?' he asked gently.

Feeling foolish, she dabbed at them with her fingertips. 'I just felt like someone was dancing on my shadow. Claire wouldn't have missed this party unless something was terribly wrong. I was all right until just now. Guess my calm wore thin when Uncle Josh left.' She looked hesitantly into his eyes and found them warm and kind. 'I don't want to inflict my despair on you — you've had enough of your own.'

His voice rippled deep and thoughtful, his words slow. 'You're very considerate, but it's been two years of slow forward movements for me, although I can appreciate what your family is going through tonight. You and your cousin are close?'

Sadie smiled thinly. 'Like sisters. Closer

than most, I suppose, because neither of us has a real sister or a brother.'

'And I'm anxious to meet her. Look, Claire may have gone to a house for shelter when the storm got bad. With the phone lines down, she probably hasn't been able to call anyone.'

'No, Claire would never stop at a stranger's house.' Sadie remembered driving off, leaving Claire staring into the ozone. Claire, so sensitive about hurting anyone's feelings, she'd feel guilty over even an inadvertent insult. Damn. Had she gone back to do that when the storm broke? At least she'd be indoors, safe — if being trapped on a mountain top with Mr what-was-his-name, Cullen? — was considered safe.

Sadie had noticed how he'd ogled her cousin, like a hungry lion. Her fine-tuned radar picked up on such things. Had Claire tried to adopt him as another of her social causes? Exactly what had transpired between Claire and the groundskeeper during their expedition out to the shed? They'd come back around the house engaged in an animated, heated conversation. One ending abruptly as they'd come within earshot of her and Uncle Josh. Sadie could kick herself for driving off and assuming Claire would follow.

Who knew anything about the man? Uncle

Josh apparently trusted him with his house. But with Claire?

She studied Ned's handsome features. 'My cousin is different than most people. She tries to be strong like her dad, but deep down she's fragile.'

'We're all more fragile inside than we know.'

Sadie shook her head. 'My aunt and uncle adopted Claire, and none of us knows exactly what kind of life she endured before then. When we were girls, I had to leave a lamp burning all night when she slept over. Once the bulb burned out in the middle of the night, and she woke up howling. Terrified.'

'Sadie, she was a kid having a nightmare. My girls used to wake up with nightmares or see monsters under the bed when they were little. They outgrew it. Chances are Claire can take care of herself better than you give her credit for. That's what makes it so hard to let your kids go; in the back of your mind you always see them as babies.'

'Just thinking of her all alone in the dark somewhere gives me the creeps. You never think about how dark the night is where there are no streetlamps. What if — ?'

He silenced her with a finger across her lips. 'Claire is lucky to have such a caring cousin. But speculation won't help either of you. For tonight, let's just roll with the punches, avoid reacting to assumptions.'

'God, you're smart.'

He gave her a slow grin. 'I'm also getting drenched. Are you flirting with me again?'

She gasped indignantly, her face heating with shame. 'I came on pretty strong, didn't I?'

'You did take me by surprise this afternoon. I haven't been so flattered in years.'

'Ned, I can't believe I'm the first woman who's come on to you.'

'If any have, I never noticed. Until you came along.'

Caught by surprise, Sadie felt her heart lurch. This man, so ordinary and unassuming, excited her far more than the race-car driver she'd once dated. More than any of the men she'd once dated.

Before she could marvel over that for long, he pressed his lips over hers. His mouth was like him — warm, tender, intriguingly spicy. He smelled of soap from a shower, but also vaguely of the diner. She'd expected him to be tentative, but his mouth claimed hers steady and sure. She clasped his shoulders, drowning in the comfort of his kiss as it deepened.

Her toes had numbed by the time he released her.

Staring down at her, he averted his glance guiltily. But she'd glimpsed the desire in his eyes. 'Now who's coming on strong?' he muttered, backing off and closing the car door. Sadie sat stunned, her heart thrumming. Confused, she eyed him warily as he settled into the driver's seat. She'd been kissed a lot, but never like this. And she wanted to be spoiled to it forever. Why the sudden change?

As they rode to the hospital across town, in silence except for locating road signs and landmarks in trying to find it, Sadie wondered if she had responded too eagerly. Was she simply needy tonight? Sadie Woolrich, expert at holding men at bay for months before deciding whether she might want any serious relationship, knocked off balance?

She'd yet to find one man she wanted to be tied down to, and she came off sounding casual in her attitudes. She didn't want anyone to know how seriously she was looking. Claire seemed to think Sadie jumped into bed with every guy she dated. Why did Sadie never deny Claire's misconceptions? Was she afraid to admit how much finding the right one mattered? That those she allowed to get close always turned out to be so wrong for her?

She'd fallen in love as a teenager, fallen too hard to consider preserving her virginity. A tragic, impulsive mistake. The boy she'd pledged herself to broke her heart a week later, forgetting he'd promised to love her forever. The son of one of her father's friends, he'd come from the right kind of family, gone to good schools. Much like Barre? Maybe that was why she distrusted him. Irrational transference?

She admired Claire for upholding principles inconvenient in modern society but sometimes she couldn't help wondering whether her cousin didn't use her standards as a shield.

★ ★ ★

The emergency entrance to the tiny hospital was a bustling place with ambulances arriving, stretchers being rolled in. Dismally, Sadie tried to avoid staring in that direction as they walked across the parking lot. The reality of what they were doing weighted her stomach like lead.

Ned, following her gaze, planted a hand on her back and steered her toward the main entrance. 'Assume she's not going to be here,' he advised.

'So many people hurt,' Sadie reflected. 'I

hope none of their injuries are too serious.'

Squaring her shoulders, Sadie walked under the arc of his arm as he held the door open for her. Approaching the information desk, where a sleepy clerk was reading a paperback, she gripped the countertop with both hands as she inquired whether Claire Woolrich had been admitted.

She felt Ned standing behind her, as if to catch her should her legs collapse. The clerk turned and punched buttons on the computer.

She eyed Sadie speculatively. 'W-o-o-l-r-i-c-h?' she asked.

Here it comes. Sadie's stomach knotted. She nodded mutely.

The clerk turned again, then shook her head and shrugged. 'Sorry. No one by that name's come in yet. Hold on, I'll check the emergency room.' She picked up the phone.

Sadie held her breath.

After a brief exchange into the phone, the clerk hung up.

She looked Sadie in the eye. 'I'm sorry . . . '

The lobby whirled. Sadie's high heels wobbled. She felt the pressure of Ned's hand at her back.

'She's not here,' the clerk finished.

Sadie exhaled deeply. Turning, she found

herself in Ned's arms. She hugged him tight, suppressing a fresh threat of tears.

Finally, she pulled away from him, self-consciously remembering his silence after their kiss. 'What now?' he asked.

'There must be a way up that mountain.'

He shook his head. 'You heard what that deputy said. Three of us lost up there won't do any good.'

She knit her brow. 'You'd come with me?'

'I'd rather talk you out of it. If even the cops won't go up there tonight, Sadie, you'd be foolish to try. And we're not exactly dressed for traipsing up a mountain.'

She sighed heavily, suddenly anxious to be free of the cloying disinfectant smell of the hospital. 'Let's go. Please. I've got to get out of *here*.'

He followed her out the door. Even the damp night air felt good to her now.

He stood behind her without touching her. She turned to look at him. 'I liked the way you kissed me a while ago, Ned. Have I done something to put you off?'

'Oh, Sadie, no. I haven't even thought about kissing a woman for the past two years, and when it happened it felt easier than it should have. Too much too fast, does that sound crazy? I wasn't prepared. Ever since Greta died, I haven't planned anything beyond getting through the next day.'

'And now you're wondering what you're doing here with me in the middle of nowhere? Feeling guilty?' She glanced pointedly at his wedding ring.

He followed her gaze, twisting the gold band on his finger. He did not pull it off. 'A little.'

'At least you're honest about it.'

'No reflection on you.'

She pressed her hand to his. 'I understand that, Ned. I'm not offended.'

'Would you have me certified if I told you I don't want to be anywhere else right now? I wish your cousin wasn't missing, but I like being with you, Sadie. I've been moving in kind of a daze for the past two years, using the diner and the girls as a tranquilizer so I wouldn't have to really live or feel anything outside my daily routine. And now you come along and suddenly the world's in Technicolor again.'

Sadie stared hard at Ned. She'd only met him this afternoon, yet she felt as though she'd known him forever. Was it possible to take one look at a man and fall in love with him? After all this time, could it happen so swiftly and effortlessly?

'I'm not thinking very well right now myself,' she admitted.

'Trust your instincts.'

She looked into those infinite warm eyes. 'Do you trust yours? I'm kind of scared about the direction mine are headed. Talk about not being ready.'

Ned bit his lip. The breeze ruffled his hair. 'I'm taking you to the hotel to meet your uncle, then heading back to Nashville. Maybe we can try this over again another time? Not let circumstances dictate our actions.'

Sadie nodded in agreement, although she did not want him to leave. 'This is happening too fast, even for me,' she admitted. 'Everybody's emotions are raw tonight.'

'Let's go. I'll wait with you until your uncle arrives.'

⋆   ⋆   ⋆

Uncle Josh and Barre were already sitting in the hotel lounge when Ned and Sadie arrived. Sadie was relieved to see her uncle sipping ginger ale, Barre hitting the stronger stuff. They appeared to be arguing, but both men fell silent as Sadie and Ned approached.

'Claire's not at the hospital, Uncle Josh,' she reported.

'Nor at the shelter.' He seemed to have regained more of his normal composure. 'All we can do is wait until morning. Bad news is, this place is full. Media's swarming around, and some families had to leave their homes. I've reserved three cabins at a tourist lodge north of town. Desk clerk here says it's the only place with vacancies.'

Ned eyed Joshua speculatively. 'I know it's not much help, Mr Woolrich, but I grew up in a rural community like this, and people tend to help each other out. I'm sure everything possible will be done to locate Claire.'

Sadie met his eyes, and she knew Ned was thinking he'd be worried witless too if one of his daughters were missing. Uncle Josh never relied on the mercy of strangers. He took care of his family and his business himself.

Uncle Josh rose. 'Good night,' he bid the three of them, raising a disapproving eyebrow at Barre, who had his head bowed over the table, cradled in his hands as he stared down into his half-empty glass. Joshua looked at Sadie. 'If you want to stay a while, the desk clerk can give you directions to the lodge.'

Stiffly, he accepted Sadie's hug. She felt his tension and blinked back hot tears springing to her eyes. People envied her uncle as the man who had everything. Everything money could buy maybe, but she knew his frustration. All his wealth hadn't been able to save the wife he'd lost, hadn't been able to wipe away his daughter's elusive nightmarish past. If he could be strong now, she would as well. Knowing he had instilled his strength in Claire provided a small reassurance. If she was as tough as her old man, she could make it through whatever was happening to her tonight. 'No. I'll come with you, Uncle Josh. Ned will be driving my car back to Nashville.'

Sadie walked to the parking lot with Ned while Josh and Barre stayed behind to double-check the directions. When she passed the desk, the clerk was drawing a map. Outside, as she pressed her car keys into Ned's palm, he caught hold of her, drawing her close and kissing her so hot and hard her head reeled. She pressed close to him, savoring his warmth against the cool mountain air.

He broke away. 'I'd better be going before I change my mind. After so long, I'm suddenly feeling like a caged lion.'

Sadie wished he would change his mind. But he had responsibilities. He couldn't just plunge into some spontaneous relationship just because stars were colliding all around them. And she would never ask a man for more than he offered.

'I'll call you when there's news,' she promised.

'I feel like a heel taking off in your car.'

She waved off his reluctance. 'You need to

get back, and I can't leave. The car's the last thing I'm worried about.' She managed a smile. 'It's not like I'll have to walk.'

He kissed her again, and Sadie wanted him to stay so badly she felt her heart would burst. This, this is what Claire had wanted — the bells and whistles and sirens. What Sadie up to a few hours ago had stopped believing existed.

Through misty eyes she watched him drive away.

★   ★   ★

The Willow Cove Lodge consisted of a cluster of tiny log cabins nestled in the woods, a cutesy tourist trap no Woolrich would ever frequent under ordinary circumstances. Under the glare of fluorescent lighting, Sadie saw a small playground off to one side. Two plaster deer grazed in front of the office.

Exhausted, Sadie said goodnight to Barre and her uncle and found her cabin immediately after they'd checked in. Her disappointment over Ned's leaving seemed irrationally selfish under the circumstances. She had her shoes off and in her hand before the door was unlocked.

Still, as she inspected the cabin's quaint interior — pine furniture, blue-and-white checked drapes and cushions, quilt and matching shams on the bed, oil lamp atop the dresser — she felt even sadder to be alone here.

Unzipping her gown, she stepped out of it and hung it in the bathroom to dry. With a folded towel, she patted the rivulets of water from her arms and chest.

In her half-slip and panties, she slipped between white sheets. Sinking back into a too-soft mattress, she closed her eyes and clasped a hand to her forehead. Claire, wherever she was, might be glad for any bed at all tonight. How she wanted this night to be over with.

The light tap at the door startled her. Had her uncle come to deliver bad news in person? 'Just a minute,' she called. Groping in the darkness, she stumbled to the bathroom and retrieved the bath towel, clutching it over her breasts as she padded to the door.

She was about to pull it open when she realized someone other than her uncle or Barre might be knocking.

'Who's there?' she asked.

'Ned. I won't blame you if you'd rather not let me in.'

She couldn't unhook the latches fast enough. The towel fell away as she swung open the door.

Stunned, he eyed her appreciatively. 'Oh, darlin',' he approved in one, long, low breath. 'Maybe I'm a little too old for you.'

Sadie drew him inside and closed the door. 'Let me decide that,' she replied, sliding into his embrace as natural as a leaf fluttering in the breeze.

'It's been so long, I feel like I'm doing this for the first time.'

She stroked his chin with her fingertips. 'So do I,' she whispered.

Kissing her, he danced her back into the room toward the bed, and Sadie really couldn't tell which of them was leading. But she knew she had been waiting all her life for this man, this moment.

★　★　★

Claire shuffled along the darkened driveway, peering anxiously through the swirling mist. At least she hoped she was on the driveway. If she lost her bearings, she could be hopelessly lost out here until dawn. Wheeler wouldn't come after her again, especially now that she'd made him angry.

'Hey!' She heard a rush of bootsteps approaching from behind. Knowing it was him, she didn't turn.

He caught up to her easily, then slowed his

pace to fall into step at her side. 'Where do you think you're going?'

'To get my phone and call Father. I'm not your prisoner, and I've had enough of your company.'

'I told you I'd get the damn phone.'

'I might be accused of treating you like the help, then. You saved me. I've thanked you. I don't need your help anymore. You're free to go wherever you like. As you said earlier, you're on your own time now.'

She kept walking straight ahead, and he took hold of her forearm and guided her to the left, steering her back onto the driveway from which she'd been veering, she realized.

'Sure about that?' he asked. 'It'd be a long, miserable night out here all alone in these woods.'

She shook her hair back and kept her head high. 'Preferable to spending the night with you.'

'Give it a try before you knock it.'

She halted, cringing at the sight of her car positioned so precariously at the roadside. Through her shock earlier, she hadn't realized she'd spun completely around. Like some crazy amusement-park ride. She acknowledged how truly lucky she was not to have careened completely off the road.

'What? Okay, sure.' She couldn't remember

what they'd been arguing about.

Wheeler gave her a funny look before he marched toward it.

'Madeline's ferns,' Claire lamented. 'They're still in the trunk.'

'That's what you're worried about?' he asked as he swung open the driver's side door. 'Potted ferns?'

The interior light shined frostily through the mist. He leaned across the front seat, fishing around on the floorboard. Claire wished she could see what he was doing. Finally, he emerged and handed the cell phone to her.

'Doesn't seem to pick up anything.'

'That's impossible.' She tried to dial. Nothing happened. Her hopes withered.

To her astonishment, Wheeler slid into the front seat and started her engine. The keys were still dangling in the ignition. The sound startled her. 'It runs,' he consoled her.

'Too bad there's no way to get around that tree.'

She always left her radio on, and on her way up the mountain this morning, she'd tuned it to the local radio station. Nothing else would come in.

Now, the announcer's voice sliced the silence of the night, sounding strange and surreal. 'And continuing our special report, rescue operations are still underway after a twister demolished much of downtown Blakesville earlier this evening.'

Claire and Wheeler exchanged astonished glances as the disembodied voice continued. 'No official damage estimate yet. We hope to bring you an update soon. Despite many local residents homeless and injured, no deaths have been reported. Among the missing is the daughter of prominent Middle Tennessee industrialist Joshua Woolrich. Claire Woolrich was last seen at a charity luncheon atop Clover Creek Mountain this afternoon.'

Thunderstruck at the mention of her own name, Claire cocked her head and listened intently. She hoped Madeline and the few townspeople she'd met in the process of arranging the luncheon were safe. They were pleasant, friendly people, and many of them had gone out of their way to help her.

The broadcast continued. 'The road up the mountain has been closed, blocked by fallen trees and a mudslide caused by high winds and heavy rains. Mr Woolrich had no comment for our reporter, but his daughter's fiancé, Barre Sutton . . . '

A chill passed through Claire. Had Barre identified himself as her fiancé or had they got that wrong? Why did that bother her? They had planned to become engaged tonight. Would have if not for the storm. He wasn't being presumptuous, yet the small detail nagged her. Couldn't he have waited for them to actually become engaged, announce it together?

She felt Wheeler's silent gaze fixed on her.

'Mr Sutton says he and Ms Wheeler's family are heartsick over the situation . . . '

She seethed, blanching. 'My God, they think I'm dead!'

Wheeler killed the ignition, shutting off the radio. He emerged from the car with her pocketbook dangling by its strap from his fist. 'You'll be back before the funeral.'

In no mood for his warped humor, she kicked at the gravel, balling her hands into fists. 'I want to go home!' she demanded, pounding her fist against his chest. Wheeler didn't flinch, just stood gaping at her.

She stood staring incredulously at her own fist, realizing she'd struck him. She'd never hit anyone in her life, and maddening as he could be, he certainly didn't deserve that.

'Oh my,' she sobbed, shaking her head.

He caught hold of her wrists, sobering her.

'It's all right, Claire. You didn't hurt me. Take a couple of deep breaths.'

His steady voice hit her like cold water. Despite her outburst, he remained unruffled.

She blinked up at him, then breathed

slowly and deeply enough to satisfy him. 'I'm okay now. I'm sorry.'

He didn't let go of her. 'From the sound of it, there aren't likely to be any buses making stops up here anytime soon. Panicking isn't going to get either one of us out of here.'

'Yes. Of course. I'm sorry. I didn't expect to hear myself being discussed. How could Barre be giving interviews? He knows how Father shuns any publicity focusing on his personal life.'

'Beats me.' Wheeler's voice was cold.

'Surely this station should be broadcasting emergency information useful to the people who have lost their property instead of talking about me. Father must be . . . '

'Your old man is tough. Why don't you worry about yourself for once? I could use your help.'

Stunned, she met his gaze. A man who smashed doors and could lug her around as if she weighed no more than a puppy dog didn't require her assistance. His generosity in trying to make her think he did touched her.

Suddenly she felt drained. With him standing so close, the heat of his hands pulsing up her arms and all through her, she resisted a fierce urge to sink against him, bury her face in his shirt front.

He set her hands down at her sides. Turning away from her, he slammed the door shut, dousing the faint light. The mist obscured any moonlight, and Claire couldn't recall a darker night. 'You might need this,' he suggested gently, pressing her purse into her hands. He stood close beside her. 'You heard what the reporter said, everything's in chaos down below. Your boyfriend's being melodramatic.'

'Why would he?'

Wheeler gave her a hard look but didn't answer. 'You should know. You're the one who's so all-fired in love with the guy.'

Claire stood staring at Wheeler through the mist, warming to his presence in a way she wouldn't were she as devoted to Barre as she'd believed earlier today. Neatly she dodged the question. 'I don't want to inflict anguish on him or anyone else. He's probably too worried to be thinking clearly.'

Her loyalty to Barre had caved. She admitted it now. Just looking at Wheeler, she longed to be in his arms. She admired his strength, his self-sufficiency, and grudgingly, his sharp wit, the gentle perception he struggled to mask. Barre was the settled, conventional husband her father wanted for her. The man everyone, except maybe Sadie, thought she should marry. Wheeler never ceased to surprise her, and she liked the way he kept her blood churning.

Far too much to be feeling for a man she could never hope to be with. A man who professed no affection for her but openly acknowledged wanting her physically. What would it be like to yield to pure, delirious passion with a strong, skillful lover? For tonight, the rest of the world, its restrictions and obligations were shut away. Up here, she was on her own with no company except Wheeler and nowhere to escape her intensifying thoughts and feelings toward him.

When he reached out to wrap an arm around her shoulders, she fleetingly thought he was reading her mind. 'Here, lean on me. You're still limping. We may as well go back to the house. It's late.'

Resigned, she slanted into his sturdy shoulder. Power radiated from his muscled body. He slowed his step to allow for her labored gait, for which she was silently grateful. Knowing Barre and her family were down below, assuming the worse and talking to the media instead of coming to rescue her, she pushed down a rising sense of loneliness.

For the first time she could recall, she couldn't count on her father to intervene. She was left to her own resources. Wheeler had accused her of having a safety net, but tonight it had been snatched from beneath her.

'We're going to have to hike down the mountain, aren't we?' she said.

'When daylight comes. Think you can make it on that ankle?'

'My ankle's all right,' she insisted, pain bolting up her leg as she stepped forward. No more whining and complaining if she expected to get herself out of here. And no more hysteria. How selfish she'd been to keep depending on Wheeler. She shot him a sidelong glance. 'I have been acting indulgently like a princess ordering around her servant. I'm used to having things happen when and how I expect them. I'm afraid you've taken the brunt of my frustration, and none of this has been your fault. If not for you, everything would be so much worse. You've been good to tolerate me.'

'What Barre said must have really thrown you to make you so repentant,' he noted. This time he didn't have trouble getting Barre's name right. In fact, he said it almost as if he knew Barre. Well, from listening to her talk about him all night, he almost did. 'Kind of scary.'

'Regardless of how we feel about each other, we both want the same thing — to get out of here. We should be working together instead of fighting.'

He agreed with a quick nod. 'There's a creek back in the woods not too far from here. Hikers have beaten something of a path beside it, and we should be able to follow it down to the highway. Soon as the sun comes up. Should burn off this fog.'

'All right.'

'It's rugged terrain, Claire. We're not talking some well-cleared state-park nature trail. I could go on ahead, send back help.'

'I'd go mad just sitting up here, doing nothing but waiting. Besides, if they can't get up here now, your getting down wouldn't make any difference. I'm no mountain climber, but I'm not as weak as you think. I play tennis, ride horseback, ski, swim. Activities more strenuous than lying around eating caviar and bonbons. I'm in good shape.'

'No question,' he said pointedly.

His suggestive remark made her belly soften reflexively. Up until a few hours ago, everything in her life had made such perfect sense. Now nothing did. She was fantasizing about stripping in the firelight, baring herself to Wheeler. Watching him undress, waiting to see whether he was really all muscle. Touching him.

Her heart rate kicked up as she contemplated his hot skin grazing her most intimate places.

Stumbling on the porch steps, she quickly recovered her balance.

'Careful,' Wheeler muttered, eyeing her strangely. She felt herself blushing. No way could he have known what she'd been thinking. What had possessed her?

She realized losing her virginity hadn't ended her waiting. She still wanted the symphony and exploding Roman candles and hot chills. In all the years she'd spent fending off men's advances, she hadn't expected to not find what she was looking for the first time. Barre was attractive and she cared for him. But the sexual chemistry just wasn't there. She was kidding herself to believe it would evolve over time. How could she marry a man who didn't drive her wild in bed?

Once she committed herself, she wanted a man she'd enjoy making love with over and over again for years to come. After all, she had those long, celibate years to make up for. Had she gotten stuck on this mountain top only to realize she couldn't, in fairness to both of them, wed Barre?

'I'll see what kind of sleeping arrangements I can come up with,' Wheeler announced once they were back inside the house. Happy to put some space between her and Wheeler, desperately needing some activity, she occupied herself collecting their muddy garments and tossing them in the bathtub. She ventured upstairs long enough to retrieve the pajamas she'd left in the bathroom. Wheeler saw her on the staircase but didn't try to stop her.

She tossed everything in the downstairs bathtub and ran the water, adding the only soap she could find, dish-washing detergent stored under the kitchen sink. She stirred the clothing with a broom handle, rinsed it the best she could, then hung it to dry on the towel racks and shower curtain rod. In the flickering candlelight, she couldn't tell whether anything was cleaner than it had been to start with. Nothing was going to dry completely in this dampness either.

Returning to the living room, she found Wheeler holding a pot over the fire, heating water — for coffee, she assumed. Orange firelight bathed his handsome features. He'd brought the mattress up from downstairs. It sat behind him in front of the hearth, the old blanket spread atop it. Tonight even mega-doses of caffeine wouldn't be keeping her awake. Despite her brief nap, she couldn't stop yawning.

Quite obviously there was one mattress for two bodies.

'Don't burn yourself,' she cautioned, alarmed at how close he was leaning into the fire to hold the pot over the flames. He poured steaming water into a cup before handing it to her. She took a sip of the acrid coffee, then set the mug on the hearth.

After pouring his own coffee, he glanced up at her. 'I figured you'd be warmer sleeping up here.'

Knowing how lame the question sounded, she had to ask it anyway. 'Where are you going to sleep?'

'I'll curl up on the floor somewhere. That ease your mind? I won't hold you to your promise to sleep with me.'

'*What?*'

'I told you not to complain about spending the night with me until you'd tried it and you said sure.'

Her mouth dropped open. 'In response to something else, count on it.' She eyed him evenly. Hours ago, she wouldn't have given a second thought to consigning him to sleep on the hard floor. Would have reveled in relief at his agreeing so easily to do so. But her perspective had changed. She wouldn't sleep knowing she was hogging the only soft place. 'Listen, the mattress is large enough for both of us. There's no reason for you to be cold and uncomfortable.'

He studied her incredulously.

'Don't get the wrong idea,' she added

hastily. 'Father's bed upstairs is ruined, and we both need rest. I'm willing to share if you are.'

'Suddenly we're equals? Why the change of heart?'

'I detest snobbery. You can believe that or not. But I grew up in a world teeming with unwritten rules and boundaries. Just because my father's rich doesn't make him or me better than anyone else. In my heart I know that. But arrogance stems from fear, Wheeler. Sometimes people who have less fail to see us as human beings and want things other than our friendship. My father's cautious about people he doesn't know. I suppose he's made me that way too. So much so at times I act without thinking.'

'Yet you're willing to cross those boundaries now?'

'This is an extreme situation. One I trust you not to take advantage of.'

He grinned brilliantly. 'As long as you keep to your side of the mattress.'

She stared into the fire. 'Tomorrow's Sunday. My aunt always serves brunch — waffles, cantaloupe, strawberries. Pretty floral-print napkins.' Realizing how self-absorbed she must sound, Claire regretted her words. Wheeler had no Sunday brunch awaiting him. From the radio report, no one seemed to have remembered he was here.

'Maybe you'll get home in time. Just pretend you're a kid on a camp-out.'

'I can't. I've never camped out.'

'You did grow up on Mars. Didn't your father ever let you have any fun at all?'

'Sure. We traveled.'

'No, I'm talking about fun like mud fights and swimming in lakes and riding your bike ten miles from home just to see how far you could go.'

'You must have given your mother fits.'

'All three of us did actually. My two older brothers were just as adventurous and obnoxious as I was.'

'It must have been fun, even if you were slinging mud at one another.' She pictured three miniature blonde ruffians wallowing like piglets in puddles, laughing their young heads off. She imagined him as a mischievous young boy, covered in mud.

'Sometimes we had fun. Not always.'

How different they were. Her worst difficulties had come when she was young, and she expected happiness now. Wheeler spoke of a relatively carefree childhood, but he lacked hope for his future.

She straightened the blanket, wishing she had a pillow and determined not to mention it. She thought of the four fluffy ones in lace-edged shams stacked against the head-board of her bed at home.

Standing opposite her, Wheeler lifted one corner of the blanket, folded it back, glanced up at her, then looked down and settled himself on the mattress. Claire stood over him, knowing he was waiting for her to climb in beside him so he could draw the blanket back up.

Tonight was supposed to have belonged to her and Barre. She'd envisioned them going home together, sealing their engagement by making love all night. Because she really needed to know before they were married that it wouldn't always be like that awkward first time. All day, she'd been mustering her courage to admit to him she didn't care to wait.

She should have been with him now instead of settling down on a makeshift bed beside Wheeler Scully. And she should have felt sad and disappointed, but oddly, she didn't. Acknowledging this disturbed her terribly. Nearly as much as did the thrill racing through her at the prospect of sleeping so close to Wheeler.

Wheeler was watching her. 'Good night, Claire.' He rolled over on his side with his back to her, scrunching over as far to the edge of the mattress as he could get without tumbling off.

Claire stretched out exactly as he had, only facing the opposite direction, hugging the edge of the mattress and putting her back to him. As she pulled the blanket over them, she immediately felt the heat of his body. She'd never slept all night with a man before.

She closed her eyes, the nearby fire warming her face. She struggled not to think of Wheeler's proximity, how his body had felt against hers earlier. A man like Wheeler was probably used to bolder, less inhibited women. Had her response to his kiss been too restrained for him to guess how much she'd liked it? Had she disappointed him? As she feared she had Barre. She doubted she'd sleep a wink. Thinking along these lines, she certainly wouldn't.

Wheeler's voice floated through the stillness. 'Of course, you're perfectly welcome to scoot over here if the mood strikes.'

'Why don't you hold your breath until I decide to do that?' She smiled secretly. This verbal fencing had become almost entertaining, now that she'd come to expect it. 'I've taken your warning to heart.'

He said nothing, but through the darkness, she sensed he was smiling too. 'Wheeler?'

'Yes?'

'When we get out of here, I want you to come back to Nashville with me. You can stay at Father's house while he sees to replacing your belongings and rebuilding the cottage, if you're determined to come back here. You'll come to brunch at my aunt and uncle's house, of course. If we get there in time.'

'Never happen. Go to sleep, Claire.'

'I mean this.'

'I know you do. Thank you. Go to sleep.'

To her surprise, she did finally fall asleep.

★ ★ ★

Wheeler waited until he heard her breathing even out before rolling over on his back and craning his neck to study her profile. Her eyelids, laced with dark lashes, were closed, her lips slightly parted as she slept. She looked peaceful, angelic, dazzlingly beautiful.

That she meant to drag him to her father's house like some stray puppy she'd found simultaneously insulted him and touched the hard place inside him he'd thought unshakeable.

Deep anger churned at the thought of her with slime like Barre. Barre probably wouldn't cast her off like cracked crystal as he had Jillian, since Claire would be useful to him as long as her old man was alive. Maybe longer — who knew? Claire was an intelligent woman. Barre had her snowed right now,

233

might keep her blinded for a while, but pretty soon she'd start to see through him.

Then what? Barre would leave her and all those perfect little robot kids she intended to conceive brokenhearted. Damn it, he had to warn her about Barre. The headstrong heiress wasn't getting his deliberately unsubtle hints about marriage in general. If she refused to believe the truth, at least Wheeler wouldn't be responsible for her misery.

How long had it been since he'd stopped thinking about wanting kids? Since shortly after he'd gotten married. Listening to Claire tonight brought that back. God, she seemed so vulnerable. Had Barre Sutton not been the intended father of her umpteen, unborn offspring, Wheeler would have wished her well. So consciencious and maybe too sensitive for her own good — he could well imagine her in a rocking chair with a baby at her breast. She wanted to give her children all the mothering she'd never had. Wheeler could appreciate that. His old man had been a wiz at making him feel lower than a mole sometimes. He swore no matter how his own children turned out, he'd never let a day go by without letting them know he was proud of them, loved them.

Jillian had always stalled him when the

subject came up. Too vain to bloat her figure with pregnancy, she'd never displayed much interest in any children she'd encountered. She'd probably lied when she'd professed she wanted a family. Wasn't the only lie she'd ever told him.

He took another look at Claire, liking the way her golden curls framed the smooth contours of her face. Firelight bathed her creamy skin. She looked sweet and vulnerable, and it was all he could do to keep from touching her. She stirred slightly. He imagined her squirming beneath his touch. Longing ached painfully. A half-smile played on his lips as he envisioned her informing Joshua Woolrich she was bringing the caretaker home to Nashville. For brunch.

Inwardly, he groaned. It was going to be a long night. He should never have kissed her, but, hell, he didn't want to miss the last chance before he died. And that second time, well, he hadn't been able to stop himself. And he was curious, too, over whether all that back in the bathtub had been an accident. Now, he couldn't shed the idea of getting her properly into a bathtub and climbing in with her. Maybe he should have bunked on the floor after all.

He sank back across the mattress. Staring at her wasn't diminishing his arousal. Missing his pillows, he locked his hands behind his head.

He listened to the fire crackling, breathed in the scent of gardenias. As much as he tried not to, he felt himself hardening inside the ill-fitting knit shorts.

The Princess was right. Barre had ruined him, and he'd slunk off like a whipped hound. He'd given up, believing he had nothing worth pressing on for. His whole life had been a sham. He'd trusted Barre as a business partner and friend, and Barre had not only ruined his business, but heightened the insult by seducing his wife.

Everything and everyone was disposable to Barre. He'd learned it all from his old man, the world's ultimate phony. All that pop psychobabble Denver spouted in his books was stuff he'd copped from other sources and translated into modern jargon, calling it original. Wheeler knew because Jillian had been a psych major, and she'd kept books and journals all over the house. He picked them up and read them occasionally.

Wheeler took a long breath, remembering the morning Jillian had come back. A Sunday morning. He'd cracked open a beer and was reading the newspaper comics when she'd strolled through the door, all dressed up but boasting dark circles under her eyes. Eyes red from crying. Instantly, he'd known Barre had dumped her.

She'd begged Wheeler to take her back, start over. Wheeler had dreamed of it, her coming back, seeking forgiveness. But when it happened, the truth settled inside him like an iceberg. She'd broken the bond of exclusive intimacy between them, allowed an intruder inside. And Wheeler couldn't get past Barre always being there with them. He wished he could love her again, but he felt only a dull ache inside. He'd sent her away. He couldn't trust her or anyone, swore to never risk himself by loving again.

'No!'

The sudden outburst startled him. But the voice hadn't been his. He looked over at Claire, who'd been sleeping so soundly. Now, she tossed restlessly, flipping over to her other side so she faced him. At first he thought she was awake. But her eyes remained closed, lids twitching.

Ah, she dreamed. What demons plagued this angel? At least he knew the faces of his.

'No, please!' Her voice was hoarse and terrified.

He hated to wake her, but he felt like a spy peering into her nightmare.

Leaning over, he set a hand on her shoulder and shook her gently. Even from his guarded stance, he felt the warmth of her breast. 'Bad dream, Claire,' he whispered into her ear. 'Go back to sleep.'

She moved again, scooting closer and snuggling up against him, nestling her head against his chest, locking her hip to his, her long, bare legs entwining with his.

He groaned inwardly at the fierce arousal pinching him, and he steeled himself to keep from acting on it, clamping every muscle in his body. Her slender arm looped across his chest. Her skin felt cool to the touch, moist with a sheen of sweat.

The sane thing to do would be guide her back to her own side of the mattress. Skulk off to sleep on the floor. But Wheeler liked the luxurious feel of her too much to manage it. He hadn't held a woman in his arms for too long. She felt smooth and small and soft. He closed his eyes.

If she woke up right now, he was hamburger. Worse, her father might arrive in the middle of the night and find them twisted together like tangled pretzels.

He stared down into her shining gold hair. The color reminded him of Indian summer and the brilliant glory of the last warm, sunny days of the year. Scared of the dark. Silly. Was she dreaming of the incident upstairs, the car wreck, the tornado striking, or something worse that had happened too long ago for her to remember when she was awake?

Lord, they'd both been through a lifetime tonight. He stroked her silky tresses. Did she know how brave she was? Most women who had been through what she'd endured tonight would have been clawing the walls by now. Especially one accustomed to luxury. Yet she maintained a quiet dignity, except for her outburst out by the car. And she'd been due that one.

Cuddling against him appeared to have calmed her. She slept soundly now.

He felt a surge of affection, a fierce protectiveness. The people who should have cherished her had tossed her away, probably after treating her badly for years. How would it feel to go through life knowing that? She had to know about Barre before he had the chance to do the same thing to her.

Wheeler considered discreetly telling Joshua about Barre. Yeah, he'd take the word of his caretaker over the son of an old friend. Woolrich would resent Wheeler stepping out of line so much he'd fire him without stopping to listen to what he'd said.

Her hair brushed against his neck like a scarf fluttering in the wind. As she breathed, the tips of her compact breasts grazed his chest.

So delicate. Each touch produced exquisite torment. He felt like a man stretched over a torture rack, the ax blade dipping lower with each swing. A woman sure of whom she wanted to spend the rest of her life with would not have kissed him with the force of a missile flying into orbit. Claire's passionate response had nearly made him forget who she was. Who he was. He'd felt her desire. He burned to explore the full capacity of her passion, push her to its height. So long since he'd taken a woman. Deprivation suddenly weighed heavily.

If Claire gave into her passion, she would recognize her commitment to Barre stretched too thin for her to actually go through with their wedding. By seducing her tonight, he could spare her from Barre without revealing how he knew so much about him. Now, while she was all hot and sleepy . . .

No.

Wheeler drew in a long, sharp breath. That solution sprang from sheer selfishness and lust. Besides, he never did things halfway and he saw no point in making love to a woman unless she was totally alert. What Claire Woolrich did was none of his business. She believed he was a manual laborer who could benefit from a few night-school courses. If not for an act of God, she would never in this millennium or the next have been sleeping in his arms tonight. Or any other night.

And he already cared too much about what happened to her. He dreaded the moment her father would come and take her away, despite the crude accommodations. He couldn't kid himself. Under no circumstances would they ever be lying together this way if the road to the outside world wasn't blocked.

For tonight, looking after Claire Woolrich was as much his responsibility as locking the mansion doors at night, and at the moment she needed comfort from some monster disturbing her sleep. She didn't belong to him anymore than this house did. He shouldn't have kissed her, not the second time anyway. And making love to her shouldn't be entering his mind. For his own self-preservation.

Making his decision, he wrapped his arms around her and closed his eyes. Mentally, he reviewed the manual on lawn-mower maintenance he'd been studying the other day when the darn thing conked out. Dry stuff, but at least it filled his head with something besides the sensory signals bombarding him. And he hoped tedium would bring the merciful oblivion of sleep quickly.

★   ★   ★

Claire awoke, burrowing her head deeper into the pillow only to discover it was warm and breathing.

In fact, her entire body was entangled between male limbs. She lay pasted to Wheeler's side, molded against this chest as he sprawled on his back.

But it was her own arm, draped casually along his torso, her hand dangling in the warmest place beneath the blanket that shocked her into full consciousness. Granite brushed her errant, prowling fingers.

Dear God. She heated uncomfortably. Had she in her sleep been stroking him into arousal?

His eyes were closed, his handsome features bathed in boyish innocence beneath the dark whisker stubble shading his jaw. Craning her neck, she studied him leisurely, wondering how without waking him she might retract her hand and disengage herself from the arm clamping her to his chest.

For a moment, she thought they'd made love during the night, but she knew they hadn't. She'd been dreaming of it. No wonder, considering his intimate hold on her. Odd, she'd never awakened in a man's arms before, and under other circum-stances, she might have liked it. Dropping off to sleep together after making love. Awaking refreshed and starting all over again.

Her body simmered at the idea, and she realized too late this was not something she should be contemplating in her present situation. She hardly knew this man. Had Wheeler held his wife this way when they slept? Although the woman had no face, Claire didn't particularly like envisioning the two of them together. She didn't want to think of anyone but herself right here.

Ridiculous. He was her father's caretaker. He didn't want her here with him. Perhaps he'd been dreaming of his wife, reaching out in the night and accidentally pulling Claire to him. By rights, she should shake him awake and demand he release her, but she liked the feel of him against her, liked watching him with his guard down.

And after all they'd been through, all the trouble having her here had caused, she owed it to the man to let him sleep undisturbed. Even if that required lingering in his embrace a while longer.

He moved against her fingertips, an intriguing yet alarming sensation. She moved to retract her strayed hand. Wheeler groaned, clamping his hand over hers, pressing her to him.

'No, Claire, don't stop now.'

Recoiling, Claire gasped. Startled, she disengaged her hand from his and snapped it free as though it had caught fire. 'How long have you been awake?' she demanded.

'Nowhere near long enough. Pretty hard to sleep with someone staring at you. You feel it, you know?'

Obviously not *all* he'd felt. Her skin singed with embarrassment. 'Sorry,' she muttered. 'I was trying to decide whether to wake you. My hand was . . . my arm fell across you while I was asleep.'

'Was I complaining?'

She realized she had grounds to be angry. 'You could have let me know you were awake.'

'Why?'

Claire froze suddenly, realizing she was lying on a mattress facing him toe to toe, belly to belly, nose to nose. The heat inside her stemmed from more than their argument. Wondering if he was still aroused, she suppressed a wild impulse to touch him again.

She tried to move completely away, but he did not release her. 'We must have gotten twisted together last night accidentally.' She feigned nonchalance.

He quirked an eyebrow. 'You don't remember any of it, do you?'

'Remember what?' she demanded, horrified. Had she not been dreaming, actually made love to him and couldn't remember it now? The dream had felt so calm, soothing. No, she knew it hadn't been real.

'You moved over to me.'

'I never.'

'Nobody's here but the two of us. You don't have to be ashamed to admit it. I swear I'll never tell.'

She knew she should roll away from him as she would to escape a burning building, but somehow, his face this close to hers in the leaden light of a silent dawn compelled her. He shifted slightly, his hardness pressing against her. Her belly warmed and softened in involuntary response. The hot dampness between her legs alarmed her. She contemplated how it might feel to lay back down and take him inside her. She wanted to.

'If I disturbed your sleep, it was totally by chance. I regret the . . . inconvenience.'

He laughed.

She moved off of him.

Throwing back the blanket, she sat up, and despite herself, she saw the answer to her question.

She pushed a hand through her disheveled

hair. 'I've got to get out of here!' she decreed.

Wheeler got to his feet and turned away from her. 'You and me both, Princess. How about I call us a taxi?' He marched off toward the bathroom.

8

Still spinning from the shock of awakening in Wheeler's arms, Claire retreated to the porch. Although her ankle remained swollen and mildly sore, she was relieved to find she could walk on it more easily than yesterday. To put distance between them right now, she would have crawled if necessary. She needed air.

After the long, dark night, she welcomed the sight of even the faintest early morning sunbeams. If the sun was shining again, surely everything would be all right. Once she reached the edge of the porch, she froze in her footsteps at the surreal sight of a world turned upside-down.

In the sunlight, most of the mist had already burned away. The air, so cold last night, felt thick and sticky, and everything felt ominously still after last night's atmospheric upheavals.

She saw the pile of rubble where Wheeler's

cottage had stood. Her heart dropped at the sight. He'd lost more than she had, but he'd yet to utter a single complaint.

Uprooted trees crisscrossed at the edge of the woods, branches broken and twisted. Not far behind the cottage a Jeep lay on its side. Wheeler's, no doubt. She hadn't noticed it earlier. He must have kept it parked out back. Dear God, and she'd been lamenting her car running off the road. All she needed was a tow.

Hearing his footsteps behind her, she turned. Awakening to find herself locked in his intimate embrace still distressed her.

'Are you all right, Claire?'

'Yes.' She gripped the porch rail more tightly.

'I'd forgotten you never do anything reckless and impulsive. I suppose you're expecting an apology?'

'No. It was my fault. Purely unintentional, believe me.'

His voice was low as he leaned over her shoulder. She felt his warmth at her back. 'A damn shame. The only thing I'm sorry for is that you said no. We'd be good together, Claire. You sense that too.'

Suddenly, she raised her head, turning and fixing her gaze on him determinedly. 'At least we woke up in time to know what we were doing. One of us did.'

'Must be my lucky day.'

'What would be the purpose? As you said, we'll both return to our old lives. And you'd be accusing me of using you as a diversion.'

'Today's a new day. You know what? Who your old man is doesn't bother me anymore. I'd love to go back inside and finish what we started.'

Her heart was hammering. She raised her eyebrows. 'Just like that?'

He moved close beside her, propping his hands on the porch railing. Against her shoulder, he felt warm and sturdy. His male scent blended with the smells of pine and rain in the open air. Her pulse accelerated, as her senses thrilled to his proximity.

'I can't steel myself to you, Claire. Holding you feels so incredible, you're so soft and warm. And your skin smells like flowers. When I get close to you, I don't think about who your old man is. I'm not going to pretend I don't want to make love to you simply to make you more comfortable. I guess that was kind of obvious anyway.'

She wanted those powerful, muscled arms around her, wanted to run her hands over his intriguingly leathery skin.

She knew what she feared most — not the physical abandonment with a compelling, skillful lover, but that afterward she would care far too much, more than she already did. And that once her heart was entwined with his, Wheeler would go away from her. They wouldn't be here together forever. He didn't want any part of her life, and she didn't know what his would be.

She cast him a slanted glance. 'You certainly don't act like a groundskeeper. I don't know who you really are.'

'One of the homeless at the moment. I could make up something more impressive, if you like. But I'm not going to lie to you. Someday, after I get things straightened out, I'll tell you the whole story. Provided you're still interested in listening.'

'We're friends at least, aren't we now? I'm never going to forget that. Not ever, Wheeler.'

'You didn't really enjoy being around all those pompous snobs yesterday, did you? No more than I did. I think as a kid you would have preferred building castles on the beach to ballet lessons. I like that sparkle you get in your eyes when you forget and stop trying so hard to be someone other than just Claire. It's there when you laugh. And I saw it there a few minutes ago.'

'I was half-asleep. I didn't hurt you, did I?'

For an instant, he looked baffled, then, comprehending what she meant, he shook his head. 'Nothing I haven't lived through before. You're the first woman who's ever given it a second thought.'

'I feel guilty enough without leaving you in a state of discomfort. I read a lot . . . ' She bit her lip.

He tilted his head, as if seeing her for the first time. She wished the porch planks would part so she could dive between them and hide.

'You have been under a glass dome.'

She swallowed hard. 'I'm old-fashioned. I've never considered sex a casual matter. I never will.' Her words drifted off into the trees.

'You won't turn to stone if you look at me.'

She turned and raised her gaze to meet his. Surprisingly, he wasn't laughing. 'You really are kind of shy, aren't you?'

'I promised myself years ago I would never have a child I wasn't equipped to care for properly with a home, a family. Only people deeply in love should become lovers.'

'No guy ever came along and changed your mind?'

'There wasn't any lack of trying. But no, not until recently.' She diverted her gaze. 'I can't believe we're standing here discussing this.'

'You're a desirable woman, Claire. I admire

you for standing up for your principles. The world would be a better place if more people took their responsibilities as seriously. But you are as inflexible as your old man.'

'Inflexible?'

'Sure. My old man was like that. When he was right he was right, and a shipload of logic wouldn't have convinced him otherwise. I work hard at trying not to be like him, but I know nothing I ever do will compensate for his mistakes. Denying yourself isn't going to undo your parents' indiscretion. Besides, Claire, if they'd never wanted you, wouldn't they have given you up at birth? Maybe something as unexpected as that twister last night happened and they couldn't take care of you anymore. There are ways of being careful. Responsible people use them.'

'They don't always work.'

He shrugged. 'Usually they do. When two people have sparks flying between 'em, tumbling into bed comes pretty natural. Somehow or another, those two people are going to wind up touching each other. Natural as the stars coming out at night. Nothing in life comes with guarantees.'

'Maybe this morning happened too easily.'

'Princess, with you nothing is too easy. Nothing happens without a reason. I don't know about you, but I'm getting kind of curious to find out what that is. Be like lightning striking dynamite.'

'An original argument, but not sufficient to persuade me.

'If you think an engagement ring or a wedding ceremony puts the stamp of security on a relationship, guarantees a happy home, forget it. People get married only to discover they can't get along. Sometimes not until after they have children. My wife didn't want children — was I irresponsible to sleep with her? I haven't made love to anyone since long before she left. Until the wind blew you in, I haven't wanted to. It's been a long, long time since I took a chance on anything. And you know what, I miss taking risks. Haven't you ever in your life done something just because your instincts tell you you should?'

She raised her eyes. 'I am sorry about your wife.'

Wheeler pounded his fist into his hand. 'Look, you were dreaming last night and slid up against me. I swear that's the truth. I should have moved you away, and I didn't. So you can stop beating yourself over it.'

'Dreaming?'

'Muttering something in your sleep. Nothing I could understand. Except when you started calling out my name.'

'Very funny. You must have been the one dreaming.'

'But you are smiling for the first time this morning. And you've got that light back in your eyes again.'

'I was angry at myself for being tempted, Wheeler. I feel like I've been locked out of the world I've always known. To just chuck everything I believe in because I'm scared and tired and confused wouldn't be fair to you or to me. Maybe when this is over with, we can see each other again and find out how we really feel.'

His handsome features constricted, a soft breeze springing up to ruffle his sun-streaked hair. 'Yeah, sure. We'll go to the symphony one night. Come on, Princess. We've got a long walk ahead of us.'

★ ★ ★

Sadie lagged wearily behind her uncle and Barre as they dashed across the parking lot at the Jackson Snow Memorial Airport, thirty-five miles outside Blakesville. Frustration wore on her this morning, and the air was thick as molasses. Not a good day and, from the look of the darkening sky, if Uncle Josh's last resort didn't work, things were about to get worse. She looked over her shoulder to make sure no reporters had followed them. They'd been swarming like buzzards ever since Barre gave that darn interview last night.

She'd done some quick, mindless shopping at a local clothing store outside Blakesville this morning to get them all a change of clothes. Apparently the merchants here assumed everyone wanted outdoor gear in drab colors and shapeless styles. In cotton shorts, a sleeveless blouse and canvas shoes, admittedly more functional than her gown, she felt wilted and frumpy. But today, she didn't much care how she looked.

Uncle Josh and Barre were outfitted like a couple of novice fishermen in their brand new canvas shorts and T-shirts.

A tall man, with dark curly hair spilling just to the collar of his chambray shirt, took brisk, clipped strides toward a hangar as he emerged from the main building.

Her uncle waved to him. 'Excuse me.' he called. 'I'm looking for Vaughn Fogarty.'

Turning, the man gave them a cursory look, viewing them with the same indifference he might have extended ants crossing the pavement. He stopped walking only briefly, not long enough for them to catch up completely. 'That's me, what of it?'

Sadie pushed down a wave of detached amusement. Obviously, this man had no idea who he was talking to.

Uncle Josh scrambled to fall in step at his side, extending an open hand sideways. 'I'm Joshua Woolrich, Mr Fogarty. You're a difficult man to get hold of.'

'I'm a busy man today. Had to airlift a kid to a hospital. And I really am in a hurry now, if you don't mind. Another storm system's moving in.'

'Exactly why I need your help. My daughter's trapped up on top of Clover Creek Mountain. She's been up there since the storm hit last night, and I haven't heard from her.'

Vaughn Fogarty skidded to a quick stop, his boot heels scraping the pavement. His angular features constricted in calm concern. 'How old is this kid?'

The hopeful glow faded from Uncle Josh's eyes. 'She's not a child. But the road is closed and I'm told the only way up there is by helicopter.'

'A lot of people are stuck on that mountain, sir. Part of the risk of living up here, a little snow, a little mud, and you sit it out.'

'Name your fee, Mr. Fogarty. I don't have time for games.'

The pilot shrugged. 'Can't do it for a million dollars right now. You'll have to wait your turn.'

'You don't understand.'

'No, you don't understand, sir. Much as I always enjoy rescuing a damsel in distress, I've got four teenage campers lost in the woods, and I'm on my way to get them back to their mamas before the next fog rolls in.'

He quickened his step, and Josh started to race after him, but Barre caught him by the shoulder. 'He's not going to change his mind,' Barre told him. 'Let's go back and see what progress they've made on getting the road open. Arguing with this guy would be like debating a stone.'

Barre looked bedraggled this morning and had been unusually quiet on the drive here. Sadie slightly regretted buying him a T-shirt emblazoned with a giant bass leaping across the front. Payback for talking to the reporter. He looked pretty silly.

Grumbling, Josh stormed on ahead toward the car. Sadie put a hand on Barre's arm. 'You holding up okay?' she asked.

'I just want to find Claire and have this over with.'

'Neither you nor my uncle look as though you'd slept at all.'

'He's upset with me for talking to that guy

from the radio station. Can't you explain to him I was just giving him something so he'd back off?'

'You'll have to settle that with him on your own, Barre. All you had to say was, 'No comment.' Look, nothing's rubbing him right at the moment. Let it slide for now.'

'How'd you sleep, Sadie? I couldn't help but notice your car showed up at the motel last night.'

'Notice as well it was gone this morning? Of course you did.'

'You're sure he didn't steal it?'

Sadie flashed a frown. 'Ned stealing my car is my most remote concern.'

'Oh.' Barre gave her a peculiar look, inviting further discussion, but she did not explain.

She and Ned hadn't spend much time sleeping last night. He was a considerate yet vigorous lover. He made her feel as though she had never really made love before. Falling in love with him was as sudden and startling as being turned upside down. She'd known she wanted to spend the rest of her life in his arms. In the early morning hours, he'd whispered in her ear he loved her, a confession even more thrilling than his caresses. She'd drifted off to sleep feeling as happy and secure as if she were wrapped in a quilt stitched from rainbows and ribbons.

She cringed now at the memory of waking up alone this morning. Ned's hastily scrawled note on the bureau on motel notepaper with a sketch of a pine tree in the corner. 'Sadie, you're an angel, I never expected to feel like this, so much more than I'm ready to handle. I'd better get home before the girls do. I'll arrange to get your car back to you. If I stayed until you woke up, I would never be able to go.'

Sadie had crumpled his message in a ball and flung it against the wall. She'd been so afraid he wouldn't love her. But the joke was he'd left because he did. So much for all those warm, sappy feelings. Truth was, if you put your heart on the line you were begging to have it broken. She'd acted like some starry-eyed teenager, and she of all people should have known better.

* * *

The swollen creek strained within its banks, frothy water rushing downstream. Where the ground narrowed, Claire clutched tree roots to avoid pitching down the steep, muddy incline into the churning water below. Wheeler's warning about this being treacherous terrain had been an understatement, she

259

understood now. He'd advised her not to look down where the slope got steepest, but she couldn't help herself.

Negotiating the rocky terrain on her weakened ankle proved especially tricky. Though she struggled to ignore the constant jabbing pain intensifying with every step, she feared it might give out on her. Muddy, sweaty and hurting, she was determined to press on. Food, a hot shower, a phone to call Father, awaited her at the bottom of the mountain.

After this morning, she had to distance herself from Wheeler before something irrevocable happened. She required time and space in which to sort her jumbled feelings. In Wheeler she'd found something she'd never realized she needed. Whatever that was, she no longer trusted herself alone with him.

Clinging to the bank, she stared down into the rippling current, licking dry lips. At the moment, she would have committed armed robbery for a glass of iced tea. Father's housekeeper flavored hers with a touch of cinnamon, then poured it over ice in tall glasses with little paper parasols on top. Claire pushed the vision from her mind.

All the while, she felt Wheeler at her back, hovering close to catch her if she fell. His solicitous presence alone bolstered her determination not to slip and land smack in his arms. The man was doing his job, she reminded herself. His watchfulness stemmed from obligation rather than personal concern.

Today, she refused to give him the satisfaction of hearing her complain. Missing brunch presented a small sacrifice in comparison to losing all your worldly possessions. She could be tough too. After all these years, she was finally beginning to understand what grit was. Starch down to your very soul, venturing into places you were afraid to go without hesitation. A self-reliance Wheeler seemed to come by naturally. So did Father. Yet Father commanded the world with a snap of his fingers. Wheeler could accomplish anything he set his sights on, if only he'd realize that.

Until now, she'd never had to venture beyond her comfortable little circle, learn what she was really made of. Wheeler had been right. She'd lived a sheltered life. Because of who her father was, she never felt insecure or worried over what tomorrow might bring. Her shadowy past disquieted her, but never the future. How surprised her family might be to see her negotiating this slick hillside.

Before they left the house, she'd taken an old sheet covering a sideboard in the basement and ripped it into strips, fashioning a long, wide scrap into a sling which she'd tied around her waist to carry their precious last can of soup and her wallet. Wheeler had advised her to leave everything behind, but she didn't want to reach town without money for some food and a place to stay. In truth, she knew if only Barre was waiting for her down there, she wouldn't feel right relying on him to provide for them when she couldn't marry him.

With a narrower strip of cloth, she'd tied her hair back, but the knot had come loose about half an hour ago, the fabric fluttering down into the water to be carried away by the current. Her long hair was hanging loose now, impeding her progress as it swirled over her face, causing her to periodically pause and toss her head back.

A clearing up ahead came into view, a shady plateau where the creek curled around the mountain. Level ground — heaven.

Wheeler touched her shoulder to get her attention. 'Let's take a break,' he suggested.

She offered no argument, clambering the final few feet to the clearing before collapsing on a large rock along the bank. With the pressure off, the nagging pain in her ankle eased immediately. Bliss. She wouldn't contemplate right now the inevitability of getting back up on it, hiking farther. But in a few minutes, they would have to go on.

The last traces of mist had burned away. Mottled sunlight filtered through tree branches bowing into a canopy over the creek. Under different circumstances, she might have found this place quite beautiful. Catching her breath, she rubbed fingertips against the tip of her nose, then swatted at a mosquito poised for attack on her arm. Pesky critters were feasting this morning. Closing her eyes, she leaned back, raising her face to let the sun bathe her skin and listening to the rippling water.

When she opened her eyes and glanced toward Wheeler, he was staring straight at her, chuckling.

'You smeared mud on your nose,' he informed her.

Glancing down at her filthy clothing and mud-streaked limbs, she guessed it was the only part of her that hadn't been dirty already. She must look about as glamorous as some prehistoric swamp creature.

Self-consciously, she attempted to smooth her hair with one hand, then dabbed at her nose with her fingertips. Her nails were broken and jagged, polish chipped.

'I wish I had some polish remover,' she mused.

'I hope no one grants you any wishes, then.'

'I didn't say it would be the first thing I'd wish for.'

She brushed hair from her face with the back of her hand and sighed heavily. 'People travel far and pay big money for mud baths. Guess I got a bargain. Once this washes off, I'll — abracadabra — be stunning as a supermodel.'

'You're prettier than any model, Claire,' he answered quickly.

She snapped her head up to assure him she hadn't been begging for compliments, but when she met his gaze, he shifted his eyes guiltily. His solemn expression revealed he hadn't meant to say that. What manner of man could look at her now — filthy, long hair tangled and windblown — and think her attractive? Wheeler did really see her, she realized. In a way no one ever had. Guiltily, she recalled her quick assumptions about him, how little attention she'd paid her father's caretaker until he'd exasperated her by arguing.

He saw beyond what everyone expected of Joshua Woolrich's daughter. Whatever degree of affection — it had to be more than sheer desire — Wheeler granted her was bestowed not because of who her father was but in spite of it. He made her feel unique in her own right, and she liked that. Getting all muddy did feel liberating in a strange way.

She poked at her hair again. 'Kind of you to say that while I'm in this subhuman state.' Involuntarily, she imagined how she might enjoy dressing up for him in a slinky new gown, hair styled into a veil of smooth, flowing curls. She saw herself spinning across a dance floor in Wheeler's strong arms. With alarm, she realized she was envisioning last night's party. Only Barre had been banished from her vision, with Wheeler usurping his place.

Guiltily, she stared at the ground, studying the pebbles protruding from the red mud. Aside from the babbling of the water, bird calls, and the occasional rustling of leaves in the wind, the woods in their stillness felt somehow tranquil, a stark contrast to last night's fury. She and Wheeler were totally alone. No one could ever guess where they were.

He sat on the bank. 'I'm happy you can joke about this. I thought you'd be begging to turn back by now. I underestimated you, Claire.'

She twisted her hands on her lap. 'And I you, Wheeler,' she said, unable to break her gaze from his. Something inside her admired this man and ached for his touch. Passion swelled as relentlessly as the creek within its banks. But love for her could never be sheerly physical. To give into desire only for one moment in time would prove her genetically programmed to be the same kind of person who selfishly and irresponsibly could create a life, then toss it away like a disposable item from the convenience store. Prove she'd never be a Woolrich. Wheeler had not pledged any degree of devotion or even affection for her. But she sensed he understood what it was like to not truly fit in anywhere. She feared tapping into the deeper understanding intimacy was bound to bring. How could she go on with her life if she fell in love with a man who didn't want her for keeps? Or was it already too late to worry about that?

'Really?' he asked.

'I thought you must be running away from something to be living up here like a hermit. Sometimes I think I'm the one who runs, hiding in the regimentation of my life. It requires more strength to be alone, doesn't it? Because then you can't deny who you really are.'

'Why should anyone want to? The only freedom in life comes from being yourself. It's other people who encroach on that.'

'Being forced to make your own way

measures your self-worth. You're a capable man, Wheeler. You don't need Denver Sutton to tell you that.'

'You never did either, Claire. There's no shame in being adopted. If your old man considered you anything less than his daughter, he would have sent you back a long time ago.'

'I've never gotten over the insecurity of wondering if some day he might decide to send me back. What I remember of my past is murky, but it gives me a cold, dark feeling of being alone and unwanted. I never want to feel that way again.'

'No kid ever should. Your father would be damn proud if he could see you right now.'

'You think so? I always feel I've let him down.'

'Nobody lives up to their parents' expectations. Unless you have an old man who tells you over and over you'll never be good enough. Easy to live up to that.'

'If your father told you that, he was wrong. But you're right about me, Wheeler. I've never had to take any real risks with my life.' She nearly admitted to the small fortune in investments Father had set up for her last year on her twenty-fifth birthday — at least, the day on which they celebrated it, the anniversary of her adoption. She seldom thought about the money. Though it was hers to do with what she pleased, she never touched it. Father had established a fund to provide security for her future, and she intended to leave it for that. Beyond the two of them and Father's attorney, only Barre knew it existed.

'When this is over, Wheeler, I'll see you have whatever you need to put your life back in order. I promise I will.' If she could find a way to make him accept her help.

'I let down people who trusted me. Nothing anyone can do can restore my reputation.'

'Intentionally?'

'No.'

'Then they'll understand, give you another chance. Surely there's some way to make things right again.'

'I think there is. I'm going to work things out on my own. I think I've figured out how now.'

'You're not going to continue working for Father, are you?'

He shook his head. 'No. When you fell asleep last night, I thought about taking off and leaving you at the house.'

She gave him a hard look. 'You stayed.'

He shrugged. 'It was dark, raining.'

'More than the storm stopped you. You're

too decent a man to have left me there on my own.'

'My disappearing might have been the best thing that could have happened to either of us,' he suggested. She read the desire in his dark eyes and understood exactly what he meant. How she ached for the feel of his embrace, the salty taste of his lips.

Quickly, she looked away, hoping to mask her own longing. Fortunately, they'd be back among civilization soon, relieved of temptation so she could sort these traitorous feelings at her leisure. She'd been wrong about her feelings for Barre — how could she trust what she felt for Wheeler?

'How much farther is it?' she asked.

He shook his head. 'I have no idea. I've never gone down by foot before. Can't be too far.'

She suspected he was minimizing the truth to keep her from giving up. She'd yet to hear traffic sounds from the highway below. 'Yes, it can. We haven't gone more than a mile or so, I'll bet. Play straight with me, Wheeler. Being patronized is insulting.'

'Sure is.'

Her mouth fell open, then she realized her protest was baseless. 'I sounded like a supercilious nitwit yesterday, didn't I?'

'To tell the truth, your unexpected

interest caught me by surprise. Gave me a wake-up call to something I already knew but didn't want to admit. I've been up here too long.'

'Why wouldn't you take the tip?'

'Seeing you hold out that money shocked me. Showed me how low I'd sunk to have people tossing me change. Especially someone like you. You made me angry with myself, Claire. Not with you. A few months ago, I might have . . . '

'Might have what?'

He cleared his throat. 'Are you sure you can make it the rest of the way? You've been limping pretty badly.'

She wondered what he'd been about to say. If Wheeler had simply accepted her money, she wouldn't have hesitated over leaving. She might have gotten down the road before the tree fell and never have gotten as close to him as she felt now. His pride and the curiosity it had sparked in her had trapped them together.

She pulled nervously at the front of her sticky T-shirt. Humidity must be about two hundred percent. With growing discomfort, she decided Wheeler intrigued her as Barre never had. While she often anticipated Barre's next action, Wheeler stimulated her mind and her body. And her heart?

'I can walk all right. This heat is dreadful though.'

He yanked off his shoes and socks and rolled up the cuffs of his jeans. 'You're right. I'm going in.'

She eyed the creek dubiously, then swung her gaze back to him. He was pulling his shirt off. She had a hard time forcing her gaze away from his broad, tanned chest. A sheen of sweat glistened on his skin.

Rising, he stepped off the bank, sinking his feet into the water and extending an open hand to her. 'Come on, Claire,' he coaxed. 'Let me get that mud off your nose.'

Her hand flew to the tip of her nose, her mouth dropping open. 'Why didn't you tell me it was still there?'

He flashed a devilish grin. Here she was covered in grime, yet obsessing over a fleck of dirt on her face?

He shrugged. 'Thought you knew. Gee, this water feels nice and cool. There's nobody else around for miles if you want to get out of those heavy clothes. And I don't mind.'

'I'm sure you wouldn't.' She struggled to sound unruffled by his suggestion, but her face burned at the quick memory of awakening all twisted up against him, his hard readiness to take her. Just the memory of it ignited a slow burning between her legs. He was raw, rugged and all male. Small wonder he inflamed her most womanly longings.

Grinning, she pulled off one tennis shoe after another and set them side by side in the grass. The prospect of sinking her aching feet into cool water was too much to pass up. An angry blister flared on the back of her right foot where the shoe had been rubbing. The shoes, Sadie's favorite knock-arounds, were nearly ruined. Claire regretted destroying her cousin's favorites, but she was so grateful Sadie'd left them behind, she'd happily replace them with ten pairs of new ones.

Aware of Wheeler watching her, she got up, still wearing the shorts and T-shirt, tiptoeing to the water's edge and noting the disappointment in his eyes. Surely, he hadn't really expected her to disrobe in front of him.

She stepped carefully into the water, refusing his proffered hand. Recalling all his talk of mud fights and noting the mischievous glint in his eye despite his exaggerately innocent expression, she suspected he planned to toss her into the stream and dunk her like a trout.

After the initial shock of the icy water, she enjoyed the blissful coolness. Invigorated by the water rushing between her bare toes and the fresh, moss-scented air, she inhaled deeply.

Wheeler stood facing her. Dwarfed by his long, powerful frame, she couldn't help remembering this morning . . . Her gaze fell to his torso — the trim stomach, taut muscle, leathery skin.

Reaching out, he rubbed his thumb against the tip of her nose. 'It's indelible,' he decreed, shaking his head.

'Indelible mud?' she asked, too preoccupied to react before he stooped to scoop water in his cupped hands. He suspended them above her head, then parted them, allowing the cold water to pour over her. She shrieked, shivering as her spine turned to ice.

'All clean now,' he declared with feigned innocence.

Spewing water and rubbing her eyes, she shot him a steely glare, plotting a fitting revenge.

'Get out of my creek or I'll shoot!' The voice drifted out from a behind a fat tree along the shore.

Wheeler jumped, then spun to confront the tree trunk. 'We're only . . . ' Nobody was there. 'What the . . . ?'

Claire grinned impishly as his brow narrowed in worried confusion. 'You'd better go see who's there,' she coaxed, her words breaking off into laughter.

Frowning, Wheeler glanced back at the

tree. 'Gotcha!' it taunted.

Turning his head, he leveled an accusing gaze on her. She shrugged. 'Tops your silly mud trick, I'd say.'

'How did you do that?' he demanded.

'I learned ventriloquism from Eric.'

'Another boyfriend?'

'Hardly. A kid I met at the hospital.'

'You've been sick?'

'Oh, no. No. The children's hospital. The one we were raising money for yesterday. I go by there on Sunday afternoons and visit the kids, read to them or put on puppet shows. I used to hire clowns and magicians to entertain them, then once I got the hang of the ventriloquism, with Eric's help, I bought some hand puppets. The younger kids really love talking to my little 'animals'. Took lots of practice before I chanced it. Kids aren't easily fooled.'

He gaped at her. 'You weren't just raising money for charity to make your old man look good?'

'My father doesn't need my projects to enhance his reputation. He supports the work I do. Lord knows I'd never be able to raise as much as I do without his connections and influence, but the hospital is my project. After seeing those kids, how brave they are, I can't not do it. They're irresistible. I could never possibly help them enough.'

'Guess you weren't the only one making assumptions. I'd have figured you never set foot in the place.'

'I got involved in a roundabout way. Father's secretary was called away suddenly when her child was injured in a school-bus accident, and I drove her to the hospital. She waited a long time, and I stayed with her in case she needed anything. Shelly's a single mother with no husband and no family in town. What I saw there tore at my heart: babies with AIDS, toddlers with birth defects, children badly burned and disfigured. Children stripped of their innocence before they have a chance in life are the most innocent of all. Most of us take growing up and living as adults for granted, part of our birthright. Yet these children are attacked by horrific diseases. I couldn't walk away and forget. I was restlessly wandering the corridor when I stumbled over Eric's radio-control car. I never encountered a boy so old and wise, and he was only thirteen.'

'Was?' Wheeler asked gently.

'He died last spring. He informed me about five minutes into our initial conversation he was terminal. Said it as casually as someone might comment on the weather. I think he wanted to let me know up front what

I was dealing with, give me a chance to bail out. Like some people close to him already had.' She sighed deeply. 'He was so incredibly brave, Wheeler. You can't imagine. He had beautiful red hair and blue eyes and freckles, and a smile that would have broke many hearts had he lived. He should have been out riding a bicycle or playing soccer instead of haunting the hospital corridors.'

She cast her eyes to the bank.

'Must have been hard on you.'

'Eric wanted to be an actor. The little ham. Father and I established a scholarship in his name. A performing arts scholarship. To give some other kid the chance he never had.'

'You were brave to risk yourself, knowing ultimately you'd be grieving. Not many people would do that.'

'Maybe I was too idealistic to admit the reality of it. Telling myself all along the doctors wouldn't allow such a horrible thing to happen. I should have prepared myself for the worst, but when he died I was devastated.'

'Nobody's ever prepared for the worst.'

'No, I do have a hard time accepting defeat because I've seldom been vulnerable to it.'

'The easy thing to do would have been to walk away when you knew caring about him was going to prove inconvenient. You didn't do that, Claire. And refusing to give up hope, not accepting defeat until you were actually defeated, wasn't a mistake. It was optimism. Something I've been needing a dose of.'

She furrowed her brow as she looked up at him. 'What's life about if you run from what your heart tells you is right?'

Wheeler quirked a brow, and she probed deeply into his eyes to gauge his reaction. She was battling her stubborn heart because falling in love with her father's caretaker on the eve of her engagement to a man who fit neatly into her life entailed major inconvenience. But what of Wheeler? Did he feel anything more for her than a vague combination of duty and lust? She had to know. But she couldn't ask. If he cared, wouldn't he volunteer that information?

He met her gaze with an intensity matching her own, shooting a fierce longing down her middle. She read in his eyes that he sensed it too, this spiritual bond between them, a force stronger even than whirlwinds and desire pushing them together. He cared for her. She sensed it in his every movement. Heard it in his voice now. But he was too much of a mule to say it.

If only he would . . .

He didn't trust her, she realized. He believed once he got her out of here, she'd dismiss him from her life, pay as little attention to him as she had yesterday afternoon.

And wasn't he right? Even if he agreed to come back to Nashville with her, Father might let him rest up at the house, give him money, offer him another job he didn't really want. But he'd draw a sharp line at Claire involving herself in a relationship with his caretaker — perhaps send her off to the French Riviera for an extended vacation? Offer Wheeler piles of money to disappear to anywhere except the French Riviera?

She was twenty-six, plenty old enough to make her own personal decisions. But Father had sacrificed for her, given her everything. Walloping him with a jolting disappointment seemed unappreciative. He wanted her to marry someone like Barre, a man from a prominent family, with enough money of his own not to be interested in hers.

Didn't he? He'd approved of Barre, but he'd never told her outright what he expected. She assumed she knew. Now, she wasn't so sure. Surely her father loved her too much to want her to enter into any loveless marriage.

Wheeler broke his gaze and spoke. 'If you like working with kids, maybe that's what you should do.'

'Quit my job?'

'Life's too short to spend it doing something meaningless. Take my word, I've been doing exactly that for months now.'

'Actually, I think I'm good at what I do. I could be better working for someone who would let me try more new approaches.'

She'd never considered not working for Father. Ever since she was in high school, he'd talked of how he dreamed of one day the two of them working together, how he wanted to teach her everything he knew about business. She'd joined the company to win his approval. At first, she'd found it challenging and exciting, but she'd been in her position long enough now that it had become routine. Father liked everyone in his employ to stick with proven methods of doing things.

She couldn't imagine Father ever doing anything to make her withdraw her love for him. Making her own decisions, living her own life, didn't mean she was ungrateful. It meant she was ready to test the integrity he'd instilled in her. Wasn't his intentional example stronger than an accident of heredity? If she couldn't listen to her own heart, she had no path to follow, nowhere to go.

A new shower of cold water snapped her from her reverie. Gasping and blinking, she saw Wheeler standing over her, chuckling as he doused her.

'You dog!' she charged, shaking water off herself like a wet retriever, then splashing him back with a triumphant laugh that echoed through the woods.

'A dog, am I?' He beat a steady shower of water at her.

She kicked back, swaying as her foot slid on a slippery rock in the creek bed.

Wheeler caught her by the waist, pulling her forward.

'Truce,' he decreed. 'Before you hurt yourself.'

His hands warmed her belly from both sides as she fell up against him. His glistening bared chest loomed inches in front of her, and she looked up into his dripping face. As he smiled down at her, the teasing faded into an intensity she understood. Her hardened nipples pressed against his chest. More than just laughing hard had turned her breathing ragged. If she didn't love him, she wouldn't be so tempted. Her principles were too deeply entrenched for her to ever entertain the possibility of making love with a man solely to experience passion, yet she felt so irresistibly drawn to him. The realization struck her with the same sobering effect as being doused by cold water.

Lifting one hand, she grazed his stubbled jaw with the back of it. He bowed his head over hers, and she memorized the contours of his fine features, studied the droplets of water glistening like diamonds between his dark eyelashes, sunlight playing in his hair.

She remembered the tangy taste of his lips, how his skin felt rough and soft at the same time. She wanted to kiss him now. But this time, she couldn't blame panic or curiosity. She well knew they'd gone beyond that.

What one more kiss would lead to was as obvious as thunder.

Cautiously, she stepped back. He released her. 'Do you think we'd be okay drinking this water? I'm awfully thirsty.'

'You might get a belly ache, but I doubt it will kill you.'

'I'll risk that.' She stooped to scoop water in her hands. 'I've got to drink something.'

'Wait!' He stopped her.

She looked up quizzically. 'You said it was safe.'

He retrieved his T-shirt, rinsing it by swirling it around in the creek. 'Here, open your mouth.'

Dumbfounded, she gaped at him.

Reaching out distractedly, he stood holding the pouch he'd made of the shirt in one fist. He cupped her chin in his leathery palm, tilting it upward. 'Maybe by the time I hand you over to your daddy, you'll finally trust me,' he muttered. 'Filtering the water is the least we can do. Might be a little safer. Say 'ahh'.'

He shifted the shirt to aim the dripping water over her mouth.

Feeling like an idiot, but too thirsty to argue, she opened her mouth and closed her eyes. A quirk spurt of icy water filled her mouth. Dismissing its strong mineral taste, she swallowed. She waited for more and none came. Perplexed, she opened her eyes. 'Could I have some more, Wheeler? Please.'

He shook his head. 'No.'

She looked startled. She was unaccustomed to being denied.

'Well, I'll just get some myself.'

Catching her by the hand, he stopped her. 'No more, Claire. I know how thirsty you are. I am too. But this isn't Perrier. We drink as little of it as possible. I don't want you getting sick.'

Wheeler took a small drink himself, then rinsed the shirt again and wrung it out.

'How many contaminants can there be on this pristine mountain, Wheeler? Some people up here must drink well water. And it really doesn't taste that bad.'

'No.' He flashed her a pointed look.

She gave it up. He was probably wrong, but drinking less of the water couldn't hurt. She could live the next few hours without more, hold out for her iced tea. Soon, she'd have all she wanted.

And she wasn't going to think about her rumbling stomach. Chicken noodle soup for breakfast wasn't a stick-with-you kind of meal. She was starving, but she knew people could survive for days without food.

Wheeler stepped up on the bank and pulled the wet shirt over his head.

'Wheeler, what will you do when we get back?'

'Something I should have done months ago instead of backing away from trouble. Something I need to settle.'

'What's that?' she asked.

'Personal business. That's all.'

'I hope it works out for you.'

He gave her a hard, penetrating look. 'I hope you get what you want too. Your fancy party, fancy clones, I mean kids . . . '

'After all this, I'm not sure I'll ever look at my life the same way again.'

'Sure you will. You'll get in the swing of it easy.'

'You're the one who doesn't trust anybody, you know,' she accused.

Wheeler looked startled, but only for a moment.

There, she thought. It was settled. No more stolen kisses, no temptations. They'd reach the mountain's base and part company, their lives no longer connected. As anxious as she was to get home, the prospect saddened her. She was going to miss Wheeler. But he didn't want to be with her once he was free to go other places. And she couldn't possibly go anywhere but home.

All for the best. The thought of leaving him behind forever without taking away the memory of his lovemaking left her bereft. It would have been glorious. Enough to carry her through the rest of her life?

'I suppose you'll be rescheduling your party.'

She shook her head. 'No. I'm postponing it indefinitely. The Barre I thought I knew would never use my absence as an opportunity to draw public attention to himself. And if he really knew me, he'd be discreet enough to understand I wouldn't want that either, whether I were dead or alive.'

'Some people are good at pretending to be what they think you want to see.'

'I've been very good at that myself.'

'Cheer up. Focus on food and a hot bath ahead.'

'I've just had a shower, thanks.'

'Will you be okay for a second? I'm going

to go find the men's room.'

'Yes, go,' she insisted.

'Be right back. Watch out for snakes.'

'Thank you for setting my mind at ease. I suppose I can kill a snake as easily as you could.'

His expression grew solemn. 'You don't kill it, okay, Princess? On the off chance you do see one, play dead. Snakes attack according to heat and movement. Don't move and it can't strike you.'

A sick feeling filtered through her as she realized he wasn't simply trying to scare her. After all the rain, a snake could very well slither by. She hoped he wouldn't be gone long, but she would have sooner beat her head against a tree trunk than admit it.

Once he disappeared into the overgrowth, she scanned the ground near her feet. No movement among the sticks, thank God. Why did he so enjoy worrying her? He was a bully. No, he used cowing her as a tactic to put her off. That she could even for an instant believe herself in love with him showed how skewed her thinking was.

The sun disappeared behind the clouds, making everything look gloomy again. Glancing at the higher ground above the incline, she spotted plump round berries hidden amid the foliage on a cluster of bushes nearby.

Straining for a closer look, she recognized them as blueberries, the kind bakers put in muffins. Wonder of wonders, lunch was being served after all.

She climbed the bank, wandering back into the bushes, plucking a berry from a branch, sniffing it, taking a tiny bite. Sweet and tart — a real wild blueberry. Happily, she raised the hem of her shirt, dropping berries into the little hammock she made over her midriff.

She, Claire Woolrich, had found food. When Wheeler came back she'd make him raise his chin and close his eyes and see who trusted who.

From over her shoulder, she heard trampling, then snorting. Finally. But what was he grunting about? Just like him, couldn't even give her credit for her discovery.

'Blueberries, Wheeler. Don't try to tell me they're poisonous, because I know they're not. Even I know blueberries. These grow on Father's property — '

He made a disgusting low blowing sound.

'For pity's sake, what is wrong with you . . . ?'

Spinning, she froze to find herself facing a bear as tall as a porch pillar. He scowled down at her, billowing and clacking his teeth.

She dropped the shirt end, spilling berries everywhere.

Inching backward, she bumped her spine against a tree trunk. Holding her breath, she closed her eyes.

Go away. Go away. Screaming inside, she couldn't make a sound. *Play dead*, Wheeler had said.

His shout shattered the air. 'Run, Claire!'

She didn't want to open her eyes and face that mass of brown fur, oily gray skin beneath it. Shaking all over, she knew she didn't have much time to decide what to do. One swipe of those mammoth claws and . . .

Something zipped through the air, striking the animal's chest. She opened her eyes and saw a rock bounce off him and fall to the ground.

Wheeler's arm was still arched from tossing it. He had another in his other hand. They'd both be killed.

Impulsively, she reached into the pouch at her waist and clutched the metal can. Squeezing her eyes shut, she threw it, surprised as it struck the animal square on the forehead. Dazed, he wobbled slightly.

'Run!' Wheeler threw his other rock, then rushed toward her like a football player making a tackle. Claire's legs flew into motion, carrying her toward him. Catching her by the hand, he pulled her into the woods.

With no path to follow, they zigzagged between trees, ducking low branches and leaping over roots. Claire thought her heart would burst, but she didn't dare stop long enough to look behind her.

Her ankle felt as though it were shattering each time she pressed it to the earth. She had no idea how far they'd gone when she was jerked back by the hair. Crying out, she skidded to a halt.

Wheeler spun, his eyes wide with alarm, relief quickly filtering through them. He propped his hands against her, one falling on her shoulder, the other covering her hammering heart.

'Your hair's snagged in the branches. That's all. He's not coming,' he said, although his breathing was as labored as hers. 'He would have caught us by now if he'd decided to chase us.'

'Can you untangle it?' she asked, her fear ebbing into painful awareness of the pressure of his palm over her chest. Her heart beat into the heat of his steady hand, pumping his touch through her veins.

'I'll try. Tell me if I pull it, okay? I don't want to hurt you.'

'Just get me free quickly, please.'

He retracted his hand, seeming to just now notice where it had landed. Working his way around to one side of her, he studied the back of her head and frowned. 'This may take a while.'

Claire shifted impatiently. She appreciated his caution, but she didn't want to be tethered to a tree here in the woods under a darkening sky with a ticked-off bear roaming about.

'You have a knife, don't you?' she asked, refusing to dwell on how she pampered her hair, buying special organic shampoos and conditioners to keep it free of chemicals, brushing it to make it shine, getting a trim from the stylist every two weeks. Her greatest self-indulgence, because her long, golden hair was uniquely her own.

'Only as a last resort,' he countered.

'We can't stay here.'

She heard a snapping, and felt her hair fall over her shoulders. He'd broken off pieces of the branch to free her, but a few thorny sticks remained tangled in her tresses. For now, it would do.

'Thank you. We're hopelessly lost now, aren't we?'

'We should be able to find our way back to the house from here.'

Claire groaned. 'Not the highway, Wheeler?'

'Claire,' he said gently. 'We're much closer to the house. Your ankle's swelling again.

Bears seldom kill anyone, but I'd sure hate to be an exception.'

'What about the neighbors' houses?'

He shook his head. 'Still farther down, back along the road. Your father owns most of the property this high up. Look, I don't want to go back any more than you do, but someone may have come looking for us by now.'

'You don't believe that, and I don't either. They're too busy cleaning up from the storm down below.'

Claire squeezed her eyes shut. She'd imagined before nightfall they'd be happily ensconced in a comfortable place, bathed and wearing clean clothes, eating hot food and sipping cold drinks. The disappointment stung. But she pushed down the rising bile of defeat.

'I've given up on things before when I shouldn't have, Claire, Not this time. We may not get down from here as quickly as we'd like, but we'll be okay.' His hands clasped her shoulders, and she opened her eyes, meeting his gaze. In that instant she knew the truth she couldn't run from: Wheeler already occupied a place inside her heart. A place Barre could never fill. She'd gambled her emotions with Eric and lost. But how lucky she was to have gotten to know him before he went on to a place where maybe no one was burdened with loss and heartache. Could she be strong enough to face her feelings for Wheeler without fearing the consequences?

Perhaps only then would he acknowledge the truth she'd read in his eyes back at the creek. The one she was seeing now.

She leaned into his arms and he held her. Simply held her.

'You're still shaking,' he observed.

'Just don't let go, okay? Not yet.'

He tightened his embrace, drawing her closer. She burrowed her head against his shoulder, nestling against him. He felt wonderful.

He kissed the top of her head. 'You packed quite a wallop with that can. I hope I never make you that mad.'

'I wasn't going to let him kill us.'

'Never play dead with a bear.'

'I'm hoping to never have occasion again to know that. Wheeler, I lost our only food.'

'Screw the food. As long as you got away from him, I don't care if it means I'll starve to death.'

'Oh, geeze, Wheeler. Why did you have to say that?'

'Because I mean it.' His cheek grazed the top of her head, and she fell into the rhythm of his breathing.

'I do trust you, Wheeler. More than anyone else I know.' She tensed briefly, realizing the implication of what she'd said. 'No one's ever fought a bear for me before.'

Pulling her closer, he buried his face in her damp hair. 'You're sweet, Princess. I don't know what to make of you.'

He smelled wild and musky, his breath falling in warm puffs against her scalp, making her tingle all over.

She needed something real to ground her. And Wheeler was about as genuine as they come. When she leaned back to look at him, he caught her lips between his. His kiss was as hot and hard as their run through the woods. Feeling breathless and wild, she returned it fervently. Never could she have enough of him.

His fingertips traced the hard nub at the tip of her breast. Claire arched her chest into his hand. Her knees threatened to buckle as the liquid fire poured through her.

He continued rubbing small circles, assaulting her with swirling sensations. It was all she could do to keep from crying out. No one had ever touched her as he could. No one else ever would.

His hips ground against hers, and she meshed her body to his. She tasted his tongue and brushed it with her own. Breaking off his kiss, Claire took hold of his wrist, pushing his hand back.

'No, Claire,' he complained in a low, raspy voice. 'I want you.'

Claire looked into the depths of his infinite brown eyes, his raw need obvious, and something more beyond that. He was as bold and rugged as the mountain itself. Who would have thought beneath that baseball cap would be this man who had captured her heart unaware? But perhaps the real treasures in life were so precious because they never came in predictable ways.

If she listened to her heart, as sure and steady yet easily muted as the rippling of the creek, she couldn't deny this was the man she was meant for, the one she'd been waiting to find. Could she refuse him what was already his by rights?

Knowing their time here was a time out of time, an interlude that, once ended, would be behind them forever, she felt an urgency to express what he meant to her the way he would understand. If she told him she loved him, he might not believe her. If she showed him, he'd have to know.

She dropped her hands to the hem of her T-shirt. After only a second's hesitation, she raised it, baring herself to his inspection.

He gaped with astonishment at the firm,

creamy mounds. With the side of his thumb, he stroked the delicate skin of one. 'You're so beautiful, Claire.' Opening his palm, he slowly covered her breast, closing his hand over it. She shimmied under his touch, his roughened palm grazing her delicate skin. An exquisite sensation. The powerful work-toughened hands she'd seen split logs touched her with a tantalizing reverence.

He moved forward, to kiss her again, she thought. But his head dipped lower, and he slid down on one knee, his mouth dropping to the swell of her bosom, his tongue tickling her skin.

She clasped his shoulders to keep from falling over. His lips captured her nipple, teasing the bud with his tongue and playing his lips over it. Kissing and nibbling before zeroing in to suckle her.

Claire tossed her head back, squeezing his shoulders for dear life. As he eased her to the ground, she was aware of her heart beating wildly, but not for one instant did she consider resisting. The smells of wet grass and male musk exhilarated her, stirred something primal in her she hadn't known existed. Taking Wheeler inside her would be the most incredible experience she'd ever known. The one she'd been waiting for all her life.

His whiskers scratched against her skin.

Wheeler knew no boundaries, his lips freely exploring and kissing between her breasts, along her midriff, down to her belly, above the center of her burning need. He moved over her, threading his own leg between hers, parting them. His thigh pressed against her womanhood. Shamelessly, she dampened between her legs in readiness for him. She wanted his powerful body, wanted to savor all of the delights he so skillfully produced.

Now.

When she felt him jerk back, heard him curse, she thought at first she'd done something wrong.

Emerging from her daze, she felt the water pelting her and knew it was raining again.

Wheeler politely straightened her shirt, pulling it down to cover her. Rising, he extended her hand to help her up. 'We should get back to the house,' he concluded. 'Too dangerous out here.'

9

Two hours later, Claire's desperate hope that they would return to find Father impatiently waiting to take them home dissolved as the house came into view. The stately old mansion remained undisturbed — abandoned and partially in ruins.

She was numb. Her body ached so badly she felt weary beyond exhaustion. At least there was water and shelter here. At least she had some time left to convince Wheeler to come back to Nashville with them for a few days to recover. Whatever it was he had to do, maybe Father could persuade him to accept his help.

'They'll come, Claire,' Wheeler, sensing her dejection, tried to reassure her. But his voice betrayed his own disappointment.

Resigned, she went inside, pulling her shoes off in the foyer. Soaking wet again, she retrieved one of the towels hanging in the bathroom. She had no change of clothes but Wheeler's pajamas. She put them on and rinsed out her muddy shorts and T-shirt.

When she emerged from the living room, Wheeler was nowhere around. The rain hadn't been all that was chasing him from the woods. He'd seemed so anxious to make love to her — why had he suddenly changed his mind?

She sat cross-legged on the floor in the living room. It would be dark again soon, and the power was still off. At least this rain wasn't as violent as last night's.

Twisting her mane of hair over her shoulder, she began trying to untangle the thorny branches still knotted in her locks. They were too high on the back of her head for her to reach easily.

'Here, let me try.'

Wheeler was standing over her. She hadn't heard him come in the room.

Letting her hands fall into her lap, she turned her back to him. She felt him bending over her, working at her hair, attempting to untangle the sticks without pulling or breaking it. The dim light in the room was fading rapidly.

'You'll have to cut it,' she decreed finally.

'There aren't any scissors.'

'Use the garden shears from the garage.'

'Claire, I can't.'

'I'll make a bigger mess of it if I do it myself.'

'All right.'

She heard him walk away and refused to think about how much she loved her long hair, how she took such good care of it. She couldn't sleep with sticks poking her in the head all night.

She felt him moving over her, lifting a long shaft of hair, and winced at the crunch of the shears biting through it. The briars fell away, along with a generous shock of honey-gold curls.

She raised her hand to the back of her head. 'I was planning to get it cut anyway,' she said.

He tossed the hair into the cold fireplace. Claire couldn't bear the sight of it. As if he knew this, he closed the fireplace doors and set the shears aside. 'Claire, I don't want to cause you any trouble.'

'Trouble, Wheeler? Apparently, you don't understand the Woolriches as well as you profess. Nobody makes up our minds for us. Headstrong, I believe is the word you used. I'm the one who has caused you trouble.'

'I'm sorry about what almost happened in the woods.'

'If there's anything I'm sorry for about

what's happened, that's not it. You don't understand, do you, Wheeler?'

'What did I miss?'

'I like you, Wheeler.'

'Suppose I don't want you to like me.'

'Too late. How many people do you suppose I'd allow to take garden shears to my hair? I feel safe with you. I like the feel of your arms around me. I wanted us to make love back in the woods. Nothing had ever felt so real and so right to me.'

'Claire, I'm nothing but the grounds-keeper. Once you're back where you belong, you'll realize that.'

'So you would have been happy to make love to me, as long as it didn't mean anything. I'm not the only one here with a safety net.'

'You were right this morning. We should wait, see how we feel later on. You deserve silk sheets and wine. I can't give you any of that.'

'Those things alone mean nothing. I'd hoped I'd deserved you. All my life, I've held out for perfection and always been disappointed. I want one perfect moment. With you. It doesn't matter what we are away from here.'

He turned away from her. She feared that now she'd opened her heart, he would retreat from her completely.

The rain outside had stopped, and a cool breeze blew in through the windows he'd opened earlier. The room felt warm to her.

Wheeler went into the kitchen. He came back, holding a small rectangular object. She craned her head, trying to see what it was.

He set it on the hearth and opened it. A battered ballerina figure popped up, leaning to one side. She wove drunken circles as music tinkled, a warbly old love song.

Claire grinned with delight. 'Wherever did you find that?' she asked, focusing on the object he held between them.

He smiled back at her. 'Buried in all that old junk in the basement. Not exactly an orchestra or even a radio, but it still plays.' He caught hold of her, pulling her into his arms and gliding her along with the music. 'You never got your chance to dance last night.'

Claire felt tears threatening. In her dream they'd worn fancy clothes and danced at the country club, not wearing rags in an empty house dancing to faint notes from an ancient music box. But somehow, this was more than she'd wished for.

Holding her close, he whispered into her ear, 'I am sorry you missed your party. Here, lean on me, so your ankle won't bother you.'

'I'm glad it never happened. Otherwise, I wouldn't be free now.'

'I'm betting you would have stopped clocks in your gown.'

Her skin warmed as she self-consciously appraised her ragtag appearance. She wished she could look beautiful for him. 'I look like a hobo,' she lamented.

'You're stunning,' he assured her in a heavy voice, as though reading her mind. 'Claire, not a moment's gone by you haven't been the prettiest woman I've ever known. Even with mud on your face, there's just something about you that shines through.'

She hugged his neck, burying her face in his shoulder. 'Oh, Wheeler. Someday I'm going to dress up for you. And we'll dance to real music.'

'Shh.' He held her tight, and her body heated at the contact with his tough muscles. He felt so solid and good against her, his hand entwined with hers, the other planted at her back.

She followed his lead, so thoroughly caught up in his eyes she could not look away as he waltzed her around the living room. He was an amazingly good dancer. Claire's worries melted away as she swayed to his rhythm. She wouldn't have minded spending the rest of the night dancing in his arms.

'You've done this before,' she noted.

'Not for a long time. Not since . . . '

'Since when, Wheeler? Tell me what you're thinking.'

He hesitated. 'Not since my wedding.'

'Never afterward? Surely you and your wife — ?'

'No. I was trying to get a business off the ground. Too caught up in it, I suppose. I should have paid more attention to other things.'

Claire gasped. 'You put your trust in the wrong people. But it doesn't mean everyone is corrupt.'

'Pollyanna,' he muttered with a heart-stopping grin. 'Not a phony bone in that beautiful body.'

'Sometimes I believe I'm the world's biggest impostor,' she confessed. 'Knowing nothing about where I came from or who I really am. Maybe you're right, that I am afraid to know.'

He shook his head. 'I was wrong about that. I see who you are without the window dressing, Claire — determined, intelligent, compassionate. Whatever you know or don't know about your biological parents couldn't change that.'

'What about you, Wheeler? You're the strongest, kindest, bravest man I've ever met. You deserve better from life than being locked away up here in some dilapidated cottage. Maybe we've both been hiding from truths too painful to face.'

'I like having you here all to myself. How do you know your name is Claire?'

'It's always been Claire.'

'So your father must have some record of where you came from.'

'No, I think I told him my name was Claire. I told someone.'

She stared incredulously into his strong features. Up here in this topsy-turvy world, nothing existed but the two of them. What had begun as a near-tragedy now struck her as a miracle. For the moment, she forgot her concern for her father and her hunger pangs. She raised her fingertips to his whiskered cheek. 'Twenty-four hours ago, I feared I was the unluckiest woman on earth. Now, I'm thinking maybe the opposite is true.'

For the first time in her life she knew exactly who she was and what she wanted. All connected to the present, separate from her past.

He clasped her upraised hand in his own. 'Everything's going to change — soon.'

Her heart whirled, as it had back in his cottage, a lifetime ago yet only a day earlier. Once again, the world was collapsing around her. She recalled the sense of urgency with which they'd kissed that first time. As then, she could no longer afford the luxury of indecision. She crossed a finger over his lips. 'They won't come before daylight, do you think?'

The music box stopped playing, and she moved to step out of his grasp, but he held her to him. 'No, please. We'll make our own music.' He leaned over her shoulder, burrowing his face in her long hair, humming softly into her ear. She smiled dreamily. Desire snaked down her spine, pressing her closer to him. The primitive rhythm she moved to stemmed from her own heartbeat. Her hips meshed to his, and she felt his arousal. This time, it did not alarm her.

When the cottage toppled down on top of them, she'd clung to him from instinct and terror. Now, with calm certainty, she knew she wanted to make love with Wheeler. In the short span of a day, she knew him better than she knew Barre, with whom she'd made love and planned to marry. She wasn't the same woman now, could never go back and do that. In such a short time, everything had changed.

Feeling woozy and warm, feverish in a pleasant way, she rested her head on his shoulder, inhaling his musky scent. His breath warmed her skin.

He stroked a broad palm over her hair. 'No

sense worrying too much about your clothes, Claire. You look real sexy in those pajamas. But you're not going to be keeping them on much longer anyway.'

Here was a man who could lift her heart, set her afire, just by walking into a room. She no longer feared him. No longer feared her reaction to him. She dreaded instead the inevitable time when the world would intrude.

Still, her instincts ran strong, and nothing could shatter something right and true. If this brand-new feeling was what she suspected, the rest of the world was going to have to come around to it. She pushed back the thought of her father, who would have a hard time looking close enough to see Wheeler as anything other than a caretaker.

Leaning back, she searched Wheeler's handsome features. He was the only person who'd ever seen her for who she really was, who didn't gauge his expectations according to her social position.

Wheeler was smiling down at her, his eyes shining with unmistakable passion. So much power focused on her took her breath away.

'I hope not,' she told him. 'Wheeler, I haven't had a lot of practice at this.'

'I caught on to that this morning.'

'Well, you've been married and probably

done this about a thousand times. Nine-hundred and ninety-nine more than me. I don't want to disappoint you.'

He gave her a slanted grin, sliding his hand under her thick mane of hair, clasping the back of her neck with his palm. The warm pressure trickled down her spine. 'I have no intention of being disappointed,' he promised her. She raised her lips, happily anticipating his kiss.

His mouth came down gently at first, prodding and teasing her lips playfully. She stood on tiptoe, clasping his shoulders for purchase, savoring the taste of him. He traced her lips with the tip of his tongue, and she parted them for him.

She shivered with delight as his tongue slipped inside her mouth. She returned his kiss without reservation, settling in to enjoy it, floating with the sensation.

Still kissing her, he unbuttoned the pajama shirt, exposing her firm breasts to the air. She squirmed as his fingers brushed her bared skin. He covered the mound closest to her heart with his hand, massaging until her knees threatened to buckle.

But he had a tight hold on her. Breaking off the kiss, he leaned back. She warmed as he inspected her.

'Oh, you are perfect,' he breathed, shifting

his grasp to her waist as he bowed, swooping to nuzzle the hollow of her throat. Her fingers curled over his shoulders. He trailed down to catch a pointed nipple between his lips. She gasped at the surge of intense pleasure, knitting her fingers through his hair and hugging his head to her bosom. He suckled her with slow, deliberate intensity.

She moistened shamelessly between her legs, aching to feel him inside her.

Her breath came in ragged gulps, sobs almost, and she thought she might weep from the sheer delight.

A wild exhilaration overtook her as he skated his hand across her midriff and inside the waistband of her pajama bottoms to caress her belly. The heat radiated down lower, where she throbbed for his touch.

He paused, casting her a questioning look. His pleading gaze tugged at her heart.

'Oh yes, Wheeler, don't stop now.'

When his hand finally slipped lower, winding through downy curls to press against her womanhood, she threw her head back and closed her eyes, trembling both inside and out. She dug teeth into her lower lip, reeling as she held on to his shoulders. His slight movement against her sparked excruciating delight.

To her distress, he broke away from her

suddenly. Falling to his knees, he rested the side of his face against her belly. His whiskers scratched against her smooth skin, an intriguing sensation. She nearly forgot what she'd neglected to tell him.

Finally, he raised up again, getting to his feet. Kneading her shoulders, he stared hard into her eyes. His were glazed with desire.

'I wish I could make love to you tonight, Claire.'

Bereft and bewildered, she furrowed her brow. Of course he could. Did he have to hear her say it?

'Please, I want you to, Wheeler.'

He shook his head. 'I want to more than anything, Claire. But we're getting a little crazy here. Neither one of us was prepared for this. Doing without every other necessity, we overlooked the fact we need protection. And after our long conversation about responsibility this morning, I can't risk getting you pregnant.'

Finally she understood. 'No. You don't have to. Hold on,' she said, rushing out of the room.

'Claire, there's not anything we can use as a substitute for — '

She rushed back, holding out an open palm, on which a square foil packet sat like a jewel on a ring bearer's pillow.

He gaped as though she'd manifested an elephant. Finally, he shifted his gaze back to her. 'Where the hell did you get this?' Then he wrapped a fist around it. 'Oh. Never mind. I think I know, and I don't want to. I'm just glad you have it.'

In one swift movement, he scooped her into his arms, lifting her into the air. Wrapping her arms around his neck, she remembered she'd earlier resented how effortlessly he'd lifted her. Now, she knew where they were headed, what they were going to do, and she thrilled at being in his arms.

He carried her into the den, where he'd moved their mattress out of sight this morning. He pushed the door shut with his back, but it refused to close completely, creaking open an inch. With no one else around for miles, their privacy was assured. For now, she'd banished the rest of the world to a remote planet. She grew aware only of him, his maleness, his powerful aura, the fierce burning inside her only he could satisfy.

Moonlight filtering through the windows highlighted the planes of his face.

'There's an energy in here. Can you feel it?' she asked.

He placed her on her back across the mattress, kneeling over her. She felt his breath on her skin as he spoke. 'If it's too dark, I can get a candle . . . '

He'd remembered, she realized, she didn't like dark places. Such small consideration, yet her heart squeezed. She brushed her fingers against his chin. 'No, don't go anywhere. I'm all right.'

'You're sure?' he asked. She knew his inquiry covered more than the room lighting.

'Very,' she answered, daring to reach down and touch the inside of his thigh through his shorts. The cloth felt hot as though just ironed. He moaned, pressing himself against her hand, his body quaking. She left her hand lingering, delighting in his obvious pleasure. Slowly, she centered her grasp. He shuddered and growled, lowering his mouth to hers, drawing her into a kiss that slung her like a tornado.

His hands glided across her skin unrestrained now, warming her breasts and her belly. He touched her as though memorizing each contour of her body. She alternated between chills and flashes of heat. His hardened manhood grazed her middle, making her dampen freely where he'd touched her moments ago. She ached to be touched there again. She wondered how he would feel inside her.

'Wheeler.' Her voice was raspy.

'Still here, darling. What's wrong? You're tense.'

She laughed softly as he raised his head to look down at her. God, he was incredible. Even as he waited for her to speak, he was tracing the hard tip of her nipple with one fingertip. She could hardly think what she'd meant to say. 'Not anything you've done.'

'Why are you freezing up? If you're having second thoughts, tell me now.'

'No second thoughts.'

He eased her shoulders back so she was flat against the mattress. Rising over her, he peppered her face with kisses, scattering pinpricks of heat, then captured her mouth in his. His hips ground against hers, and she arched her back to feel his hardness.

Suddenly he paused. 'Tell me what's bothering you. Your muscles are in knots.'

She tried to dodge his gaze but, with his face hovering so close over hers, that proved impossible. 'You're a big man, Wheeler.'

He froze for an instant. 'Oh, Claire, I'm not going hurt you. Okay, I swear.'

She blinked her assent, believing he must think her a coward now. Still, the unexpected sharp stab of pain last time lingered in her mind. Barre hadn't meant to hurt her. Her body was reflexively bracing for a repeat. And Wheeler was so much bigger and stronger.

Inching downward, Wheeler suckled each of her breasts in turn, driving Barre far from her mind. Slackening as her breasts swelled in his mouth, her nipples pinching, she focused only on Wheeler and the intense pleasure he sparked.

Rising up, he slipped her pants down over her ankles and tossed them aside. She felt the air hit her skin, cool the dew between her legs. His hand skimmed her hip, tracing its slope. Then he slipped down to press his lips to the spot he'd just touched, nipping at her skin. So hot they were ice.

Claire closed her eyes, giving herself up to the sensation and wriggling beneath him and knowing he would make love to her in any unexpected way he chose. Wheeler was too much for her to anticipate. She lay back, luxuriating in his masterful caresses. She relaxed, lulled by the gentle restraint in his deft hands, the deep timbre of his voice.

Totally vulnerable, she realized she trusted Wheeler at this moment more than she'd ever trusted anyone in her life. Something deep inside told her she could. At some long-ago juncture she couldn't remember, she'd learned to steel herself, hide the vulnerable part of herself away. So afraid, afraid of being hurt too deeply to bear, of not being wanted.

Now, she risked everything. Wheeler

wouldn't allow her to hold anything back.

She opened her eyes, smiling as she watched him tugging at his clothes, making short work of shedding them and tossing them across the room. Sitting up, she pulled the tangled pajama shirt over her head and threw it aside. She watched him, appreciating the symmetry of muscle over his trim form.

He came back to her, kissing her deeply as his hands raked over her, as if ensuring no part of her would be left untouched.

She opened her legs, bursting for his intimate touch. He wedged himself between them, his manhood nudging her.

But he pulled back. 'Touch me,' he requested.

Reaching through the darkness, she tentatively caught hold of him. He pasted his hand over hers, molding her fingers to him. He took his hand away, allowing her time to acquaint herself. Gradually, she grew bolder. He shuddered, emitting a low groan, then to her surprise, gently disengaged her hand.

He dropped down to kiss her on the mouth. 'Not yet, darling,' he whispered. 'But hold the thought.'

He buried his face in her shoulder, blowing softly against her neck, tickling her so she wriggled against him. His bare skin and hard muscle felt wonderful against her skin.

Moving his mouth over her breasts, he blew a stream of air against her nipple. The heat hit her as though he'd taken a torch to it.

Claire sank back and closed her eyes, letting the hot sensations flow through her like the current of a raging river. She'd hated how he'd called her Princess all the time, but he kissed her and touched her as though she were royalty.

Opening her eyes, she found his face hovering over hers. The corners of his mouth lifted, and she smiled back at him. He raised a hand and pushed the hair back from her face with the backs of his fingertips, and she remembered how touching that gesture had struck her back on the porch after they'd escaped from the rubble of the cottage. Only yesterday? She felt as though she'd known this man forever — somewhere in her heart, in her soul, she'd known him.

She couldn't think now about letting him go. This was fate.

He leaned down and kissed her softly on the lips. 'I have a confession to make,' he told her. His rumpled hair gave him a wild look.

'Should I be afraid to ask?' she said.

'I had no intention of caring about anybody ever again. And now ... Don't be afraid of me — '

He broke off the statement she so

desperately wanted to hear him finish. He played his fingers over her flat belly, shooting off sparks. She knit her fingers into the hair on his chest.

Still looking into her eyes, he dipped his hand to the patch of curls below her belly. As Claire gasped, he caught her open mouth in his kiss. His finger slipped easily into the moist juncture between her legs. Each deliberate movement radiated tidal waves of pleasure. 'You're so incredibly soft inside,' he whispered, probing further. 'I love touching you. I want to touch you everywhere. This is good, Claire.'

Claire didn't require more convincing of that. Pleasure speared her, unbearable as the jolt of a lightning bolt.

Slowly, he rolled over, pulling her on top of him. Pressing her to him with one hand at the small of her back, he caressed her intimately between her scissored legs. She scarcely remembered her earlier impatience with the leisurely pace at which he did things. As he stroked, she gave herself up to the intriguing pressure. Heart racing, she closed her eyes, burrowing her face into his neck. Her universe narrowed to a pinpoint where her soul met his.

Just as she believed she could endure no more, the pleasure boiled over. Whimpering, she shimmied against him, surrendering to the waves of ecstasy. A fireball exploded inside her.

Wheeler held fast to her, pinning her against him as she spent her passion. As her senses gradually returned, she raised her head to see him smiling at her in the pale light. He looked appreciative, as though she'd been the one who had taken him to paradise.

'You have a glorious smile,' she said breathlessly.

'I enjoyed that,' he stated without apology. Disengaging one hand, he groped along the floor for the foil packet. For an instant, she feared it had gotten lost, but no, he had it now. He handed it to her, then stretched out on his back beside her, his manhood standing like a majestic oak. He was a big man, all over.

She realized what he meant for her to do. She tore open the packet, getting to her knees and sheathing him, trailing her fingers up and down the length of his manhood. She memorized the feel of him, wanting desperately to possess him in the throes of pleasure as he had done for her.

She caressed him more boldly, cupping her hands between his legs, rubbing the sensitive tissue. He moved in her palms.

Reaching out, Wheeler caught her by the

waist, lifting her so she straddled his hips. Unsure of what he expected, she glanced down at him.

'So you can move away if you need to,' he said, brushing her long hair with his hand. 'Okay?'

His eyes widened in appreciation as she moved, then guided him inside her. She slipped over him gradually, easing downward.

'Oh!' she exclaimed, marveling at the fullness, the fire radiating through her from the center outward. She clamped tightly around him. Instantly, she forget her apprehension. His power permeated every nerve in her body, and she felt her spirit meshing with his. She slid down fully over him, limp with desire, biting her lip to keep from crying with joy. She possessed him too now.

He coaxed her forward, capturing her breast in his mouth and suckling as he thrust his hips higher. Her head swam. He released her breast and reached down into the tuft of curls between her legs, stoking the desire she believed she had spent. He was merciless. Reflexively, she molded her hips to his and rotated them to deflect unbearable pleasure. A tidal wave of release split her in two.

She trembled in his arms as he rolled her onto her back, thrusting with a rhythm as relentless as last night's rain. She raised her hips, clasping his buttocks and pushing into him, feeling his mounting urgency and playing to it.

She wrapped her legs around him, whispering his name into his ear. He wove his fingers between hers, pinning her hands to the mattress. An animal growl escaped from low in his throat, and with one final drive, his whole body quaked as he gave himself over to her. The tremors coursed through her again. She held him tightly, until he lay motionless, his head buried in the crook of her shoulder.

His heart was beating wildly in his chest. His breathing, ragged as her own, gradually evened out.

Finally, he raised his head and kissed her solidly on the mouth. 'Are you okay?'

'Gosh, yes.'

He chuckled mildly. Politely disengaging himself, he got up and disappeared.

Instantly deprived, Claire wondered how he could leave her so quickly, then she realized he had to dispose of the prophylactic. He returned quickly, stretching out on the mattress and bundling her into his arms. She nestled her cheek against his chest. The muscle was hard, the hair soft as feathers.

'Cold?' he asked, skimming fingertips along one side of her breast. Even through her

318

sleepy contentment, she felt fresh stirrings of desire.

'No.' She liked lying here naked in the moonlight with him.

'I figure we're either dreaming or hallucinating from hunger.'

'I hope not. Not such an incredible moment.'

He held her tighter. 'I don't want to let you go, Claire.'

She squeezed her eyes shut. His words provided an invitation, not an ultimatum. Two unlikely souls as theirs would never have collided in the real world, a world by which they'd soon be swept away. And yet their spirits fit together as neatly as their bodies. She had never felt for any man what she was feeling now for Wheeler Scully. If true love equated to passion beyond reason, this was the first time she'd felt it. Yet he hadn't said, 'I won't let you go.' The decision was hers.

'I can't imagine going on with my life without you,' she admitted. 'It's hard to imagine I ever considered marrying Barre.'

His chest sagged. 'Are you sad about that?'

'If I'd really loved him, I wouldn't be here with you now. I'm not like that, Wheeler.'

He brushed her hair with his strong hands. 'Then don't mention his name again. And by the way, thank you.'

'For making love with you?'

'That too. But I meant for the dance.'

'Imagine dancing in the thick of disaster. And yet it felt so completely right.' She kissed his chest.

He was rubbing her shoulder, stroking her as though they were about to make love rather than having just finished. 'Whatever happens, Claire, try to remember how wonderful we both feel right now. I'd forgotten I could feel anything until you forced me to. You have a way of doing that, you know.'

'I knew what I was doing, Wheeler. I'm not sorry. I'm glad this happened. You make love beautifully.'

He tightened his grasp on her. 'I could make love to you all night, darling.'

Claire knew this might be the only night they had. She refused to think about it. Her father wouldn't be pleased, but he was going to be angry once she broke off her relationship with Barre anyway. She had to live her life, and as much as Father had done for her, he had to accept she was no longer the lost orphan who relied on him to prop her up.

She scooted lower, kissing Wheeler's firm stomach, licking and nipping at his skin as he had done to her.

'You never cease to amaze me.'

'I'm surprising myself.' She raised her gaze to meet his. 'I stayed a virgin for a ridiculously long time.'

'That's not anything you need to apologize for.'

She pulled in a sharp breath. 'Maybe I do. I was holding out for the man I wanted to spend the rest of my life with. The joke was, when I finally thought I'd found the person I was safe with, I guess I'd been looking so hard for him, I deceived myself. I couldn't admit I'd made a mistake.'

'Nobody makes perfect choices all the time.'

'Father.'

'I bet if you asked him, he'd admit he experiences doubts just like the rest of us mere mortals.'

'Doubts about me, probably.'

'He's said that?'

'He'd never say it. I can tell when he looks at me I disappoint him. If you think about it, I must.'

'Rash assumption. Especially the way he was bragging the other day about how you'd done such a terrific job of setting up the fund-raising deal, mostly by long distance, and what a great idea having it up here was. Some of those people came just because they were curious.'

'He didn't say anything like that to me.'

'He probably doesn't think he has to.'

'Once, when I was little — it must have been shortly after my mother died — Father took me to visit some friends of his. Their house was beautiful, white upholstery, white carpet, glass-top tables without a smudge on them. On the coffee table was this red glass candy dish, and I took a piece of candy while Father was talking to them.'

'What kid can resist candy?'

'That wasn't the bad part. The bad part was it was black licorice, something I'd never tasted before. I spat it out right on the cushions, and it fell on the carpet. When Father saw what I'd done, his face turned a deep shade of eggplant.'

Wheeler was laughing.

'You're supposed to be offering sympathy.'

It was pretty funny, now.

'So the moral is, if you'd been born his daughter you would have read *Emily Post* in the womb? I've been trying to tell you no kid starts out perfect. We all start out pretty much as idiots, then the world and experience molds us into what we are. I'd love to see you with a real baby.'

'No time soon, I hope.'

'Where'd the condom come from, Claire?'

'My purse.'

'Do you always carry one around with you?'

'I had it because of the party.'

'Oh.' He did not sound pleased. 'Pretty much what I figured.'

'Wheeler, I packed it in there before I even knew you. I was thinking afterward — '

She felt his muscles tense.

'That was in another lifetime for me,' she explained. 'It didn't happen and it's never going to.'

He kissed her cheek. 'No need to explain.' He rubbed circles over her flat tummy, then raised her hand and kissed her fingertips. 'At the moment, the last thing I want to do is think of you with anyone else.'

'You're devouring me.' She tried to make it sound like a complaint.

'Good. My main interest in the condom is not why you had it, pretty self-explanatory, but whether you have any more.'

'Hmm.' She grinned as he pressed his nose and forehead against hers. 'As a matter of fact, I tossed a handful into the purse a few weeks ago.' She did not mention she did this right after she and Barre made love. Barre no longer existed.

'And I was afraid we were going to have to waste time sleeping.'

10

Wheeler opened his eyes to the gray light of dawn, hugging Claire, still sleeping soundly with her head on his chest, closer against him. He never wanted to let go of this angel.

She nestled one side of her face against his skin, her lips moving slightly. He trailed his glance down the length of her naked, lithe body, relishing the contrast of the rose-colored buds tipping her creamy breasts, the golden tresses spilling over her shoulders, fanning across the mattress, the tuft of curls between her long, sleek legs.

The tug in his loins made him yearn to touch her there again. Even after making love to her nearly all night long, he hadn't had his fill. They had collided like two meteors crashing in space. Her odd combination of tentative touches and abandoned daring sent him reeling.

In the semi-darkness, the morning quiet, he

didn't want to think about anything except having her here with him.

He stroked her long hair, memorizing its texture. Reaching down, he pulled the blanket over them so she wouldn't be startled, upon awakening, to be immediately confronted with their nakedness.

But her only movement was to snuggle against him, expelling a small, contented sigh. Watching her face, he saw her eyes were still closed. But he sensed she was awake now.

'Good morning, Princess,' he greeted her.

'It can't be morning yet,' she complained without opening her eyes. 'Please tell me it isn't.'

The intrusive sunlight in the room was brightening steadily. 'Don't worry about getting up. Stay right where you are.'

He skated his fingertips down her belly, liking how she squirmed at his touch. Working downward in a long, meandering line, he played in her downy hair, dipping down to stroke the soft place he'd been hungering to touch.

She gasped, tensing briefly. He watched her face as her features slackened. She curled against him, locking one leg over his to provide him better access. He watched pleasure bathe her features, gauging his motions to repeat what pleased her most.

He covered her lips with his, drinking in her desire like a sweet wine. A distant buzzing intruded into his consciousness. Power saws, he realized, his heart catapulting.

Still, he couldn't stop. Gliding on top of her, he captured her nipple in his mouth, suckling as he moved his fingers both inside her and out. Never in his life had he felt anything as soft and warm. She went liquid in his arms, whispering his name in a way that would echo in his mind forever.

She doesn't hear, he thought, trying to shut the intruders from his mind. Dear God, how he loved this woman. If he had his way, he would spend every minute of his life making sure she never again lapsed into wondering whether she was truly loved. He would help her make those babies she wanted so badly and laugh with her as she learned how they spit up and dropped crumbs on the furniture and tore their clothes. Then she would understand no one has to be perfect to deserve love.

Still caressing her, he pressed his cheek to her bare belly, then kissed her skin. He couldn't remember when he had felt so painfully alive. Hurting inside and yet rejoicing to feel so much. She bucked and whimpered, shaking beneath him as he brought her to the crest of her passion for what he feared would be the last time. He held her, savoring this one moment when she was completely his.

He slid up to watch her face as she opened her eyes. She grinned up at him. 'I could come to look forward to morning if I always woke up this way,' she told him.

'Well, since I can't offer you bacon and eggs — '

'I'd forgotten about being hungry.' She raised a hand, pressing her hand against his bristly jaw. She studied him with such open adoration he felt ashamed. Breakfast wasn't all he couldn't offer her.

Last night, this room had seemed magical and enchanted. Now, in the harsh daylight, the shabby mattress across the floor mocked him.

She reached up, locking her hand around him. Wheeler groaned. His own stamina astonished him.

'There's no time, Princess. I think we're about to be rescued.' A thousand colors swirled in her flaring eyes, like the pattern of oil in water. Quickly they cleared, and she raised her chin with the look of determination he'd glimpsed before. Tightening her grip, she pumped him. His loins wrenched.

'Maybe I won't leave.'

He fell on his back, giving himself over to

both her determined ministrations and his own white-hot pleasure. Stroking tentatively, alternately shy and then deliberate, she produced searing sensations beyond anything he'd experienced before. Gleefully, she delighted in bringing him to his release.

Mercifully, the whir of the saw remained faraway and steady. As long as the saw was still running, he realized, no one would come. He sank into the mattress, giving her a long, deep kiss before laying his head back. 'Look around you, Claire. And this isn't even mine. I'm in no position to make promises.'

Fire flashed in her eyes. She drew back, tensing. 'After last night, you'll just watch me go back to Nashville and that's it? I suppose I am more naïve than I thought. I wouldn't think you could.'

He raked a hand through his hair, propping himself on one elbow and gathering scattered garments. 'That's not fair. You know I care about you. Last night wasn't anything ordinary for me either. All I own is a pair of blue jeans and a shirt.' He tossed her her clothes. 'You'd better get dressed, people will be coming soon.'

'You have a future if you want it. Father — '

'I don't want anything from your father, especially not now. You think he can solve everything. Has it occurred to you he'd probably rather see me dead than with you, honey? You think the world is some enchanted garden because he's always given you every little thing your heart desires.'

He expected fury. Instead, covered now by her pajama shirt, she hung her head contritely and stepped closer. 'You are what my heart desires, Wheeler. I love you, and I'll never love anyone else. If we're calm and don't argue, I'm sure we can find a way to be together. If you want that. I haven't asked, have I?'

'You don't have to ask,' he said.

He kissed her on the mouth. She tasted sweet, felt small in his arms. She opened her mouth, pressing her tongue to his. Her total intuitive faith jarred him. Simple. Sure.

If he'd thought this through, he wouldn't have made love to her. He'd known, he'd always known morning would come. He'd spared her going back to Barre, but now he realized that wasn't enough. He didn't want to let her go at all.

'I'm going to get decent before the troops arrive,' he said, marching naked from the room and heading toward the bathroom. He took care of his morning ablutions, washing with cold water before putting on his jeans and T-shirt.

He raised his face to the mirror and saw the world's biggest fool. He was mad for her, willing to do anything to keep her in his heart and his bed. What he felt was as real as the blood rushing through his veins. She'd resurrected him from the numbness he'd resigned himself to, given him back his life and his hope.

Claire must love him. She wasn't a woman who came to a man's bed on a whim.

For starters, he owed her the truth about himself.

He rushed from the bathroom and found her, dressed in the rumpled pajamas, staring into the cold, dark fireplace. She turned to face him as he entered the room.

'Claire, I haven't been completely honest with you,' he said.

Her features knotted into a stricken expression, bombarding him with guilt. He stepped close in front of her and took hold of both her hands, anxious to explain.

The sound of voices outside wafted through the gap where the front door was supposed to be. 'Claire?'

She cast Wheeler a reassuring look. '*Father?*'

Joshua Woolrich and Barre Sutton, dressed in campers' outfits, rushed through the doorway. Both had dark circles under their eyes and looked like they'd been on a long binge.

'Thank God you're all right,' Woolrich said.

Barre's gaze locked on Claire's hand sandwiched between both of Wheeler's. His eyes widened, his mouth curled into a sneer.

Looking past Barre, Claire cried with joy as she rushed to hug her father. 'I've been so worried about you!' she exclaimed.

'Worried about me?' he asked, looking at her harder. 'Are you all right? Your car's out in the ditch, and the sheriff's department is combing the roadside for a body.'

She paled.

Seeing her distress, Wheeler wanted to go to her and fold her into his arms. Barre made no move to comfort her. Instead, he riveted his gaze on Wheeler. Wheeler caught hold of her wrist. He had to touch her. He could already see the hostility rising in Barre's eyes.

'What are you doing here, Ben?' Barre demanded.

Joshua and Claire both leveled bewildered glances at Wheeler. He felt his face heating. Claire wore a worried, questioning look.

'Wheeler's my father's caretaker,' she answered for him, sounding as though she assumed Barre had mistaken him for someone else. She cast Wheeler a fond glance. Although warmth surged inside him,

Wheeler saw Barre's scowl deepen, and he knew revealing her affection would prove a fatal mistake. 'He saved my life.'

Barre was staring through Wheeler. Confused, he glanced over his shoulder and saw the door to the den had swung open. Through the narrow slit, the mattress on the floor and the disheveled blanket atop it were visible.

Barre stepped closer to Wheeler. 'So you finally found a way to get back at me, did you, Scully?' He shifted his attention to Claire, striding toward her menacingly. 'And dragged Claire into it. Even for you, that's low.'

'No one has dragged me into anything,' Claire protested. 'You've been out in the fresh air too long, Barre. Whatever are you talking about?'

Barre swung his gaze to Joshua Woolrich, Claire, then defiantly back to Wheeler. Wheeler recognized the too-familiar way Barre's brow dipped when his mind was concocting a story to make himself look good. 'Ben here and I were partners, until he ran our business into the ground, bullied his wife until she came to me for help in getting away from him. He's blamed me for his own mistakes. I suppose I can't fault you for going by your middle name these days.' He glared at Claire. 'You should be more careful, darling, before you start getting chummy with the hired help,' he demanded.

Claire shrank back indignantly. Wheeler, facing Barre, stepped between them. 'Leave her alone!'

'Things look too cozy up here if you ask me,' Barre said, eyeing Wheeler darkly before taking an unexpected swing at him and catching him smack on the mouth. Reflexively, Wheeler coiled his fist, snapping his arm back.

Joshua restrained Barre, pulling him out of striking distance.

Wheeler rubbed fingers over his mouth, then drew back his hand to stare at the scarlet stain on his hand. Claire moved toward him, shooting Barre a killing glare. But before she touched him, something changed in her expression, and her hands fell to her side as she halted.

She gaped at Wheeler, devastation embroidered into her features. Why shouldn't she believe Barre? He'd bypassed plenty of opportunities to tell her the truth, to tell her Barre was the man who had ruined him, who would happily ruin anybody for his own gains. Damn it, she hadn't been ready to listen until maybe this morning. And this morning was too late. He'd waited too long to try to tell her.

'I'd sure like to know what the hell's going on,' Joshua Woolrich snarled. 'But we're all tired and on edge. Barre, take Claire to the emergency room.'

'No, please. No hospital. I'm just tired and hungry.'

'To the motel, then. Get her something to eat and have Sadie run out and pick up some clothes if she didn't get her any this morning.'

'Come on, baby,' Barre coaxed in a soothing tone.

Claire, still watching Wheeler with wounded eyes, didn't move. 'Wheeler needs some food,' she insisted, her voice low.

Barre took hold of her arm, pulling her toward the door. 'Your dad will take care of him,' he crooned.

Claire stood rooted to the floor, then shook her hair back and broke free of Barre's grasp. 'I have something to say to Mr Scully privately.'

Barre eyed her speculatively.

Surprisingly, Claire's father pulled him toward the door. 'Give them a minute, Barre,' he said. Wheeler marveled Woolrich had remained so calm.

As they left, Wheeler entertained a dim hope she was going to give him a chance to explain.

But that hope shattered as she whirled to

face him. Her stricken expression indicated she'd already formulated answers of her own. Her hands were poised on her slender hips.

She didn't speak until Barre and her father were outside. 'You couldn't even tell me your real name?'

'Wheeler is my real name. My middle name. Barre knows me by my first name. Ben stuck in college, because that's what the professors read off the roll.'

'So, you've known each other since college? Why did you do this? Nothing is ever going to be the same for me again, don't you understand? Why did you put me between you and Barre?'

'I didn't — '

'It's the only reason I can think of for your not telling me you knew him.'

Wheeler heard shuffling outside. Her rescuers anxiously waiting for her. He should have known nothing would really change between them. He'd tried to tell her from the start. Then he'd begun letting himself hope.

He leveled his gaze on her, hating the hurt in her eyes. 'Maybe you should think harder.'

'Don't talk to me in riddles.'

He swept his hair back with one hand. Knowing he needed a shave and a haircut and probably looked like a cave dweller, he realized he hadn't a dime or a change of clothing to his name. And he was about to profess his love for the daughter of one of the richest men in North America? 'Look, Princess, we both knew from the start I'm not the kind of guy you should ever be with for keeps. Sorry if you misunderstood that last night. I never lied to you about that. Or about anything. Go with Barre. He's what you really want. Go have your party.'

She blinked back tears.

Wheeler steeled himself.

'Just like that? As though nothing had ever happened? You deceive me, tear my life to shreds, knowing all the while it wouldn't work that way because I don't work that way. Last night, I thought we'd found something precious and special.'

'The storm skewed everything. Short of a disaster, last night never would have happened. And all that's behind us now.'

'I hope you feel real smug, Wheel — whoever you are. You've ripped the heart right out of me.'

He winced. 'Nothing I say will make any difference. You decided to believe Barre the minute he walked in. Go on, sweetheart. They're waiting for you.'

Flashing one final accusing look at Wheeler, she went outside to Barre. Wheeler stood in the door frame, his chest caving inward as he watched Barre coil an arm around her waist, watched Claire slant against him as he limped her toward an official-looking white Blazer. He might have been able to tolerate losing her to anyone but Barre. No, he never could have stomached watching her leave. Watching her go with Barre felt like acid in a wound.

Only the sound of footsteps from the far end of the porch reminded him of Joshua's lingering presence. 'You didn't think I'd take off before I decided whether I should be shaking your hand or taking a swing at you myself, did you?' Joshua said in response to Wheeler's startled expression.

Woolrich was carrying a soft drink can in one hand. Wheeler tried to avoid staring at it too greedily. To his amazement, Woolrich transferred the cool can to his hand. Even this small compassion came as a surprise from a man with every reason to assume his daughter had been compromised. Woolrich did have many layers to him, just like Claire.

'Thank you.' He popped the top, frothy cola spewing on his hands. Woolrich waited patiently as he gulped down half the can in one long swig.

'Let's find some place to sit down. My nerves are stretched pretty tight, and I'm anxious to get back to my daughter. So let's

337

get to the point. Exactly who are you and why has your mere presence disrupted my family?'

★ ★ ★

Claire closed her eyes, floating in hot water amid a mountain of bubbles in the claw-foot tub. She would have preferred a nice Hilton to this quaint little motel. In the past few days, she'd had her fill of rustic accommodations. But at least this place had electricity, a real bed and a door that closed. Her muscles ached, and she grew drowsy as exhaustion closed over her. She'd never felt so thoroughly depleted. A ton of soap and hot water could never wash away Wheeler Scully's deception. Benjamin Wheeler Scully. He'd even so much as told her he wanted Barre to pay for what Wheeler accused him of doing. He'd conveniently neglected to mention her fiancé was the target of his revenge.

As shrewd as the devil himself, he'd planted doubts in her mind until she didn't know what she was thinking. And he'd left an indelible imprint. She loathed him.

Tit for tat.

What a nitwit she'd been. Surrendering her mind and heart and soul to him, while all the time he was using her to settle a score. She could have died from shame.

She was going to have to tell Barre every detail of what had happened. Considering the circumstances, she hoped he would forgive her.

Through the bathroom door she heard the drone of the television set, Barre's pacing footsteps as he waited for her. He looked as frazzled as she felt. How frightening the past thirty-six hours must have been for him. But now he was here, taking care of her, defending her honor. What honor? She'd tossed aside everything that had been between them. Now, she could only pray he would understand.

She bolted upright as the door opened — she hadn't thought to lock it. Barre stepped in, and modestly, she sank deeper into the bubbles. His eyes lingered on the line of white fluff over her cleavage.

He held up a shopping bag by its handle. 'Sadie reports this town suffers from a severe dearth of clothing stores, but she hopes this will do until you get home. I brought your order — cheeseburger, French fries and cola. You're sure that's what you want?'

'Yes.' She was hungry enough she would have eaten dirt, but the burger and fries were what she craved. Involuntarily, she thought of Wheeler and hoped Father had fed him. Despite everything that happened, Wheeler had kept her safe. Tears stung her weary eyes as she acknowledged that, although he'd as much as violated her, certainly her trust anyway, she was idiot enough to keep caring about him.

Barre stepped closer to the tub, giving her an encouraging look. 'Hey, it's over now,' he cajoled.

Was it?

In her compromised position, she didn't want him coming any nearer. Until she sorted things out in her head, she didn't think she could bear being touched by anyone. And Barre was the last person whose sympathy she deserved. His present attentiveness made her feel more guilty.

'I'd like to get dressed now,' she announced.

Barre glanced toward the door as though the cause for her hesitation had just dawned on him. 'I'll be right outside if you need me.' He shuffled toward the door and left.

Claire relaxed once he shut the door. Except for his sharp accusation back at the house, he'd been nothing but kind. Why did she feel so defiled by his innocent intrusion? She pushed in the knob to drain the tub. Stepping into the bath mat, she felt a chill, even though the air inside the bathroom was warm and steamy. She thought of the steamy air in the mansion last night and squeezed her eyes shut, shivering. Wheeler Scully and what happened last night would not haunt her. It was a mistake she would get over.

She grabbed the towel off the rack and dried herself. Delving into Sadie's shopping bag, she unearthed a simple shift, a pair of sandals, a knit-shorts set and — God bless her cousin — underwear. Everything except the sandals was lilac, her favorite color. The hair brush was still encased in plastic, and there was a twistie to hold back her hair — what was left of it. Self-consciously, she felt the gaps where Wheeler had cut away the branches. Oh, good, lipstick. Claire shook her head. Sadie always said she'd just as soon go out in public naked as be seen without her lipstick.

Where was Sadie? She wanted to see her cousin. Ushered away in Barre's close keeping, she felt like a prisoner, confined for debriefing.

Chucking the lipstick back into the bag, she slipped into the underwear, feeling civilized again. The shorts set reminded her too much of the makeshift clothing she'd worn on the mountain, but she put it on anyway, saving the dress for the trip home. She wondered whether she would be able to drive her car.

Her head teemed with questions, but she

was too tired to search for answers. She brushed her wet hair, then tucked it back into a loose ponytail, making the choppy haircut less obvious. She slipped her feet into the sandals and opened the door.

Barre, standing at the window, turned and smiled. 'Feeling better?' he asked.

'Yes, thanks.' She folded her arms across her chest. 'It's freezing in here.' He had the air conditioner blasting.

He pulled the quilt back on the bed and patted the sheet. 'Get under the blankets. You can eat in bed.' As she complied, he moved to adjust the thermostat setting.

'I'm afraid I might fall asleep before I finish.'

'When you wake up, I'll buy you a proper meal.'

'You're being nicer to me than I deserve.' She read the alarm in his eyes before he masked it.

He handed her her the icy soft drink. 'We don't have to talk about any of it now, baby. Whatever that bastard did was my fault. I'm the one he hates. If he'd left you alone, I'd almost feel sorry for him.'

'Did you sleep with his wife?'

Barre flinched as though she'd slapped him, but he answered calmly. 'He convinced himself I did, because he resented my friendship with her. She begged me to help her. She was scared of him. Man's got a hairtrigger temper. Some people must blame someone for the bad luck they make themselves.'

Her thoughts were murky, veiled with fatigue. Wheeler bad-tempered? The same man who had calmly allowed her to beat on his chest like a punching bag?

'Why did she go to you?'

'We were partners. She knew I was aware of the situation, thought maybe I could talk some sense into him. He's the one who wouldn't let her come back.'

His offhand statement bothered her in a way her tired mind couldn't pinpoint. 'Why did she want to go back if he was cruel to her?'

Barre propped the pillows against the headboard. 'Here, sit back so you can eat.'

She leaned against the pillows and accepted the food he handed her, balancing the wrappings on her lap and attacking the hamburger like a greedy child. He watched her, smiling approvingly.

Hungry as she was, after only a few bites, she felt full. She set the hamburger down.

'Isn't it cooked right?' he asked. 'I ordered it well done.'

She shook her head and handed him the

343

plate. 'Eyes bigger than my stomach, I guess. I'm feeling kind of queasy, and I'm really sleepy, Barre.' He set the plate on the nightstand. 'Scoot up,' he commanded.

She leaned forward. He began kneading her shoulders. At first, she tensed at the unexpected touch, but his steady motions quickly relaxed her. She grew limp and drowsy. 'Today's Monday, isn't it? I'm keeping you from your work,' she protested. 'If you need to go back, Barre, Father and Sadie will get me home.'

'I let you too far out of my sight already, Claire. If I'd come to the luncheon Saturday as you wanted me to, none of this would have happened.'

'For Pete's sake, I'm not a child who needs constant supervision, Barre. I only wanted you to come so you could see Father's house. Nobody's to blame for my getting stranded.'

She opened her eyes. Glimpsing his wounded look, she realized she'd snapped at him. Why?

'I'm too groggy to be civil, Barre,' she apologized. 'Where's Father?'

'Still up on the mountain settling up with Ben, I imagine.'

'And Sadie?'

'Just in the next cabin.'

'I'd like to see her.'

'Why don't you sleep for a while first?'

'Which side? I'll go there.' She started to get up, but he held her back.

'Stay put. I only thought you needed some rest. I'll get her.'

He shot out the door, and she cursed herself for being so short with him. She had only herself to be angry with.

Sadie appeared within seconds, as neatly groomed as if she'd spent the morning in a salon, although she was casually dressed.

Barre trailed her through the door, and Sadie stopped, blocking his path. 'Why don't you go for a walk, Barre? I want to talk to Claire alone.'

Barre eyed her speculatively, casting Claire a worried parting glance before he spun on his heel and left, softly closing the door behind him.

Sadie sat on the edge of the bed, smiling warmly. 'Well, you gave us all a good scare. I imagine you had quite an adventure. What is with all this secrecy? Barre's worried me silly, doing everything short of placing an armed guard at the door to keep me out.' She took a hard glance at her. 'You seem to be in one piece.'

Claire sighed heavily. 'I'm fine — a little frayed around the edges is all, Sadie.'

'What did you do to your hair?'

'Wheeler had to cut it.'

'I can see why he's not a barber.'

Claire laughed, surprised she could.

'What happened up there?'

Claire avoided Sadie's interrogating eyes.

Sadie's harsh expression softened. 'Haven't we always been able to tell each other everything? Did I snitch to your dad that time you sneaked off to that Bon Jovi concert with Jamie Trumble?'

Claire, laughed softly. 'The black leather jacket and the earring. And that gorgeous curly hair. I loved his defiance, then I found out he felt that way toward everybody and everything. But I was a starry-eyed teenager. I'm afraid this is more serious.' She drew in a deep breath and squared her shoulders. She needed to vent, and Sadie was the only person in whom she could confide. Painfully, she related what had happened on the mountain, offering as few details as possible.

Sadie listened patiently, waiting until Claire finished before commenting, 'Oh, honey, you're not the first woman who's slept with a guy only to find out later he's scum. Write it off. You screwed up. It's nothing you can't live past. God knows I would have been struck dead if that weren't true.'

Claire rolled her eyes miserably, gnawing her lip. 'What am I going to tell Barre?'

'Sounds like he's guessed something close to the truth already, and he's still here.'

'I don't want to hurt him.'

'You're half-asleep. I should go now. Once you get some rest, your mind will be clearer. Then don't put off saying what you have to say to him. Delaying it will only blow everything out of proportion. Do you want him to come back or would you rather be alone?'

But Claire hadn't confessed the worst, what bothered her most. 'Sadie, I keep remembering the time up there, and something inside of me refuses to accept Wheeler was using me. Everything was exactly the way I always dreamed love should be. If he was insincere, wouldn't I have felt it?'

Sadie grinned gently. 'You finally got your bells and whistles, huh?'

Claire nodded glumly. 'The entire marching band. Maybe I should go back up there and give him another chance to explain.'

'You're not in any shape to go anywhere right now. Honey, it sounds as though he had a chance to explain and couldn't. He didn't even tell you his real name, for cripe's sake. Or mention he knew Barre. Thank your stars you got out of there when you did.' She gasped, clasping one hand to her face. 'You did use protection, didn't you?'

'Of course, I'm not that gullible. And Wheeler insisted on it as well.'

'He's not a total louse,' Sadie commented, her brow wrinkling thoughtfully. 'Look, you two were thrown together in rather desperate circumstances. Some men can be very intense, give the impression at intimate moments they'd rather stop breathing than live without you, when actually their mind's already on tomorrow's baseball game.'

Claire swallowed hard. 'I'd bet my diamond necklace he wasn't calculating batting averages. Barre's hovering over me, treating me like I'm made of eggshells, and instead of feeling grateful, I'm wishing Wheeler would march through that door and explain how it was all a mistake. Wheeler's a liar, an impostor, and even though I know it, I hate believing it. I want to be with him. I want him to be the man he convinced me he was.' Her tears flowed freely. 'He's a devil, but I'm afraid I fell in love with him.'

Sadie gave her a worried look. 'Keep that up and we'll have to send you on the talk-show circuit.'

Claire sputtered a laugh through her tears.

Sadie tilted her head and asked suddenly, 'Did you love Sam, Claire?'

Confused, Claire struggled to remember Sam. 'Not like this.'

'But I know you cared for him.'

'He gave up on me because I wouldn't sleep with him.'

Sadie raised an eyebrow. 'That's what you thought? No, I chased him off when things were getting serious. Threatened to stop showing his work in my gallery. He'd just started selling some of his sculptures. You were all bright-eyed and fresh out of college and refused to listen to me about the problems I saw coming for you. I'm sorry, Claire. I never should have interfered in your life. Ever since the day your mom and dad brought you around, I've had this instinct for wanting to protect you. Keep seeing you as that scrawny, lost little kid. Maybe you needed that back when we were kids, but we're grownups now and it's time for me to butt out of your life. You're the little sister I never had, and I love you, Claire, but it's past time for me to let go. Otherwise I'll end up a meddling spinster and you'll resent me, the way you resent your dad and now Barre.' Sadie brushed a tear off her cheek.

'You make me feel spoiled and ungrateful.'

'You were never a brat, Claire. You obviously love and respect your dad. If anything, maybe you've gone overboard in being too grateful.'

'How could I ever be too grateful? If he

and Mother hadn't adopted me, who knows how I might have ended up?'

'Isn't that as much a circular question as what if I'd never been born? Uncle Joshua and Aunt Anita made a personal decision to adopt a child before they knew you'd existed. They wanted to be parents. You happened to be the kid they picked, a fortunate accident of fate. You don't owe your father molding your adult life to please him anymore than I do my parents for conceiving me. If I did, Mom would be working me on strings like a marionette. Have you ever considered what you've already given your father? The joy you brought into a life otherwise centered totally around his businesses? And when your mom died, having you to raise gave him a reason to keep living. You alternate between leaping over skyscrapers to please him and begrudging the hold you've given him over your life.'

'I'd never want to hurt him.'

'I know. But he's not going to wake up and realize you're old enough to make your own decisions independently of him unless you flat out tell him. It won't kill him. He has the same problem I do, only a worse case of it. Over-protectiveness.'

Claire stared miserably into the pillowcase.

'You know I'll always help you any way I can. But I can't tell you what to do this time.

After what's happened to me this weekend, I'm hardly qualified. You're going to have to deal with Wheeler Scully on your own terms. He had his chance to tell you his version of the truth. Get some sleep. You're in too much of a stupor to think straight.'

'What happened to you, Sadie?'

'For now, let's just say you're not the only one who made a mistake.'

'How long do we have the cabin?' she asked drowsily.

'Take as long as you need. Your dad's paying the bill, and he can afford it.'

Sadie was halfway to the door when Claire called out to her. 'Sadie?'

'Hmm?'

'I love you. It's okay about Sam.'

'It'll all be okay.'

'Can you find Madeline? Make sure her shop's still standing. I need to explain to her about the ferns.'

Sadie laughed, shaking her head. 'Nobody in this town was concerned with ferns Saturday night. Madeline's shop escaped damage. I'll call and tell her you're okay. She was worried.'

Claire fell asleep without hearing her close the door. She slept thinly, disturbed by the rumble of passing trucks, the strange hard bed, and dreams of Wheeler Scully.

11

Claire stood in front of the travel lodge, contemplating the last fiery orange streaks of sunlight blazing across the sky. Her heart was sinking with the setting sun.

'Up already? I thought you were out for a long while.'

Turning, she smiled at Barre as he approached. 'I won't feel settled until I'm home.' But deep inside, she feared nothing would ever feel right again. 'Sharp T-shirt.'

He glanced down at his chest ruefully. 'Sadie's warped humor. She never has liked me.'

'She wouldn't bother playing jokes on you if she didn't.'

'Shame she can't seem to settle down. She seemed wild about the guy who came up here with her. Spent the night, then took off and ditched her.'

Claire raised her eyebrows. No one ditched

Sadie. No wonder she'd sounded so defeated. And despite Sadie's bold front, Claire knew spending the night with a man wasn't something her cousin fell into casually.

'Who was he?'

Barre shook his head. 'Older guy. Ned somebody.'

Claire folded her arms over her chest, rubbing her arms even though the air was warm.

'Do you want some coffee or something? A cup of tea maybe?'

She shook her head. 'No, thank you.'

'Sadie checked out a couple hours ago. Said she'd see you back in Nashville. Your father drove back to Nashville with her, and I've got a rented car waiting if you're ready to go.'

'Father's gone already?'

Barre shrugged. 'Said he had business to take care of and you're welcome to come and stay at his house for a few days if you need to. Well out of the way of the media.'

'I've scarcely gotten to speak to him since — My God, if he's done anything to Wheeler — '

Barre frowned. 'If he has, I'm sure it's not half what that scoundrel merits.'

She leveled her gaze. 'Regardless of everything else, I owe him my life. I promised

353

he'd be compensated for the belongings he lost when that shack Father housed him in blew over.'

'He did his job.'

'And more.'

Barre's eyebrows arched in astonishment. 'Wheeler has never been our kind of people, Claire. His old man was a farmer, peddling tomatoes at the roadside.'

'But that didn't stop him from attending the same college you went to. Who are our kind of people, Barre?'

'I didn't mean that the way it sounded.'

'Sure, you did. Just like your mother and her none-too-subtle barbs about my background. I wonder, Barre, if we got married and had a family one day whether she'd be drilling it into our children's heads they were inferior because my biological parents were probably poor, most likely unmarried. I wonder about that because she made me feel that way. Whatever would she say if we adopted a child?'

His mouth dropped open. 'Why would we — ?'

She'd thought she knew this man. Now, she understood he was too selfish to ever open his heart and let anyone in far enough. To Barre, all things were conditional. He was considerate and attentive not because he cared about other people, but because it reflected flatteringly upon him.

'You're overwrought, Claire. We'll have plenty of time to discuss everything once we're back in Nashville. Let's not wait, get married as soon as possible.'

She closed her eyes and drew in a deep, bracing breath. 'Just like that? You still want to marry me? You haven't asked what actually happened with Wheeler.'

His jaw clenched, and Claire loathed herself for the genuine hurt in his eyes. 'I have a pretty fair idea. Whatever it is, we can work it out.'

'You're automatically willing to forgive me?'

'I don't want to hear about it.'

'You're going to have to sooner or later. We made love last night.'

He cradled his forehead in his palm, shaking his head. Then he raised wounded eyes. She couldn't have felt worse if he'd cursed her. 'Why, Claire? You wanted us to wait. I respected that.'

'You never asked what I wanted. And it wasn't something I did to betray you. By the time it happened, I'd already realized you and I have never been right together. We were okay, Barre, but we never had the fire to keep us together the rest of our lives. Maybe

Wheeler took advantage of the situation for his own agenda, but even David Copperfield can't manufacture a tornado. And no one but me determines what I think or how I feel inside. I acted of my own free will, and that's what I have to deal with now.'

'You're not the same woman you were.'

'I am, Barre. You never really knew me.'

He took hold of her hands in both of his. His touch felt cold to her. 'Claire, I'll do whatever you want. I'll talk to my mother, point out how she's offending you without meaning to.'

She shook her head. 'It wouldn't change the way she feels about me. Nothing on the outside changes people's attitudes. Those come from inside the heart. And it's not just your mother.'

'I love you, Claire. Doesn't that count? It wasn't in the plan, but — '

Claire stepped back. 'Which plan was that?'

His face reddened. 'Figure of speech,' he muttered.

'I'm sorry, Barre.'

The desk clerk shot out of the office, running toward them and waving. 'Pardon me,' he said, panting breathlessly as he reached them. 'Has Mr Woolrich left town?'

'Yes,' Barre answered, eyeing him skeptically. 'Why?'

'There's a man on the phone. Said Mr Woolrich was real anxious about hiring his helicopter and he's available now.'

'No. He's too late,' Barre answered.

Shrugging, the man turned toward the office.

'Wait!' Claire called, racing after him. 'If he's available I'll hire him.'

She cast an anxious look behind her at Barre, standing alone, looking handsome and bereft. 'Oh, Claire,' he said heavily. 'Tell me you're not going back on the mountain.'

Instead of telling him, she rushed on toward the office, still hobbling slightly.

⋆　⋆　⋆

By the time she walked into Father's living room that evening, she was furious. He was at his desk in the study, sorting through a stack of paperwork with the familiar gold Cross pen he'd owned for years poised in his right hand, beneath a circle of yellow light radiating from his green-shaded banker's lamp. Claire had given him the monogrammed pen the Christmas she was twelve.

Catching him in such a familiar pose temporarily blunted her anger. She recalled entering his bedroom at the mountain mansion and looking at his vacant reading chair by the window, wishing she'd told him earlier how much she loved him.

He glanced up at her casually, seeming unaware of the steam that had to be spewing from her ears. 'Where's Barre?' he asked, craning his neck to peer behind her as if expecting Barre to be trailing behind her.

'I sent him home. Your helicopter pilot flew me back.'

A flicker of amusement played in her father's eyes. 'That obnoxious guy. Pleasant ride?'

'He's not much of a conversationalist. He'll be sending you his bill.'

'All right. Barre could have turned in the rental car and come back with you.' He didn't blink an eye over a whopping bill for chartering a helicopter. His only concern was why she wasn't with Barre.

She drew in a deep breath, firm in her resolve now. Might as well get this part over with. 'I didn't want him to. I can't marry Barre.'

'Did you two have an argument?'

'Where's Wheeler, Father? The pilot took me back up on the mountain, and the workmen boarding up the house said they hadn't seen him. You sent him away, didn't you?'

Joshua dropped his pen on the blotter.

'Wheeler's not working for me anymore. But I didn't have him shipped to the Antarctic, if that's what you're implying.'

She clenched her hands into fists. 'I was depending on you to see he got food and a bath and a place to sleep. And medical attention. A board or something fell on his head. And instead you fired him? I should have stayed and seen to him myself. I promised him I wouldn't abandon him. I told him he'd be rewarded for going beyond his job to keep me safe. He did that.'

'Hold up, Claire. You're not obligated to wild promises you made during a crisis.'

'You were the one who taught me there's honor in keeping your word. Does that apply only to your word? Is mine too insignificant to count?'

His sharp, distinguished features narrowed into a frown. 'You were the one who was angry with Mr Scully this morning. I got the impression you didn't want to have to deal with him.'

Claire hung her head. Placing her complete trust in Wheeler had frightened and exhilarated her. When reality encroached in the cold light of morning, she'd been too quick to believe her worst fears realized. Father was right this time. She shouldn't be shifting the blame to him.

Father's voice remained steady and calm. 'I didn't fire him. He quit. And I've seen to it he'll get what's due him.'

'Where did he go?'

'Actually, he didn't tell me. Matter of fact, the man's pretty damned reserved. When I asked him what all that flak was between him and Barre, he told me it was none of my business.'

Claire surpressed a laugh. That sounded exactly like Wheeler. 'He speaks his mind.'

'I never should have hired a man without investigating his background. But it was only a caretaker's position and there weren't that many takers. The cottage wasn't big enough for a man with a family. Why are you so anxious to find him?'

'I need to hear his side of what happened between him and Barre, know why he didn't tell me he knew Barre. Apologize for Barre hitting him.'

'Barre was defending your honor.'

'No, his own, I think.'

Father looked worried. 'Claire, when I walked in the house, it was obvious to me Scully hadn't harmed you. In fact, you seemed fond of him, which is, I'm sure, what set Barre off. Sometimes people do crazy things in desperate situations, things they wouldn't do otherwise, like forge unlikely relationships. Alone up there, it's natural you and Mr Scully might have developed some temporary bond out of necessity. But aren't you reading too much into this sense of indebtedness, letting it come between you and Barre?'

'Barre's not real, Father. He's all pretense. Wheeler is genuine, strong, and self-sufficient. He's not afraid to be his own person, and his example has given me the courage to listen to my own heart. I let him down by listening to Barre first.'

'Maybe once everything settles down, you and Barre will work things out again. In my unbiased opinion, you're a beautiful young woman, and you've always been sensible. Unfortunately there will always be men out there to whom your money and social position are a stronger attraction. You have to be cautious.'

'Apparently, I haven't been cautious enough. Have you considered what a happy coincidence it was Denver Sutton got himself introduced to you, took such an interest in me, and then brought around his handsome son who instantly fell madly in love? You, the one who told me fairy tales were nonsense? Even you can be fooled. Barre inadvertently acknowledged they had a 'plan'.'

The temporary closeness struck up

between them dissipated like a summer fog. Over the years, Father had more frequently let down his guard around Claire, occasionally softened his stoic stance on minor issues. But inevitably, major disagreements always boiled down to the ongoing power struggle between them. Until Claire acceded to his wishes. But not this time.

She lowered her voice. 'I'm tired of always jumping to conclusions about people based on appearances. I'm tired of being afraid to trust anyone who doesn't drive a sleek new car. Maybe I've just never been a whole lot like you, Father. Maybe being a Woolrich is too hard for anybody who doesn't have the right blood running through her veins.'

His features constricted. 'I had no idea you were so unhappy, Claire. Do you think it's been easy for me to keep from voicing my objections about Barre? I've nearly bitten my tongue off trying to get along with him, because I thought you loved him. In my opinion, he's spineless. I could tell him it was raining donkeys and he'd agree with me.'

'Help me find Wheeler, so I can talk to him just one more time.'

'You won't be seeing him again, Claire.'

'You can't stop me. I'll find him on my own.'

Her father shook his head. 'Claire, I can't

stand to see you hurt. Ever.'

'Everyone gets hurt. It's unavoidable.'

Joshua Woolrich shook his head sadly. 'Honey, I didn't send him away. I offered to put him up in Blakesville or here in Nashville, and he turned me down. He said he thought you'd be better off if he wasn't around. And although I am sorry, I happen to agree.'

★ ★ ★

Claire lurched in the passenger seat of Madeline's van as the florist sped over yet another pothole in the road through what remained of downtown Blakesville. The buzz of saws and pounding of hammers from the storm cleanup on this clear, sunny morning reminded her all too well of her last morning with Wheeler, before the outside world intruded. Had it only been a few short days ago?

'Sorry, honey,' the older woman apologized over her shoulder, slowing the vehicle slightly. Today, her brown hair was pulled up in the same tight bun she normally wore, but decked in overalls and a striped T-shirt instead of a tailored suit, she more resembled a teenager than a widow in her fifties. 'It's great of you to come down here to help, especially after all you went through, being trapped up on the mountain. When you called and volunteered, I didn't realize you were this serious. Having a celebrity out at the Wilders will give everybody's spirits a boost.'

Claire smiled thinly. The Wilders were an elderly couple whose home at the edge of town had been demolished. The local residents were all pitching in today to help sift through the debris in hopes of salvaging many decades' worth of family mementos. 'No more than others are doing. And I'm hardly a celebrity,' she countered.

'You and your daddy are this burg's only claim to fame.' Madeline nodded approvingly at Claire's jean-clad legs. 'Glad you came dressed in work clothes. This place is a mess.'

Claire shook her head back. 'I don't mind getting dirty. I just wish there was more I could do.'

'This is plenty. Your new haircut looks real cute, by the way. Maybe I'll get mine chopped off — save me pinning it up every morning.'

Still unaccustomed to the shorter hairstyle, Claire brushed her fingertips against the nape of her neck. Sadie's stylist had done a remarkable job, considering what she'd been given to work with. The curls feathering her hair to the base of her neck framed her face flatteringly. 'Thanks.'

Staring out the window, Claire caught sight of a crew of construction workers digging through the rubble of what had been the corner hardware store. A tall, tanned blonde man stood among them, issuing orders and looking comfortably in charge. Her mouth fell open as he raised one hand to pluck the baseball cap from his head, revealing longish sunstreaked blonde hair and sharp, handsome features. He mopped his brow with the back of one sleeve. Wheeler.

Her heart lifted as though the sun had finally come out. She nearly cried for Madeline to stop the van so she could jump out and run to him.

Briefly, he stared so intently toward the street, she thought he must see her. But without showing any sign of recognition, he quickly looked away and resumed his work. She realized he hadn't seen her. All for the best?

He'd told her to leave him, told her father he didn't want her to know where he was. Her heart went cold. Now at least she did know, saw for herself he was fine without her. How ironic they should both follow the same impulse — to return to Blakesville and help others stricken by the storm.

Silently, she watched through misty eyes as

the van pulled farther down the street and he disappeared from sight. She'd found him by accident, but he'd known these past days where to locate her. If he'd wanted to.

'Something wrong?' Madeline asked. 'You're awful quiet.'

Claire shook her head. 'The storm took away so much from so many people,' she answered quickly.

'But just look at all these folks pulling together. Rebuilding instead of worrying over what's gone. Takes more than a little twister to extinguish that kind of spirit. Some people might say a disaster changes everything, but mostly it brings out the good things inside us that we leave sleeping when we're comfortable. A reminder of our own strength, compassion, how we all need each other.'

Claire forced a smile. 'You make catastrophe sound like a stroke of luck.'

Madeline shrugged. 'Luck is what you make it. How long you plan to stay in town?'

Claire glanced back down the street. 'Oh, just today. There's no point in my lingering here.'

★ ★ ★

Finally realizing she'd been staring at one page of the novel in her lap for half an hour without comprehending a word, Claire snapped the book shut, gazing across the grounds surrounding her father's estate. Sunshine cut diamonds into the clear water of the swimming pool beside her. The glass of lemonade his housekeeper had brought earlier sat untouched on the glass-top table beside her, now diluted with melted ice.

Why was she sitting here lounging by Father's pool like a slug instead of doing something productive? For two weeks now, ever since she'd seen Wheeler in Blakesville. The idle rich, she reflected. Some people would have thought her foolish to do anything other than spending all her days languishing by the poolside, sponging off her father's wealth with servants anticipating her needs. But loafing had never suited her.

How much more alive she'd felt when she'd been hungry and thirsty and crawling through the mud. And making love with Wheeler. No matter what happened afterward, he'd loved her that one night, loved her in a way so wild and wonderful her heart had threatened to burst with joy. She knew this in her heart and would always remember and treasure her time with the one man who set her soul on fire. She had thrown that away by turning against him. Just as he'd predicted she would.

She smiled sadly as she recalled how he'd danced her around the living room, humming into her ear, holding her to him then elevating her again and again to passionate bliss. She wanted that forever, but obviously, it wasn't to be. He'd let her go. And she'd given him a reason.

Perhaps one night was all he could give. He'd been sheltering his heart for a very long time. What happened that night could have astonished him as much as her. Even if he'd started wanting her for some devious scheme of revenge, it hadn't ended that way.

She missed Wheeler — his strength, his raw wisdom, even his biting sense of humor.

And she remained angry with herself for accepting Father's invitation to return here to 'recover' instead of going back to her own apartment. Ever since the night she'd angered him by admitting how hard living up to the Woolrich standards was for her, they'd maintained a cool politeness, avoiding any discussion that might lead to an argument while remaining tense and uncomfortable in each other's presence.

She'd meant to stay longer in Blakesville, doing what she could to help, checking on the repairs on her father's house. But knowing Wheeler was there, she couldn't do that. He'd assume she'd tracked him. And Woolrich or no, she had too much pride to chase after a man who had rejected her. Just as she refused to claim the parents who'd deserted her.

Setting down her book, she rose, adjusted her bathing-suit straps, and dove into the pool, surfacing with a splash and orchestrating her own little water ballet to burn off energy.

She must forget Wheeler Scully and move on with her life despite her lack of enthusiasm. These past weeks, even after seeing him in Blakesville, she'd been waiting for him to come back, to say he'd made a mistake and couldn't live without her. But she'd hurt him badly and his pride was too big for that.

Who was she kidding? Wheeler didn't want the spoiled fickle 'Princess' she'd proven herself to be. He'd made that clear.

She trod water, spewing chlorine and rubbing water from her eyes.

'You must be feeling better if you're swimming.'

She made out a blurred image of Sadie standing at the poolside. Side-stroking, she swam to the ladder and pulled herself out.

'Hi, Sadie. I feel fine,' she lied, dripping onto the concrete as she reached for a folded beach towel. Sadie picked it up and handed it to her. 'Thanks.' She dried herself, meeting her cousin's worried gaze. 'Where have you been all week? I tried to call a couple times and got the machine.'

Sadie just shrugged. 'You must have kept missing me. I've had all this running around to do planning tonight's party at the gallery. When are you going back to work?'

'I'm not sure I am.' Claire toweled her wet hair.

Sadie frowned. 'Honey, this is serious. You've got me worried.'

Claire flashed an elfin grin. 'Thought you'd sworn off the doting mode. Honestly, I've been needing some down time to get my bearings. I've had a chance to spend a couple extra afternoons at the hospital and worked on a new puppet show. I had a long talk with a psychologist who works there with the kids. She says remembering so little about my life before I was adopted isn't so strange as it seems since I don't have the usual reminders of it most people do, baby pictures, family members relating anecdotes. I'm going to talk to her again.'

'Do you realize you've never said that before?'

'Said what?'

'That phrase, 'before I was adopted'.'

'Haven't I?' Claire shook her hair into place.

'I still can't get used to your new haircut.'

'Neither can I.' Claire set one hand to her head. She reached for her terry beach jacket and put it on over her bathing suit.

'Have you seen Barre?' Sadie asked.

'No, and I don't intend to.'

'I hate it that I was right about him.'

'Yeah, me too.'

'Is this a private conference?' Claire looked up and saw her father striding toward them. He must have just come in from work. Immediately, she tensed. She couldn't stop believing he too had treated Wheeler unfairly. Still, he was her father, the single stabilizing factor in her life, and she had a nagging sense of needing to right things between them. Only she wasn't sure how.

'Hi, Uncle Josh.' In her usual, breezy manner, Sadie stepped forward to kiss his cheek.

He was smiling, but dark half-moons underscored his eyes. As if he'd been under a lot of stress. Claire wondered whether something had gone wrong at the office.

'I just stopped by to remind both of you about the big bash at the gallery tonight,' Sadie told him.

'High time you got that place off your hands, Sadie,' he approved. 'No money in promoting amateur art.'

'I've enjoyed it,' Sadie countered. 'I've got to run — I still have a trillion errands to run this afternoon. But you will both be there, won't you?'

'Sure,' Claire assured her dispiritedly.

Sadie studied her. 'Why don't you come with me, Claire? Bring your clothes and change at the house and we can go to the party from there.'

Claire shook her head. 'Thanks, but I have some things I want to do here. Besides, I'm not dressed to go anywhere. I don't want to make you late.'

Sadie checked her watch. 'I am running behind.' She leveled a worried gaze on Claire. 'Wear something stunning tonight. You'll be surprised how much better you'll feel. *Ciao*.'

Claire shook her head as Sadie sprinted off. Maybe pretty clothes bolstered Sadie's spirits, but Claire didn't think even the sleekest designer creation could chase away the heaviness in her soul. She did marvel how Sadie seemed to have gotten over Ned. Sadie's heart was broken, but no one would have ever guessed. Unless they stopped to wonder why Sadie was suddenly giving up a gallery she'd lovingly established, nurtured and built a reputation for over the years. Sadie had never operated her business for the money. Closing the place signaled a fierce upheaval in her life. But she was moving on, an example Claire resolved to follow.

Suddenly, Claire felt self-conscious at being left to deal with Father alone. He stood beside her as if waiting for something.

'Let me get you some iced tea,' she offered.

'Ethel's been bringing me one every afternoon for the past ten years, Claire. That's what I'm paying her for. If you're feeling useless, we could certainly use you at the office.'

Guilt rippled through her. 'I'll only be going back long enough for you to find a replacement for me. I'm enrolling in some college classes for the fall.'

'You never mentioned going back to school.'

She shrugged. 'I thought I might go into another field eventually.'

'Really? I'd prefer to keep you in the company. A man my age starts wondering who will take over some day . . .'

'You're not far past fifty. And I can't see you ever retiring.'

'You do a good job, Claire. Maybe I haven't stopped to say that often enough.'

'I wasn't fishing for approval. I want to do something I love as much as you love running your businesses. Something of my own.'

'There's no rush to have to decide about doing anything. I'm not trying to pressure you.'

'I appreciate that, but I am sure about this.'

'Vegetating around here can't be much of a vacation. Why don't you get away for a while? My travel agent has a great bargain right now on a Mediterranean cruise.'

Claire shot him a knowing half-smile. 'And you just happened to be chatting with her about it? I'll be all right. Going away isn't the answer. But how about you? Maybe you could use a vacation.'

'You're trying to change the subject, Claire.'

'You must get lonely in this big house with Mother gone. Sometimes it feels empty even with both of us here.'

'Lately it has.'

Claire dropped her gaze guiltily. 'I'd better go pick out something to wear tonight.'

He stopped her. 'That won't take you but a few minutes, Claire. Sit down. Let's talk. Something you said the other day has been bothering me.'

A sense of dread rippled through her. Father had a way of making an invitation to chat sound ominous. The last time this had happened was after he'd found out she'd attended the rock concert he'd forbidden her to go to with Jamie, a boy he'd forbidden her to date.

She dropped into one of the pool chairs.

Father sat facing her, looking out of place at the poolside in his suit and tie.

He cleared his throat in a rare gesture of hesitation. 'We've never really talked enough, you and I. That's my fault. We were closer when you were a little girl. Do you remember?'

'Yes.'

'Then you were growing up and wanting to do things that didn't make any sense to me. I didn't know how to talk to you. And sometimes it's hard for me to talk to people without ordering them around, out of habit. Your mother would always call me on that, make me see I was doing it. Without her, I didn't have that gentling factor in my life any longer. When I tried, you'd seem upset or angry, and it was easier to send you to your aunt or Sadie. I wasn't writing you off. I was out of my league and afraid of doing or saying the wrong thing.'

Astonished, Claire smiled softly. 'You, Father? I've never known anyone more confident.'

'Yes, well, business makes sense. Raising a teenage girl requires certain instincts I lack. I don't like to fail, Claire, and I felt I'd let you down in ways I didn't understand. Until the other night, I didn't realize how far apart we'd drifted. You're grown up now and capable of fending for yourself. Wheeler told me how you spent the whole time worrying about me instead of yourself, how you hiked through the woods on your injured ankle without complaining and even found wild blueberries.'

And tactfully had not scared him to death by relating their encounter with the bear, she thought. *Oh, Wheeler.* 'Did he tell you he went out in the storm to find me after my car wrecked?'

'No. And neither did you. You and I should be more direct with each other. Apparently, my opinion isn't the only one any more, and I've been slow in recognizing that.'

'You're not single-handedly to blame. I haven't always been forthright in expressing my opinions. I see everyone around you jumping to attention when you click your fingers, and sometimes I assumed you expected the same of me.'

'But you're my daughter, Claire. I may not always approve of everything you think or do, but I'd never love you any the less because of it. It's not something I could take back any more than I could say Ted was no longer my brother or Sadie had ceased to be my niece.'

'That's not the same, and we both know it.'

His features froze. Claire had never seen him look so stricken. Certainly, she hadn't meant to blurt that. Yet, now, her words hung between them like a storm cloud.

'I'm sorry,' she fumbled to retract her statement. He didn't deserve to be hurt.

He tugged at the knot in his tie, waving one hand at her. 'No, let's get it out on the table. I'm beginning to understand. Or I did when you made that comment the other night about lacking Woolrich blood. When we stopped communicating, somewhere along the line, you assumed I distanced myself from you out of disfavor because you were adopted rather than my biological child. Is that it, Claire?'

The lump in her throat was strangling her. 'I don't want it to be. You're the only parent I've ever known, and you've always been good to me. Sometimes, I wondered whether I was disappointing you, whether you resented my getting in the way of your life, whether we might be closer if I was your natural child. Yes, it has bothered me.'

He blanched visibly, and Claire felt a stab of recrimination at upsetting him. Little jolted Father. 'I've always known you must have questions, Claire. I'm just surprised it's taken you this long to ask them. You deserve honest answers. So let's put this subject to rest forever.' His gaze shifted briefly to the concrete. Her heart clenched. For years, she'd wondered about this, but now she feared she might not like hearing what he was about to say.

He looked up, rubbing his temple. Anything this hard for him to say would be doubly hard for her to hear. 'I wish you'd had time to know your mother better. She was never so happy as after we brought you home. After she died, the doctors said she might have been walking around with that aneurysm for years, a walking time bomb. It's a miracle she lived long enough for us to adopt you.'

He paused, seeming to grope for words. Finally, he glanced in the direction where his T-Bird was parked. 'You see that car?'

She nodded impatiently, fearing he was going to compare her to a piece of machinery.

'I'm not the original owner. In fact, that car has had several owners, but it was never cared for properly, never restored to its original beauty until I bought it. It's one of a kind. I never think of it any other way than as mine, never consider replacing it with something newer. In the same way, I forget Anita and I didn't give birth to you ourselves. If your mother had lived, she would have been telling you over and over all your life how special you were. As her adoptive parents had done for her. I've never been very good at communicating that. You were my daughter, so I expected you to know.'

She fought a childish impulse to cry. When it came to finances, her father could easy discuss mega-figures, but he was seldom so forthright about his emotions. She stumbled over her words. 'Most people would have wanted an infant. My past is so sketchy. It seems unlikely I would have been the one you adopted unless there were unusual circumstances.'

He stared at her so hard, his features narrowing in such devastation, she feared he would turn away without revealing anything.

He spoke slowly. 'Did we know your biological parents? No. No secrets have been kept from you, although I always tried to spare you dwelling on the circumstances of your early life. Do you remember the hospital?'

'Yes,' she answered, surprising herself. She remembered herself as a little girl, confined to a hospital bed. 'I had meningitis when I was little. You've told me about that.'

Her father stroked his jaw thoughtfully. 'You were so sick. That's probably why you don't remember distinctly a break between your old life and your new one here. You were found abandoned, so weak and listless, you weren't expected to live. The police tried to track down your parents or any other relatives you might have and came up with nothing. Someone from the hospital told Anita about you and all she could think about was how hopeless and scared you must be, all alone like that. You were in so much pain, Claire, you wouldn't even let anyone touch you.

'Your mother and I had talked about adopting a baby, but we hadn't been married long and had decided to take our time. You see, we'd known before we got married she could never give birth to a child. Then suddenly, she wanted to adopt you. Said you needed a family. She thought we could ensure you'd get the best medical care. Yes, I opposed it. I was afraid she'd get too attached, be heartbroken if you didn't make it. Even if you survived, you could have been deaf or paralyzed. The franker the doctors were, the more determined she was you needed us. I suspect your . . . whoever was taking care of you didn't know what to do when you got sick. Until we knew you were going to make it, until we could bring you home, we didn't even tell anyone about the adoption although it was legal. I had connections, and I used them to hurry things along. But you were getting worse instead of better, your fever soaring. We camped out, waiting to hear. I tried to remain detached because I thought you would die without ever coming home.

'Late at night even a hospital gets kind of quiet. I was pacing back and forth under those hideous bright lights, bracing myself so I could be strong when your mother fell apart. The doctor came out and told us the antibiotics were working, and this wild relief gripped my heart, made me realize I hadn't readied myself for anything less. He said you were pulling through by sheer willpower, and your mother looked over at me and said, 'See, our daughter's as tough as you are.' You'd already become a part of me, a part of my family. Anita had automatically accepted you as her child, and I loved her too much not to share that. How we happened to acquire you was incidental. There were no contingencies. And there are none now.

'Maybe I've gone too far in trying to shelter you. God knows you'd had enough upheavals in your life, especially after Anita died. It was never my intention to confuse you or prevent you from leading a normal life. I got so accustomed to determining what's best for you, Claire, I never realized when the time had come to start asking how you felt. If you want to locate your birth parents, it's perfectly reasonable.'

Claire couldn't stop the flow of tears

streaming down her cheeks. She shook her head vehemently.

'You're sure? I've always dreaded the day you might ask, but I accepted it would come eventually. Back then, I was glad they'd vanished. Now, I'm sure more advanced methods of tracking them are available.'

She shook her head. 'What could I possibly say to people who left me to die? In their hearts, I must be dead to them. Maybe someday I'll feel differently, but for now, I'm perfectly happy for them to stay lost.'

'What they did was wrong, but then if they hadn't given you up, we wouldn't have found you. In their minds, it could have been the only way they saw to get you the help you needed. They did leave you near the hospital, probably hoping someone would take care of you.'

'Thank you for taking me out me of that hospital, for raising me as your child. In many ways, I am like you. You taught me to be strong, stronger than I ever realized. Even if it means opposing your wishes.'

'Wheeler?'

'I love him.'

Her father gave her a long, appraising look. 'Damn. Claire, I believe he's a decent man. I'm indebted to him for keeping you safe. But he has nothing.'

She smiled. 'Except his own incredible strength and resourcefulness. Qualities lacking in other men who are supposedly successful.'

He cleared his throat again. 'I did some research, Claire.'

Her head snapped up defensively. 'Oh, no. You had Wheeler investigated? Nothing you can tell me can change the way I feel. In fact, I don't want to hear it.'

His tone was even, calm. 'Research on Barre. Scully's name came up because he and Barre were partners in a land-development project that went belly-up. Seems improvements promised to the individual buyers never got done. Lots of angry people.'

'Wheeler told me he had a failed business, that his partner sabotaged it.'

'I don't know whether it was intentional or just negligence. Barre made all the promises, then bailed out and Wheeler went broke trying to make good on them. He tried to do the right thing, ruining his own finances in the process.'

'Barre had never mentioned a land-development project.'

'Apparently, Barre failed to mention a lot of things about himself. I should have checked his background as soon as you became involved with him.'

'Father, I don't want you investigating my friends!'

'Wheeler had good reason to be angry with Barre.'

'He never acted out of anger. I'm sure of that now.'

'It's understandable you developed some fondness for Wheeler. The two of you survived intense circumstances. Emotions get confused. Hostages have been known to believe they love their captors. Granted, the two of you grew close through your ordeal. Wheeler assumed responsibility for you. Maybe you mistook his protection for something else. His feelings may have been skewed as well. But all that's over now. Money can be a powerful temptation to men who have none. He was wise to move aside.'

'Wheeler doesn't know I have any money of my own. And if he cared about that, wouldn't he be here now? If I picked up the phone, Barre would be here in a heartbeat.'

'You have your pick of young men. Ethel says you've gotten a stream of phone calls since the news got out you'd broken things off with Barre. I want to know you're with someone who will be good for you, Claire.'

'Wheeler's the only man I've ever met who failed to be impressed I was your daughter. He was good to me in ways that really matter.

Don't you remember what it was like when Mother was alive? Could you have set her aside in favor of someone else?'

Joshua Woolrich shook his head. 'I haven't been keeping Wheeler away, if that's what you're thinking. He wouldn't take anything more than a couple sandwiches, a change of clothes, and the wages he had coming. After he saved your life, I wouldn't just turn him out because of some disagreement between him and Barre. He left me his brother's address in Franklin to forward the insurance payment for his belongings.'

'Franklin?' she asked at the mention of the outlying town.

He shook his head. 'No, he's not there. I sent a messenger by earlier with a check in the amount of the adjuster's appraisal.'

'Why a messenger?'

He flicked an eyebrow. 'I hoped to get a firsthand report on how he was doing. I do feel responsible. And I knew he'd be needing his money.'

'He's in Blakesville, Father. Or was. I guess I've finally gotten it into my hard head he doesn't want to see me. As you tried to tell me. I've accepted staying away is his decision. I'm not blaming you.'

'Too many people have let you down in your life. I hate to be so blunt, but he didn't waste any time retreating from your life.'

'Because I was too quick to believe he'd deceived me. What if by some miracle he did come back? Knowing how I feel, would you interfere? I know how easily you could, in a way I'd never be aware of it.'

Her father shook his head. 'I won't lie to you, I don't know what I would do. Fortunately, that's not an issue.'

$$\star \quad \star \quad \star$$

At the last minute, Claire reconsidered Sadie's suggestion — to primp might have some merit. She reached into the closet and came up with the new sling-back dress she'd planned to wear to her engagement party, still packaged in the dress shop's plastic bag. Inspecting it, she admired the beauty of the sleek gown, then quietly hung it back on the rack. She would never wear it.

Shifting through the handful of dresses she'd brought over from her place, she selected an elegant, deep rose-colored gown. She'd been seen in it at many events, but it was one of her favorites and she wanted to wear it tonight. What she wore didn't matter as much as who she was. A Woolrich in her own right.

She brushed her curls and decided this

style looked more sophisticated than her old one. She refused to dwell on her losses. The present and the future were what mattered. That resolved, she put on the diamond earrings that had belonged to Anita Woolrich, liking how they made her feel closer to the mother she'd scarcely known but remembered with fierce affection.

'You seem astonishingly cheerful,' Father commented as they left for the party. 'You always have been resilient.'

'I'm going to have a good time tonight,' she vowed. 'This party means a lot to Sadie.'

As soon as they entered the gallery, a business acquaintance hailed him and he disappeared into the crowd.

The tiny gallery overflowed with well-wishers. Sadie had many friends. A waiter handed Claire a flute of champagne, and she struggled to avoid spilling it as she navigated through the mass of people.

'You look wicked tonight, kiddo,' Sadie cajoled as she passed. She glanced over her shoulder toward the door as if expecting someone important.

Claire grew suspicious. 'Listen, Barre's not going to show up, is he?'

Sadie raised one palm in the air. 'Hey, I've sworn off the interference, remember? Not a Sutton on the guest list. Relax, I'll have

Bruno toss him out if he shows.' She nodded toward a uniformed security guard. 'I am glad you came.'

Sadie was swept away into the crowd, leaving Claire on her own again. Briefly, she feigned interest in an oil painting.

'Claire, good to see you came tonight.'

She turned. 'Hello, Uncle Ted.' Sadie's father was an older version of Joshua Woolrich, although more outgoing and jovial and slightly taller and heavier, his dark hair speckled with more gray. He was standing alone, looking a little awkward and forlorn. This wasn't Ted Woolrich's type of party.

'Run into any more whirlwinds lately?'

'No.' She rolled her eyes and smiled despite her low spirits.

'Probably sent it spinning back the other way, if I know you. We Woolriches are pretty sturdy stock.'

'Yes, we are,' she confirmed. 'And a pretty all-around terrific family.' Father was right. None of them — him, Sadie, or her aunt and uncle ever hinted at her not truly being a Woolrich. Where had all those doubts come from? Aurora Sutton's cutting remarks? Certainly, they'd fueled her doubts. Wheeler had been right. No self-help technique Denver recommended equaled hearing things only Father could have told her, things they'd both avoided discussing for fear of hurting each other.

Claire surprised her uncle with an impulsive kiss on the cheek. 'Where's Aunt Martha?'

'She was right over there — '

Sadie came up beside them. 'Make sure you get something to eat. The stuffed jalapenos are going fast.' Suddenly, her head snapped up, and she stared toward the door, one hand flying to her jaw. 'I don't believe it.' Her pretty features narrowed into a furious glare.

Claire turned to look. A tall, reedy man wearing glasses had come in and paused near the door, scanning the room as though he were lost. As he spied Sadie, his worried expression melted into a broad, handsome smile. He wove his way determinedly through the crowd toward them.

'Ned,' Sadie offered, still eyeing him darkly.

'Hello, Sadie. I never crashed a party before.'

'How did you even know about it?'

'Heard some talk around the diner about your closing the gallery.'

'That's why you've come, to try to stop me from closing the gallery?'

'No. I don't care much about art. I realized you might be moving away or . . . I had to see you before you left.' He took hold of her hands. 'I know I was a grade-A jerk, and I wouldn't blame you for having me bounced out of here. I was hoping maybe we could back up and slow down. I acted badly. Never in my life have I done anything so despicable . . .'

Uncle Ted cleared his throat. Sadie seemed to suddenly remember he and Claire were standing there. Stepping back, she introduced them.

Ned clasped Claire's hand for a moment when she reached to shake his. 'I'm awfully glad to finally meet you. And to see you're safe and sound.'

'Any friend of Sadie's is a friend of mine,' she said, liking him despite her annoyance over how he'd hurt Sadie. She could tell by the way he looked at her he loved her. But this time he'd better not break her heart again. Claire smiled, realizing this protective streak ran two ways. She and Sadie simply wanted the best for each other. And so did she and Father.

Ned glanced around the crowded room. 'Can we talk somewhere?'

Sadie hesitated, then relented with a heavy sigh. 'Come on back in my office, Ned.'

Claire watched them as they walked off, exchanging anxious, rather heated whispers.

Sadie might not give him another chance easily, but he seemed sincere and determined. At least one of the Woolrich cousins would have the man of her dreams. Feeling lonely and empty, no matter how hard she struggled not to, Claire decided she needed a breath of fresh air.

She walked outside, glanced briefly at a man standing at the curb smoking a cigarette, then watched a beat-up dark blue sedan pull up to the curb, jerking to a halt like an ambulance arriving at an accident scene. At first, she nearly didn't recognize the tall, broad-shouldered, clean-shaven man who jumped out.

Then she drew in a sharp breath, and warmth flooded her heart. Wheeler looked more dashing sporting a suit and fresh haircut than she'd imagined.

Marching toward the doorway, his gaze riveted on the gallery's front door, he was alongside her when he suddenly halted and turned. His eyes widened. 'Claire?' he asked in astonishment.

'Wheeler, you look fabulous.' He did.

'Your hair. Oh, well, you had to cut it, didn't you?'

'You don't like it?'

'Are you kidding? Listen, I didn't come here to swap compliments. I came here because of this.' He waved a sheet of paper in the air.

'Perhaps if you'd hold it still, I could read it.'

He presented it for her inspection.

She squinted, leaning forward. 'Sorry. Come over here, where the light's better.'

He followed her under the overhang. Claire instinctively heated as he hovered close. So close, yet not touching her. She could hardly remember where she was, let alone read. The scent of his aftershave speeded her pulse, and the fragments of her broken heart were splintering. Rational thought vanished. She could scarcely think, let alone read. All she wanted was to be in his arms.

'Well?' he asked. 'This was delivered to my brother's house with your father's check.'

'Well what?' The embossed white stationary was identical to the invitation to Sadie's gallery's closing that he'd received. An offbeat celebration, she had to admit, since most galleries have openings, but she couldn't understand why being invited angered him. 'I didn't write Sadie's guest list.'

'Claire, you can't marry Barre.'

Her mouth fell open. 'Well, who says I am?'

His brow creased. 'This does.' She peered more closely at the paper and began to understand. His invitation differed from hers.

It said this party was being held to announce her engagement.

'False alarm, Wheeler. My cousin's warped attempt to bring you out of hiding. I won't be seeing Barre again.' She looked up at him, her eyes flaring as she comprehended he had come to stop her from marrying Barre.

He gave her a long, hard look. 'Oh. I should go, then.'

She eyed him evenly. 'Don't you dare.'

Taken aback, he stared incredulously then cast her a slow, slanted grin. 'Snobbery in reverse, isn't it, not telling a woman you love her because of who her father is?'

Before Claire could react, he pulled her to him, kissing her hot and heavy, nearly lifting her off the ground.

He drew back, leaving her dazed and breathless.

'Oh, Wheeler, I'm so sorry. I didn't for an instant actually believe you'd used me to get back at Barre. I love you so much. I was so afraid everything would go wrong, I made it happen.'

'I'll be honest, Claire. I can't give you the lifestyle you're accustomed to. I don't have much. Just a little money from some land I sold. I'm better at building things than selling them and that's what I'm doing. I've been in Blakesville, helping rebuild. Once I get enough money, I'm going to get some bigger jobs, hire more men. I messed up before, concentrating too hard on my business instead of my marriage. A mistake I don't intend to repeat.'

'I'd love the challenge of getting a new company off the ground. If you had a trained professional to help you with the marketing and sales you might be able to . . . Wheeler, you're proposing!'

'Waking up without you is agony. I thought all I needed was to get a business going, then I realized none of it meant any more to me than working up on the mountain did unless I had you. Should I be on my knees?'

She glanced at the already curious passersby. 'No!' She laughed. 'No!' Standing on tiptoe, she kissed him as urgently as he'd kissed her.

'Umm,' he agreed, still holding her. 'Is that a yes?'

She gazed into his eyes, feeling his warmth and loving his familiar features, yet still disbelieving he'd come for her.

'A-hem.'

Claire glanced sideways. 'Father.'

Wheeler did not release her.

'Hello, Wheeler.' Joshua greeted him with a quick nod.

'Mr Woolrich.' Shifting slightly, he extended

his hand, a glint of resolve darkening his eyes.

'Wheeler's asked me to marry him,' Claire announced, praying Father would gracefully accept her choice.

'Yes, I have,' Wheeler confirmed.

Joshua Woolrich cast them both a low, deliberate look. Claire knew she would hate forever turning her father away from her. Yet even for him she could not give up the one man she would always love. She could only pray he would not ask as much.

She wanted to believe Father when he said he accepted her for whatever, whomever she really was. Now she would truly know.

'You didn't waste any time putting your life back in order then,' he observed. 'Especially after you refused my help.'

'I do things my own way. Always have.'

Joshua swung his glance from Wheeler to Claire, then back. Raising his hand, he grasped Wheeler's firmly, accepting his handshake. 'Apparently your ways made a big impression on my daughter. I know coming here couldn't have been easy after the reception we gave you the other morning. I admire your gumption. Welcome to the family, son.'

Claire blinked back tears. His blessing was more than she'd hoped for.

She gave her father a quick hug.

He shuffled with embarrassment. 'Don't you two want to come back inside and share the happy news?'

Claire shook her head, stepping back to Wheeler's side. 'Not just yet.' She leveled an adoring gaze on Wheeler. 'Plenty of time for that later.'

Her father nodded and went back inside.

Wheeler gave her a questioning look. 'Does that mean your answer's yes?'

'First, we have to settle one more thing.'

'Why I didn't tell you about Barre?'

'No. You tried, didn't you? I thought you were terribly bitter, but you were trying to warn me, knowing I wouldn't believe you if you mentioned him specifically.'

'Barre ruined me. I'm not proud of having allowed that to happen. I thought the entire world viewed me as a failure, an opinion I wasn't anxious to have you share. Truth was, I saw myself that way.'

'Oh, Wheeler. I know who you are. Doing the right thing is important to you. You tried, but Barre made that impossible. What happened in the past doesn't matter. It's taken me a long time to realize whatever has happened doesn't have to rule the present or the future. Recognizing what we have now is all that matters. Starting over is never so easy as Den — as some people make it sound.'

'Nothing worthwhile ever is. The only real failure is giving up. Something I never intend to do again.'

'I thought you'd given up on me.'

'I wanted to. I couldn't. Not a minute didn't go by I didn't want to see you again. Thinking you were actually going to marry Barre was the last straw.'

'Regardless of everything else that happened, I realized back on the mountain I didn't love Barre, never really had. Nothing could have changed that. I hated what it took for me to discover that, but I had to tell him the truth. My concern now is about children.'

'I want kids, Claire. As much as you do.'

'Adopted ones?'

'Be more fun to make our own.'

'I'm serious, Wheeler. I mean, maybe we'll do both or neither or one or the other. But I need to know up front, and I know you understand why.'

He shrugged. 'Either way they'll be complete brats and I can't wait to watch you cope with real kids who cry in the middle of the night and get their clothes dirty and splash in mud puddles.'

She raised one eyebrow. 'Do you think I can't?'

'The woman who fought a bear with a can of soup? Wherever they come from, Claire, I'll love them like crazy. And be wild for their mom.'

'The answer's yes, then, Wheeler. I've missed you more than you can imagine.'

He held her tighter. 'I can imagine it exactly.'

★ ★ ★

Out on the lawn of Joshua Woolrich's now fully repaired and restored mountaintop mansion, Sadie paused to brush a handful of birdseed from Claire's hair.

'You're the one who threw it at me,' Claire accused as pellets rained down the shoulder of her white satin and lace gown.

'Brides are supposed to be pelted with birdseed,' Sadie reminded her. 'It's tradition.'

'I've got to get this stuff out of my hair before crows start perching on my head.' Glancing up at the steely blue-gray winter sky, she shivered and hugged herself.

'Get inside. It's freezing out here.' Sadie gave Claire a long, last look, tears filling her eyes as she hugged her cousin's neck. 'I feel like I'm losing my little sister.'

Claire blinked back hot tears of her own. 'You're the one who's moving away.'

Sadie shrugged. 'A few hours' drive. Not all that far.' She held one palm in the air. 'Look, this time I swear, I am through meddling in your life.'

Claire glanced toward their parked vehicles. They'd said goodbye here another afternoon on a day that had changed both their lives forever. Now, Ned sat in his Trooper, engine running as he waited for Sadie. Claire waved at him. 'I'll forgive you that one last time.'

'He would have been back eventually anyway.'

'I know. But you spared us the waiting. It's not easy being bullheaded. You'd better go. Ned's waiting.'

Sadie shook her head and huddled deeper inside her faux fur coat. 'You and Wheeler had better hurry too. I heard some rumblings about snow in the forecast. Besides, the bride and groom are supposed to be the first to leave the wedding, not the last.'

Claire turned at looked toward Wheeler, leaning against the porch railing. Tall and trim in his tux, he looked incredibly handsome.

Turning back to Sadie, Claire shrugged. 'We still have to change, and I promised Father we'd lock up. With the new caretaker living down in town, he didn't want him to have to make a special trip.'

Sadie shook her head. 'Ned and I could have done that. Or Uncle Josh would have stayed and done it himself. Where are you two spending your honeymoon anyway?'

Claire shot her an evasive grin. 'Go, Sadie. You're keeping a terrific guy waiting.'

Sadie glanced toward the house, waved at Wheeler, then gave Claire a final hug. 'So are you, little cousin.'

'We are like sisters, aren't we?' Claire asked.

'Better,' Sadie countered. 'Be happy, Claire.' She rushed off, and as the Trooper pulled out of sight, the first fat snowflakes began to fall. Claire turned and strode happily toward her waiting husband.

'Gosh, this place looks magnificent finished and furnished. And with a backup generator now too.' Smiling up at Wheeler, she blinked melting snowflakes from her eyelashes.

Wheeler grinned as he locked his hands around her waist and drew her close. 'Do you think they really bought it that we're leaving?'

'Well, everyone's gone. Let's see . . . the fridge is stocked, we've got our luggage, champagne, what else do we need?'

Wheeler pulled her closer and gave her a long kiss teeming with promise. 'Not a thing, darling. Not one more thing. Are you really all right with not getting away for a real honeymoon? With the construction business picking up like it has . . . '

She cast a worried glance over the landscape. 'Do you think we'll get snowed in?'

Wheeler grinned. 'With any luck.' He scooped her into her in his arms, lifted her as effortlessly as he always had, and kissed her deeply. 'Let's go inside where it's warm. I intend to show you how thoroughly I adore you, Mrs Scully. Someday, I promise, I'll make this up to you. We'll take a long trip anywhere you want.'

Claire luxuriated in his strong grasp and crossed one finger over his lips. 'Believe it or not, there's absolutely nowhere else I want to be. Now, I believe you mentioned you wanted to show me something . . . '

He flashed a smooth grin as he carried her toward the door.

At last, Claire knew she was exactly where she belonged. She'd had to look only as far as into her own heart to find that place, always had. She planned to stay for a very long time.

We do hope that you have enjoyed reading this large print book.

Did you know that all of our titles are available for purchase?

We publish a wide range of high quality large print books including:
Romances, Mysteries, Classics
General Fiction
Non Fiction and Westerns

Special interest titles available in large print are:
The Little Oxford Dictionary
Music Book
Song Book
Hymn Book
Service Book

Also available from us courtesy of Oxford University Press:
Young Readers' Dictionary
(large print edition)
Young Readers' Thesaurus
(large print edition)

For further information or a free brochure, please contact us at:
Ulverscroft Large Print Books Ltd.,
The Green, Bradgate Road, Anstey,
Leicester, LE7 7FU, England.
Tel: (00 44) **0116 236 4325**
Fax: (00 44) **0116 234 0205**

Other titles published by
The House of Ulverscroft:

KEEPSAKES

Jan McDaniel

How could she want a man she detested? Simon's warm hands brushed her bare shoulders, radiating a ripple of warmth through her chest. For a split second Yardley forgot that he hated her and her family, that she was doing this only as a punishment. For an instant, she was the fair maiden from a fairy story, finding her prince . . .

FRESH AS A DAISY

Valerie-Anne Baglietto

Daisy's feet have barely touched the ground since marrying Ben Kavanagh after a passionate, whirlwind romance. But she's soon brought down to earth with a bump when she meets her in-laws in their impressive Jacobean manor house. Ben's father and stepmother are suspicious of her motives, and she instantly feels like an outsider. As the bloom fades from her marriage, Daisy finds herself turning to the charming and enigmatic Jerome. But when her past comes back to confront her, she realises she's not the only one harbouring a secret or two.

THE BEST-KEPT SECRET

Mary De Laszlo

Cornelia, an innocent seventeen-year-old, is to leave the sheltered atmosphere of her Catholic boarding school and spend a year in Paris. First, though, she must meet the redoubtable Aunt Flavia, who proceeds to transform the schoolgirl into a beautifully presented young woman. Next it is school at Mademoiselle Beatrice's, where Cornelia meets other English girls, most of whom are just as naive as she is. Then there is Laurent, without whom Paris would never be Paris. So begins the happy initiation which will change her life forever.

NULL & VOID

Catherine Barry

When it comes to ending a marriage, there's the easy way, the hard way — and the Catholic way . . . For Ruby Blake, there seems to be no happy ever after. Her marriage to Eamonn was a sham from start to finish. Was it a marriage at all? Or one that existed only on paper? To find out for sure, Ruby must apply for an annulment. Her life — and Eamonn's — are taken over by the authorities, as question after question are heaped upon them. Has Ruby got what it takes to see this through? Is their marriage really over? Or could it be just beginning?

ELEGANCE

Kathleen Tessaro

Browsing in a second-hand bookshop, Louise Canova stumbles across a faded grey volume. Written by the formidable French fashion expert, Madame Genevieve Antoine Dariaux, *Elegance* is an encyclopaedia of style that promises to transform plain women into creatures of grace and poise. And there's nothing Madame can't advise upon — including inattentive husbands, false friends, and the powerful bond between mothers and daughters. When Louise vows to follow Madame's advice, her life is transformed. Within the book's pages lie clues to her own past, and as she begins to unravel them, she discovers a courage she never dreamt possible. However, everything — even elegance — has its price.

TOO LATE FOR LOVE

Lisa Andrews

When Gemma Davenport hears that Blake Adams is going to buy her glass company, her heart sinks. Ten years ago they had a passionate affair which left Gemma broken-hearted and with a permanent reminder of Blake. As soon as she sees him again, it is clear that Blake is enjoying every moment of the take-over. He makes it apparent that he has never forgiven her for what he sees as her 'betrayal' in marrying another man. Gemma is soon wondering (and hoping?) if Blake is so intent on getting his own back that he's trying to rekindle their once 'fatal attraction' . . .